THOMAS WILDUS AND THE BOOK OF SORROWS

J. M. BERGEN

ELANDRIAN PRESS

For Mikey, my wingman and the reason these stories exist.

THOMAS WILDUS AND THE BOOK OF SORROWS

ONE

"HEY WILDUS, YOU READY?"

The voice cut through the buzz of kids hustling to class. Thomas closed his locker and turned, smiling. A strand of blond hair slipped out of place, stopping just above the sharp blue eyes that overshadowed his prominent nose. "Enrique! Ready for what?"

"To lose, knucklehead," said Enrique. "Doodle war. You're going down. Again."

"In your dreams, Rodriguez. That was all me yesterday. Besides, Jameel says there's a stack of papers on Dilstrom's desk."

"Another pop quiz?"

"Probably."

"Lucky for you. I was going to throw a beat-down today," said Enrique. "If there's no quiz, it's on."

"If it's on, then I'm going to make it four in a row." Thomas turned and started down the hall toward class. "Come on, let's go."

"Four? What? Uh, uh," said Enrique. He nudged past Thomas. "No way. Yesterday was not a win."

"It was a total win. You laughed. That's the rule."

"At that ridiculous scribble? No way. I was laughing at my own masterpiece. You just showed yours at exactly the right time."

"I'd hardly call it a masterpiece." Thomas barely remembered the doodle at all. Something to do with the drama teacher and a unicycle. It was uninspired work, far from Enrique's best stuff.

"Please. You crazy." Enrique took a half step sideways as a cluster of older kids approached, laughing and jostling at each other. A mischievous smile crinkled the dark skin at the corners of his hazel-green eyes. "It was art, and you know it."

Thomas opened his mouth to retort and froze, slack-jawed. Peggy Epelson appeared right behind the older kids, clutching her laptop and talking to one of her friends. Carla or Clara or something like that. They were walking straight toward him. Thomas hardly noticed the other girl, but Peggy's auburn hair shone under the fluorescent lights, her smile—

A sharp thump jarred his shoulder. "Ow! What the heck?"

"Cut it out," said Enrique.

"Cut what out?"

"The googly-eyed staring. You're like a puppy dog. It's not healthy."

Thomas grimaced and rubbed his shoulder. Peggy and her friend disappeared around a corner. He had to force himself not to stare after her. "Really? Is it that bad?"

Enrique ignored the question and tilted his head sideways. "Hey, is that—?" He dabbed at the corner of Thomas's mouth. "Is that drool? You might want to take care of that."

"What!?" Thomas's eyes went wide. He swiped a hand across his lips. It came away dry. "Drool? Seriously?"

Enrique laughed. "Hey, come on. I'm just trying to keep you from embarrassing yourself. It's not easy, you know."

Thomas walked toward their classroom, still rubbing his shoulder. Enrique had a point. The staring was probably too much, but he couldn't help it. Peggy wasn't just incredibly cute. She was also the smartest girl in their grade and a talented pianist. He tucked his backpack under the desk and plopped into his seat.

The bell rang, loud and jarring. For the hundredth time, Thomas wondered why they didn't play a snippet of music instead of blasting that awful sound through the building. Practically anything would be less annoying and probably better for learning, too.

"All right, class, take your seats, please." As usual, Mr. Dilstrom's voice was monotone, his eyes droopy and tired. "We have a pop quiz today, covering material from your reading last night. Please put away your laptops and take out a writing utensil. We'll start as soon as everybody is ready, umkay?"

Enrique shook his head. "You're lucky, Wildus. I was going to crush you."

"That's big talk from a guy who's lost three in a row," said Thomas. "Work fast and we'll battle while everyone else is finishing."

"It's on."

"Bring it," said Thomas.

"Oh, hey, you want to come over after school and hang out?" asked Enrique, his voice not quite a whisper. "Coach Davis is out, so we don't have volleyball today. My sisters won't get home until at least six, maybe later, so the house shouldn't be too crazy."

"Ahem!" said Mr. Dilstrom. "Is there something you'd like to share with the class, Mr. Rodriguez?"

"No, sir, Mr. Dilstrom," said Enrique. "I was just checking to make sure Thomas did his reading last night. You know how he is."

A hot blush lit up Thomas's cheeks as the class laughed. He managed to keep himself from kicking Enrique's leg, but it was an exercise in self-restraint. Mr. Dilstrom stared for a long moment, eyebrows raised, then turned and went back to passing out quizzes.

"What do you think?" asked Enrique, his voice hushed.

"Can't," whispered Thomas. "I've got Kung Fu tonight. It's my last class before Sifu leaves town."

"Whatever. Slacker."

Thomas accepted the dwindling stack of quiz sheets,

took one for himself, and set the last one down on the empty desk behind him. He looked at Enrique. "Tomorrow, all right?"

"Deal," whispered Enrique. "Now quit looking at my quiz and do your own work. This much brilliance can't be copied."

"Knucklehead," whispered Thomas. He glanced up and saw Mr. Dilstrom staring in his direction. He wiped the smile from his face and read the first question. *In the battle of Gettysburg, what did . . . ?* He skimmed through the rest of the questions. It was all basic stuff, requiring only that one had done the assigned reading. He had, and so had Enrique. Mrs. Rodriguez was even more hardcore about grades and studying than Thomas's mom, and that was saying something.

In a battle with Enrique, every second counted. Thomas finished the quiz as quickly as he could and started doodling. The room around him faded as he focused in on his idea—an Enrique-saurus with short T-Rex arms and a perplexed look on his half-lizard face. Thomas was putting the finishing touches on his drawing when something nudged his foot.

"Hey," whispered Enrique. He kicked Thomas's foot again. "Hey, check it out."

Thomas glanced out of the corner of his eye. Enrique was staring forward, a finished doodle dangling from the side of his desk. Thomas half-turned. The details resolved into a picture of Mr. Dilstrom standing on his desk in a tutu, his knees pointed out like a ballerina. The eyes were perfect, baggy and heavy-lidded, his lumpy body horrifyingly on target.

Thomas tried to fight it, but the laughter bubbled up. He covered his mouth, trying to fake a cough. A half-choked squawk erupted.

"Bam!" Enrique lifted his hands over his head and dropped his pen like a microphone. The plastic clattered to the floor. "Who's the champion?"

"Excuse me?"

"Sorry, Mr. Dilstrom. It's just the pop quiz, you know. I totally crushed it. It's like BAM! I'm the champion. You know what I mean?"

Mr. Dilstrom stared at Enrique, his eyes bulging and forehead furrowed. Thomas chortled so loudly he had to act like he was choking. Stinking Enrique.

• • •

Five hours later, Thomas clasped his right fist in his left hand and bowed his head gently. A bead of sweat dripped from his nose and splashed onto the studio floor. "Thank you, Sifu."

Sifu gave an answering bow. "You worked hard, but your form is still terrible. Maybe you should come with me, study in the temple."

"To China? But it's the middle of the school year."

"I'm just kidding, Thomas." Sifu smiled, his crinkled

eyes twinkling with amusement. With his accent, kidding sounded more like *keeeding*. "Your form is not terrible anymore. Very bad, but not terrible. You need more practice before visiting temple. Otherwise, your teacher will look bad."

"Thanks," said Thomas. The subtle jab wasn't lost on him, but with Sifu, moving from terrible to very bad was big progress. The hard work was starting to pay off.

"Okay, time to go. Be a good student while your Sifu is away. Practice. Don't get soft and lazy, okay?"

"I promise," said Thomas. It was still strange to think of the old master having a teacher of his own, but every year, Sifu went back to the temple to study with his uncle Cheng, the grandmaster of his Kung Fu family.

"Remember. Practice, Thomas," Sifu repeated. "Move right, breathe right, think right. Every day, practice. All the time, practice."

"I will," said Thomas. "Have a great trip, Sifu. I'll see you in a couple months."

Thomas shrugged his backpack onto his shoulders and stepped outside. The sun hung low in the afternoon sky, a glob of golden butter melting between the spires of two tall buildings. Long shadows covered the sidewalk and climbed the brick walls at his back. A breeze ruffled his hair and made the lines of sweat on his cheeks feel almost chilly. He turned toward the bus stop at 7th and Main.

The line of customers snaking out of the coffee shop

next door was longer than usual, stretching almost to the street corner. Practically everyone was tapping on a phone or tablet. Thomas felt a familiar twinge of envy. All he had was a stupid flip phone. No games. No Internet. Nothing useful at all. He couldn't wait for his birthday. His mom had all-but-promised an upgrade.

Thomas angled toward a thin gap between two of the older patrons. They separated as he approached, allowing him to pass without bothering to look up from their devices. A cute redhead with even brighter red headphones was on the other side of them. She smiled at Thomas as her head bobbed to music he couldn't hear. He blushed and sped past, crossing to the other side of the intersection just as the light changed from green to yellow.

At the corner of 16th, a musical note cut through the rumble of traffic. Thomas paused, looking down the narrow, alley-like street. The sound grew louder, a humming that rose and fell in an arrhythmic cadence, drawing him forward. A man sat on the sidewalk, his threadbare olive overcoat pressed into a bent parking meter. Thomas's feet moved of their own accord, drawing him inexplicably closer to the source of the music.

The man looked up, staring through tangles of dark hair that shrouded his face and merged with an unkempt black beard touched with streaks of gray. The music stopped mid-stream. Green eyes locked onto Thomas's, wild and unblinking. Thomas's legs locked in place. A feeling of unreality descended, a strange déjà vu that bent the moment into something dreamlike but vaguely familiar.

Thomas was frozen. There was nothing in the world but those wild eyes. A rushing sound filled his head, a waterfall thundering through his brain even as an invisible hand squeezed his gut. *I know him.* His inner voice sounded distant, as if speaking from the bottom of a deep well. *How do I know him?*

The angry blare of a car horn shattered the moment. Thomas's head swung instinctively toward the intersection. A BMW peeled past, the driver laying on his horn and flashing a rude gesture at the slow-moving car next to him.

Thomas turned back. The sidewalk was empty. He looked around, but the man was nowhere to be seen. He'd only looked away for a second, but there was nobody on the street, no sign that anyone had ever really been sitting against the parking meter at all.

"What the heck?" Thomas's whispered question was swallowed by the rush of traffic and a soft gust of wind. He ran to the bent parking meter and leaned over, peering between the tires of the rusted-out delivery van parked along the curb. He stepped into the narrow street, looking at doorways and windows up and down the short block.

The man was genuinely gone. If he'd ever been there at all. Thomas turned back toward Main Street, suddenly wondering if he was losing his mind. As he turned, a blinding light caught him square in the eyes, a flash of purple that was gone even before he finished flinching.

For the second time, Thomas froze, this time blinking furiously. When he could see again, he found himself staring at a shop on the other side of the street. A sign hung above a wooden door with slightly faded red paint. The lettering was too small to read, but there were splotches of purple around the edges. It was the only purple Thomas could see anywhere. He looked both ways and jogged across the street.

The sign came into focus. *H&A Booksellers, Purveyors of Fine Books and Rare Manuscripts*. The words were painted in chipped gold leaf, with tiny purple flowers nestled in the arcs and whorls of the lettering. Thomas stared at the sign, his eyes following the path of the thin green vine that wound through the gold letters.

Was it possible that a bookstore in this area had escaped his attention? Not a chance. Not one that was listed on the Internet anyway. But the shop was here, every bit as real as the humming man a moment earlier. Thomas felt an uneasy excitement in his chest. Cars zipped past on Main, but this street was practically deserted. He looked at the red door, at the plastic placard dangling from the nail in the center. *Open*.

He contemplated his next move. The options were simple. Forget what had just happened and turn around in time to catch his bus home or go inside and risk being laughed at for the hundredth time.

He reached out and pressed on the old-fashioned handle, forcing himself not to think about the disappearing man or the prospect of pending humiliation. The door swung open. The wide wooden counter and oversized green cash register looked as ancient as the faded lighting and worn carpet. The place was bigger than he would have expected, though, with shelves running far beyond the point where they logically should have ended.

The size was just the first curious thing about the shop. Everything else was different, too. There were no racks of shiny best-sellers, no big display cases promoting glossy fiction. Instead, cloth and leather-bound volumes were stacked and piled and crammed together in an endless sprawl of dusty texts. Every shelf was chock full of unrecognizable old books. The place was a goldmine. *Jackpot!*

Thomas looked at the placard at the end of the nearest row. The inscription stamped in tarnished bronze was faded but legible. *Alch. Hist. 1127–1490.* He reached for the nearest book, a tall, narrow volume wrapped in faded red leather, wondering what the inscription meant.

"Ahem."

The forced cough originated behind Thomas's left shoulder. He turned, startled, and found himself eye to eye with a man who had thin graying hair, a sharp nose, and hazel eyes flecked with specks of gold. The man stood with his hands behind his back and wore a yellowed apron with the words *In Liber Veritas* stenciled on the front.

"May I help you, young man?" The shopkeeper was only a few inches taller than Thomas himself.

"I, uh, I hope so." Thomas looked around the shop, his eyes wide with wonder. "This place is amazing."

"Thank you," said the little man, inclining his head in a slight bow. "Is there something in particular you are hoping to find?"

The wonder receded, replaced by a wrenching anxiety that knotted his gut and made his palms turn clammy. He could hear the scornful responses of the others he'd asked. *Are you messing with me, kid? What, are you some kind of idiot? There's no such thing as magic, dummy. Go on, get out of here.*

He pushed the voices out of his head. "I'm looking for books about magic. Magic books, really."

"Back of the shop and to the left." The man pointed a finger past Thomas to an even more dimly lit part of the building. "We have a wonderful selection of collectibles in the fantasy genre and more than a few New Age texts as well. I'm sure you'll find something to your liking."

Fantasy and New Age? Really? Thomas's shoulders slumped. He took a half-hearted step toward the back of the shop and paused, the knot in his gut tightening. As much as he hated getting laughed at, the idea of digging through piles of worthless books was as unexciting as the prospect of scrolling through another online "magic" forum. If ever there was a place that might have what he really wanted, this was it. He sucked in a deep breath and turned around.

The man looked at Thomas with one eyebrow raised. "Yes?"

"I, uh, I'm not really looking for those kinds of books," he managed. "I was hoping for something different. Something more unusual."

"What do you mean by unusual?" the man asked. "Be specific, please."

This was it. The part where he got laughed out of the building. Thomas looked at his feet, wondering if he should even bother. He considered turning around, but the words on the man's yellowing apron caught his eye. *In Liber Veritas.* Veritas meant truth, right? He looked up, his eyes locking onto those of the little man. "Unusual as in magical. Not fiction or fantasy or New Age. Magic. Real magic."

"Real magic? What makes you think there's any such thing?"

Thomas's body tensed, preparing for a swift retreat from the store. His dad's last words flashed into his mind, the final fragment before everything changed. *"Magic is real, Thomas. No matter what happens, always remember that magic is real."*

He sucked in a deep breath and forced himself to stand still. The air rushed out in a whoosh. "I-I just do."

"But why?" The man's expression was curious, focused, his eyes boring into Thomas like a drill. "And even if there were such a thing, what would it have to do with you?"

"Never mind. Just forget about it." Thomas spun toward the exit, his cheeks flushed and heart racing. Halfway to the door, he paused. The man wasn't laughing. He was asking questions. That, at least, was different. Thomas turned around. The man's unwavering eyes reflected the overhead lights, glinting with fragments of gold.

"It's, uh, it's something someone told me a long time ago," said Thomas. "Someone I trusted."

The man tilted his head, his expression almost curious. "Somebody told you magic is real, and you believed them?"

Blue eyes stared at Thomas out of a distant memory, sincere and earnest. He felt the roughness of his dad's calloused hand on his cheek, the tickle of soft beard as he pulled Thomas close and kissed his forehead for the last time. *Magic is real, Thomas.* Magic is real.

Thomas drew himself up to full size and met the man's stare directly. "Yes. I did. I do."

"And now you want a magic book, but not the make-believe kind?"

Thomas nodded. The shopkeeper's eyes were ageless, his stare unsettling. Thomas stood tall, refusing to break the connection even though his insides had turned to jelly.

"What is your name, young seeker of magic?" The hint of a smile crinkled the subtle features of the man's face.

"Thomas," he answered. "Thomas Wildus."

The smile lines smoothed, and the man's face took on a serious expression. "You're late."

TWO

"LATE?" THOMAS ASKED, suddenly confused.

"Indeed. We have been expecting you. How is it that you finally found us?"

Expecting me? Finally found us? Thomas wasn't sure if he should take the man seriously, and even less sure how to explain what had just happened outside. "I, uh, I'm not really sure. I was walking by and there was this guy sitting on the sidewalk across the street—I think maybe he was homeless—and he was humming or singing or something, but then he disappeared and there was this flash, and then I saw the sign outside and decided to come in."

"So, nobody told you to come here?" The man's expression was quizzical, almost surprised. "How very curious. I suppose the important thing is that you're here now, only how can I be sure you are who you say you are?"

Thomas fished in his backpack and came up with his school ID. The picture wasn't his finest, but it was the only form of identification he had. "I have this."

"Very well, Master Wildus." The little man handed the

ID back and was moving toward the door before Thomas could think or react. He flipped the sign from Open to Closed, pulled the door shut, and slid the heavy deadbolt sideways. The bolt snapped into place with an audible thunk. "Wait here. I have something for you in the back."

Why did he lock the door? Thomas's mouth went dry. He stared after the little man as he headed to the back of the shop and disappeared between a set of tall bookshelves. A door creaked open and then thudded shut. Thomas waited, an anxious buzz tickling the skin of his palms, questions spinning through his head. *Something for me? What is going on here?*

Minutes passed, a lifetime each, and finally, the door creaked opened again. Footsteps padded softly along the carpeted floor. The little man came back into sight, a caramel-colored wooden box in his hands. He held the box gently, almost tenderly, as if a living thing were hidden inside.

Thomas's eyes locked on the keyhole. Something stirred in his chest, heavy and foreign and powerful. Desire. Longing. Something even deeper. Need. He *had to* see what was inside. He reached for the box, but the man took a half-step backward.

"Patience, Master Wildus. Before I give you this box, we must discuss the price of the book it contains."

Thomas's excitement crashed. *Price? Of course, it has a price.* He stared at the little man in disbelief. Was all this a setup? Was the whole we've-been-expecting-you thing just a way to extract money from dumb kids with silly dreams? He swallowed down a mouthful of disappointment and forced himself to ask the obvious question. Maybe the number wouldn't be too ridiculous. "How much is it?"

"You misunderstand me," the man answered. "This book is *not* for sale."

"I—I'm not sure I follow." Thomas searched the man's face for a sign of mockery, for a hint that he was being pranked, but found his eyes unwavering. "But you just said something about price."

"I did indeed," said the shopkeeper. "The book is not for sale, but it can be borrowed."

"How does that work?" asked Thomas. "Do I need to sign up for a membership or leave a deposit or something?"

"Not exactly." The man looked almost amused. "No, the price must fit the prize, as the saying goes, and the prize is priceless."

"What does that mean? Can I borrow the book or not?" Thomas tried to keep the annoyance out of his voice but wasn't sure he quite succeeded.

"It means that money isn't valuable enough." The man looked at Thomas appraisingly, as if sizing him up in his head. Finally, he nodded. "Time. For you, the price will be time."

"Time? I don't—"

"Yes, time. Your time, to be precise." The man ran his

hand over the lid of the wooden box, gently, almost lovingly. "In exchange for access to this book, you will grant me five hours per week of your time, to be used as I see fit."

Thomas forced himself not to stare at the box too desperately and did a quick mental calculation. The book couldn't be more than a few hundred pages. He'd read it in a couple days, a week at most. Five hours was probably extortion, but it wasn't the end of the world. Even if the whole thing was a sham, he'd wasted time and money on far less promising leads. He nodded in agreement. "Okay."

"We are agreed then? Five hours per week, for as long as the book is in your possession?" said the shopkeeper.

"Yeah." Thomas held out his hands, ready to take the box. "It's a deal. I'm in."

"Not quite yet, Master Wildus." The man kept the box in his hands. "Time is the price, but the terms are just as important. Before I hand this over to you, you have to promise that you will follow our rules precisely and unfailingly. In matters such as these, one simply cannot be too careful. Especially now, when the stakes are so high."

Thomas stared uncertainly, not sure what to make of any of it. The little man stared quietly back. There was no laughter in his expression, no obvious hint of deception in his eyes. Thomas struggled to wrap his head around the possibility that this wasn't a joke, that maybe there was something special about the book. "Okay. What are your rules?"

"The rules are not mine. They pertain to the book and are for your benefit as well as our own." He paused, meeting Thomas's eyes. "The first rule is absolute secrecy. The fact that the book is in your possession cannot be known outside of this room. Not to your friends. Not to your family. Not to anybody. Is that clear?"

Thomas took a breath. Keeping secrets wasn't his thing, especially not from his mom and Enrique, but now he had to see the book. *Had to.* "Crystal clear."

"Good. The second rule is that you may only read one chapter at a time, and never more than a single chapter in a given day. No exceptions."

Thomas groaned inwardly, but forced himself to keep a straight face. Finishing in a few days was off the table, but he was committed now. Unless the rules got totally ridiculous, he was going to say yes. "Got it. One chapter per day, max."

"Very well. The third and final rule is that you must only open this box in the privacy of your home, and only when you are completely alone," said the man. "There must be no exposure of the book to anybody but yourself for the entire time it is in your possession. The process must be allowed to unfold without interference."

A chill ran up Thomas's spine. *Process? What's that supposed to mean?* He forced himself to take a breath and act calm. "No problem. My mom works late half the time anyway, so that should be easy."

"Wonderful." The man shifted the box a few inches closer to Thomas's outstretched hand. "Now, I will ask you one last time. Do you agree to follow the rules exactly as they have been described to you, in spirit and in practice, and to uphold your end of our agreement in good faith and as a matter of personal honor?"

Thomas felt like he'd stepped into an alternate universe, but he didn't need any time to think. "I do. Yes."

"Good. I will ask only two more things of you, Master Wildus." He took an oddly old-fashioned key from his pocket and set it on the wooden lid. The handle was looped, the shaft dotted with prongs. The metal had a strange, almost luminous quality to it, as if fashioned of silver and moonstone. "First, please do everything in your power to keep this book safe."

"Yes, of course," said Thomas. "I will."

"I trust that you will." The man locked eyes with Thomas once again. "There are only three copies of this text in the known world. It would be a genuine tragedy if the book were to become damaged, or worse, fall into the wrong hands."

Thomas looked at the box, his heart beating a thousand times per second. *Three copies in the known world? The wrong hands?* He nodded, not trusting himself to speak.

"My final request is that you return the book as soon as you have finished the last chapter. I repeat, immediately after reading it. Are we agreed?"

Thomas tried to answer, but the sound caught in his throat. He forced a cough and tried again. "Mmm hmm. Yes. I agree," he managed.

The man stared into Thomas's eyes for a long moment, then extended the box in his hands. The key slid forward. Thomas's hand shot out instinctively, catching it as it fell toward the floor. A shock jolted up his arm as soon as his fingers touched metal, forcing his fist to clench shut and jarring his arm with the force of an electric eel. A thrill of fear and excitement rippled through Thomas's body even as the shock dissipated. He looked from the key to the man, his eyes wide.

The shopkeeper raised an amused eyebrow and handed Thomas the box. "Tuck this into your backpack and keep it hidden until you are safely alone. I'll expect to see you here for the first of your five hours before the week is out. For you, Thomas Wildus, the interesting things in life are only just beginning."

THREE

"HEY, SWEETHEART. How come you're home so late?"

"Hey, Mom. I missed the bus after Kung Fu." Thomas returned her gentle hug.

"Again? Why didn't you call? I could have picked you up on my way home."

"Waiting isn't so bad. And anyway, I wasn't sure you'd be done with work." Thomas felt strange not telling her the whole story, but how could he explain the bookstore without talking about the book? He wasn't about to flat-out lie. Not to his mom. "Sorry I didn't get here in time to make dinner."

Susan Wildus laughed and squeezed him tighter. "Not even thirteen years old and already you're taking care of me. How did I get so lucky?"

Thomas wriggled out of her grip as she started to ruffle his hair. His eyes landed on the pile of papers balanced on the corner table his mom used as a workstation. He felt a familiar swell of disappointment. "Is that all for tonight?"

"Afraid so, kiddo. Due tomorrow," said Susan. "Would you mind popping something in the microwave for us? If I don't keep going, it's going to be morning before they're all graded."

Most professors had TA's—or teaching assistants—to do their grading for them. Susan Wildus refused to let anyone else assess the quality of her students' work. The personal attention was one of the reasons her classes were always full. An unfortunate side effect was that when she wasn't buried in her own research, she was up to her eyeballs in papers and tests. Not ideal.

Thomas checked the freezer. It was almost empty. "Is turkey and mashed potatoes okay? That's pretty much all we have left right now."

"Perfect," his mom called back. Her voice was already distracted.

Thomas peeled the cellophane wrapping and slid the tray into their microwave then set out forks, knives, and napkins. The rustle of papers and the scratch of a pen filtered out of the living room. He sighed and looked in the cupboard for dishes. Empty. Everything was in the sink or on the counter. Thomas turned on the water and grabbed a sponge. By the time he'd scrubbed a few plates and loaded the rest into the dishwasher, the microwave was beeping.

Thomas carried his mom's plate into the living room and set on the desk next to her stack of papers.

"Smells great," said his mom, quickly glancing up. "Thank you."

"You're welcome," said Thomas. "If it's okay, I'll be in my room. Yell up if you need me."

"Mm-hmm. I will," said Susan. "Dream beautiful dreams."

"I'll try. Don't stay up too late."

"I'll try." Susan flashed a smile. "I love you, sweet boy."

"Love you too, Mom." He kissed her on the top of her head, then picked up his meal and headed toward the stairs. He paused in front of the lone photograph on the mantel. Familiar blue eyes stared out at him, clear, twinkling. In the picture, John Wildus looked exactly like he did the night he walked out the door for the last time. Thomas had only been five years old at the time, but the memory was as fresh as if it happened yesterday.

Magic is real, Thomas. No matter what happens, always remember that. He walked out the front door a few seconds later, never to be seen or heard from again. That was seven years ago, and his mom still wouldn't talk about what happened. Thomas didn't remember a funeral. He wasn't even sure there had been one. His dad was simply gone. No longer on this earth, as his mom would say. It was a silly euphemism, but it painted a clear enough picture.

Thomas turned away from the photograph, a cool shiver running up his back. *"Magic is real, Thomas."* The words were as clear as if his dad were once again kneeling in front of him, his blue eyes staring into Thomas's own, smile lines crinkling the edges of his face. His dad was gone, but to Thomas, John Wildus had never seemed closer.

FOUR

IT WAS MIDNIGHT before Thomas finally resigned himself to the fact that sleep wasn't coming. His brain wouldn't turn off. The little wooden box seemed to whisper his name, calling to him from its hiding place under the bed. Thoughts of the afternoon bounced in his skull. Already, he could tell that the rules would be way harder to follow than expected. Not being able to open the box unless he was home alone was rough. Keeping it hidden from his mom and friends was going to be brutal.

He switched on the reading light and reached under his bed. His fingers met wood. A thrill of excitement sped through his veins.

Thomas ran a hand over the lid, letting his fingers slide down toward the metal clasp. Electricity leaped across the space, a tiny arc of bright blue that zapped Thomas's finger. He jerked his hand back instinctively. The bedside light flickered. Dark shadows ran across the ceiling, a flood of sudden movement twisting through the room.

Thomas leaped to his feet, adrenaline pumping through

his veins. A splash of color caught the corner of his eye. He whirled to face it, hands raised in self-defense.

Dirty laundry lay in a pile on the floor in front of his closet, his red tennis shoes tossed lazily on top. Nothing moved. The light was steady, the room empty. The only thing out of the ordinary was his overactive imagination. He could almost hear his mom telling him to pick up the mess.

The breath whooshed out of Thomas's lungs. He flopped onto his bed and lifted the box by the wooden edges. His fingers paused, the edges catching tiny ridges and contours. He lifted the box into the light. It was a slightly darker color than the slats of the top bunk and made of a higher quality wood.

A line of miniature symbols ran around the edges, carved so finely as to be nearly invisible. The shapes weren't quite letters or pictures but something closer to hieroglyphs. Maybe that's what they were. He turned the box, focusing on the lid. A delicate pattern emerged, hardly visible even in the light. There were dozens of shapes and symbols, the etchings almost completely hidden beneath layers of varnish.

The box felt suddenly heavier, the patterns more visible. Without thinking, he reached for the bedside drawer, groping for the key he'd tucked inside. His skin grazed metal and a shock jolted his arm, burning a trail to the top of his head. He jerked his hand out of the drawer.

The key came with it, the metal attached to his fingertip

like a magnet. Thomas stared, eyes wide, as the buzzing slowly subsided. He reached out, hesitantly, and grabbed the white metal with the nervous fingers of his other hand. The key came away without further shocks or jolting. He held it up to the light. The material looked and felt almost ordinary. Almost.

The urge to open the box was overwhelming, but the shopkeeper's rules were fresh in Thomas's mind. *Only when you are completely alone.* With a sigh, Thomas dropped the key back into the drawer and slid the box out of sight behind a stack of comics under the bed. He climbed between the sheets, clicked off the light, and stared at the glowing star stickers under the top bunk. Eventually, fatigue won out and his eyelids fell heavily shut.

FIVE

"THOMAS, HONEY, are you up yet? Thomas?"

Thomas groaned and pulled a pillow over his head.

The knocking on his door grew louder. "Thomas. It's almost time for school. If you don't hurry, you're going to be late again."

Thomas's eyes flew open. "I'm up!"

He was out of bed before the last syllable was out of his mouth. Last time he was late, Mrs. Maybury made him stand in front of homeroom and recite the pledge of allegiance by himself. Others had suffered the same humiliating fate as punishment for their tardiness, and he did *not* want to go there again. Thomas dunked his head under the faucet, globbed on deodorant, ran a brush through his hair, slipped into clean clothes, and flew down the stairs.

"Hi, Mom."

"Good morning, sweetheart." His mom spoke from behind her morning newspaper. They were the only house on the street to still get an actual newspaper delivered. Everyone else had gone digital. "How'd you sleep?"

"Okay, I guess." It was a partial truth. He'd slept fine, but only for about half as long as usual. "How about you?"

"About the same," she answered, still reading the paper. "Have some breakfast."

Thomas glanced at the headlines as he peeled the wrapper on a protein bar. *Explosion Destroys Historic Cavern, At Least Seven Dead.*

Thomas quickly skimmed the text. Armed attackers had taken over a historic natural cavern in Western Canada. The assailants had locked up the tourists and park employees before disappearing into an off-limits tunnel. An explosion closed the entire site, collapsing huge sections of the cavern and injuring dozens of hostages. Two park rangers had disappeared under the collapsed mountainside along with all the assailants. The writer speculated terrorism, but the motive for the attack was under investigation.

Terrorism? In a cave in Canada? The idea struck Thomas as strange. He wanted to read more, but there wasn't time. Maybe later. He chugged his glass of orange juice and hopped up from the table.

"Love you, Mom." Thomas kissed her cheek, grabbed his backpack, and sped toward the front door. "See you tonight."

"Have a great day, sweetie." Her words followed him out the door as his feet pounded down the sidewalk.

Thomas made it to the stop just as the bus pulled up. He climbed the steep black stairs with a sigh of relief and started down the narrow aisle. Without warning, his feet tangled with something large, and he tumbled to the floor, his backpack landing heavily on top of him.

"Chump." Sean Parker and his cluster of oafish friends sniggered cruelly.

Heat flooded Thomas's cheeks. He gritted his teeth and took a breath, fighting the urge to lash out. A hand touched Thomas's shoulder, interrupting his darkening train of thought. Thomas looked up. Peggy Epelson was right in front of him, staring down at him. His blush deepened, but she didn't seem to notice. She took his hand and helped him to his feet. "Are you okay?"

The laughter and embarrassment vanished from Thomas's awareness. All he could see was Peggy. Everything else disappeared. He tried to speak, but his brain refused to send the proper signals. Somehow, he managed to nod.

"Good." Peggy flashed a smile, spun around, and hopped into her seat. Her friends went back to their conversation as if nothing had happened.

Thomas resumed his walk toward the back of the bus, hardly noticing the wad of paper that hit him in the back of the head. He'd trade a little harassment for a moment like that any day. In a heartbeat. He flopped down into one of the last empty seats. It was one of the hump seats, with the wheel well taking half the leg room, but he didn't care. He set down his backpack and looked around.

Across the aisle was a skinny kid in a checkered shirt.

Akhil had transferred at the start of fall term and already had a reputation as one of the smartest kids in school. Unfortunately, intelligence didn't hold much weight with Parker and his dunderheaded friends. There was a spitball in Akhil's tousled hair and an ugly red welt on the back of his neck.

"Hey," said Thomas, flashing a friendly smile.

An answering smile surfaced and retreated in a flash. Akhil turned to stare out the window. A second welt lit up the other side of his neck, wider and angrier than first. Thomas clenched his teeth. Parker! It wasn't right. Nobody deserved to be bullied like that, especially not a new kid. As the bus pulled into traffic, Thomas set himself a new mission. Akhil would have at least one friend to watch his back before the school year got out. It was a done deal.

SIX

THE MORNING SWAM BY IN A BLUR. Thomas tried to focus on his classes, but his thoughts bounced back and forth from Peggy to Parker to the bookshop, inevitably circling back to the wooden box under his bed. He was so distracted that it took all of his lunch break to finish the homework he hadn't gotten to last night.

Mr. Dilstrom assigned so much busy work in history class that he and Enrique hardly had a chance to say two words to each other, much less rematch their doodle war. The inability to avenge his loss prickled at Thomas, but he didn't have time to dwell on it. He wanted the day to end so he could get to the bookshop.

When the last bell finally rang, Thomas grabbed his backpack and sprinted out the front door. He caught the 3:15 city bus headed downtown and managed to finish his English homework before reaching his stop. He stepped off the bus and onto the sidewalk.

A sudden prickling sensation tickled at the back of his

neck. The hairs on his arms stood on end. Someone was watching him.

Thomas looked around, scanning the nearby shops, but didn't see anybody looking at him. He turned toward the bookshop and ran straight into a woman whose head barely reached the top of his chest.

"I'm so sorry," said Thomas, as the woman grabbed his arm to steady herself. "Are you okay?"

The woman gently squeezed Thomas's arm. There was no effort in the gesture, but he found himself suddenly rooted in place, completely unable to move. He stared at the woman. Wisps of obsidian hair with silver-white streaks fell onto thin shoulders draped in a dark cheongsam. Although a visor hid her features, Thomas had a sense that the woman was old, maybe even ancient. He tried to take a step back. His body refused to respond.

A glimmer of light drew Thomas's eyes to the dragon pendant resting against the top of the woman's black silk dress. The dragon was carved from a rich green stone, jade perhaps, with a gold fixture connecting it to the chain. He stared, hypnotized by a sudden feeling of déjà vu. The pendant was eerily familiar, as was the woman herself.

Thomas tried to place them, reaching for a memory that shifted just beyond the edge of his awareness, like the last fragment of a dream that doesn't want to be caught. With a start, he realized that the woman was speaking, her voice so soft it blended with the rush of cars and wind. He looked up, trying to make out the movement of lips behind the visor.

". . . a great treasure," she said, her voice suddenly clear. She squeezed Thomas's arm again, a deep grip that defied the appearance of age and fragility, then let go and stepped past his still-frozen form. She glanced back, her face hidden behind the visor. "We are watching you."

A great treasure? We are watching you? Thomas's reality shifted subtly on its axis. He watched the woman disappear around the corner, his heart pounding in his chest. With an effort, he forced himself to turn around, lifting first one foot and then the other. The bookstore was waiting. Perhaps he would find answers there, with the strange man and his gold-flecked eyes.

The shop came into sight as soon as he turned on 16th. The faded red door was propped open, a broom and dustpan leaning against the outside wall. Thomas stepped inside, hoping to be greeted by the shopkeeper. Instead, he was met by a woman with deep brown skin and a beautiful, ageless face.

"Hello," she said, looking at him with eyes that sparkled even in the dim light. "You must be Thomas. I'm Adelia."

Thomas shook her hand. It was as warm as her smile, and he found himself smiling back, in spite of his still-spinning head. "It's nice to meet you, Adelia."

"It's very nice to meet you, too. I've been expecting you."

Thomas nodded and looked around. Like yesterday, the

shop was completely devoid of customers. "Is he here? The man I met yesterday?"

"Huxley? Do you mean to tell me that my husband gave you one of our most prized possessions without bothering to introduce himself properly?"

"I, I guess so?" stammered Thomas. He hadn't really thought of it like that, but when she said it out loud, it did sound a bit odd. Odd name, too. Huxley.

"How very like him." Adelia laughed, gently, and put a hand on Thomas's shoulder. "I'm sorry to disappoint, but he's out on urgent business this afternoon. You're stuck with me."

Thomas's face fell. "He's not here?"

Adelia shook her head. "I'm afraid not, but he did give me an assignment for you. He said that you're to dust the back wing of the shop, where we keep some of our oldest and most interesting books. Most of the material is mundane, but there are a few unique volumes hidden amongst the others. Huxley thought that section would hold a particular interest for you. Was he right?"

Thomas nodded. It did sound like a good first assignment, but he couldn't fully shake the feeling of disappointment. Adelia looked at him, as if searching through the silence for his thoughts. He had the disconcerting feeling she might actually be able to find them. Her dark eyes caught the overhead lights, revealing flecks of gold reminiscent of those in Huxley's eyes.

"You have questions," said Adelia. "Is there something you'd like to talk about?"

Is this some kind of test? A challenge to see if I'm keeping my side of the bargain? He had lots of questions, but he'd promised Huxley he wouldn't talk about the book with anyone else. No exceptions.

Thomas decided to play it safe. "No, I'm fine. Just a long day at school is all. Is there a special cloth or duster or something like that?"

"Right behind you, on the counter next to the cash register."

There was a microfiber duster exactly where she described, though Thomas could have sworn he hadn't seen it when he walked in. He grabbed the plastic handle, wondering if he was losing his mind or just his attention to detail. "Got it. Thanks."

"You're very welcome," said Adelia. "I'll come get you in a couple of hours. Have fun."

"I will." Thomas meant it. After years of searching for anything resembling a real magic book, the thought that there might be more material as interesting as the book under his bed was exhilarating.

The aisle Adelia had indicated was enormous, filled with thousands of books wrapped in various shades of faded leather. There'd be no time to look at any of them in detail—not if he wanted to get home before his mom—but the section would definitely get future attention. He climbed the sliding ladder and ran the duster over the first few books on the top shelf.

"Perfect. Just like that." Adelia flashed a thumbs up from the other end of the aisle. "Nice and light, just enough to get the dust off without putting pressure on the paper."

"Got it." Thomas gently feathered the tops and spines of the books as he worked his way from one end of the aisle to the other. Titles caught his eye as he went. *Fables of Avalore. Fairies of Western Europe. Ghost Magic of the Bimini Tradition.*

Mixed in with the titles he could read were others written in unfamiliar languages. Some were marked with curious shapes and symbols, and a few didn't have titles or markings at all. Thomas imagined reading them all. It would take years, maybe decades, and that wasn't counting the time it would take to learn all the languages.

The ladder reached the end of the track. Thomas stepped down to the lower rung and started on the books on the second shelf. A small sound rang out from the set of books where he had just dusted, almost too soft to hear. Cha-che-choo.

Was that a sneeze? He listened, duster poised above the next book. Thousands of tiny particles floated in the air, catching the light like so many specks of fairy dust. He waited, head tilted, ear angled toward the top row. The silence of old leather and crisp parchment was broken only by the distant sound of Adelia shuffling through papers.

Thomas went back to work. A soft scuffling sound filtered down, pulling his attention back to the same spot. His eyes flitted up, catching a hint of movement between the heavy books at the end of the row. He stepped up the ladder for a better look, focusing on the shadow in the space between thick volumes. There was nothing but a thin triangle of open shelf between a pair of freshly dusted books.

A subtle illustration on the taller of the books caught his attention. Pixie-like creatures danced across the red border, their forms only slightly more detailed than stick figures. A thick metal clasp wrapped around the binding, holding the book closed at the middle. Thomas reached for the latch at the edge of the clasp, hoping it didn't require a key.

Purple-blue electricity arced out, zapping his fingertip. The shock was no bigger than a jolt of static after walking on carpet, but it surprised Thomas so much he practically fell backward off the ladder. He barely managed to catch himself on the wooden rail. The bookshelves rattled but held strong.

"Is everything okay back there?" Adelia's voice drifted from the other side of the shop.

"Fine," called Thomas, though he clung to the ladder so tightly his knuckles had turned white. "I just slipped a little. No problem."

"Okay, be careful, and let me know if you need help."

"I will," called Thomas. Heart racing, he reached for the top edge of the book and tilted it forward. *Why is it that the interesting things in this place want to shock me?* The metal clasp had a keyhole hidden around the front. He sighed and let the red book tilt back onto the shelf. Maybe another time. For now, there was work to do and an even more intriguing book waiting at home. He rolled sideways.

The ladder slid smoothly along the grooved tracks as his duster swished back and forth. He slid into a rhythm, his worries fading like so many particles of settling dust. Before he knew it, Adelia was tapping on his shoulder.

"It's six o'clock. Time to close up shop." Adelia ran a finger over one of the books and held it up, dust free. "Nice work. If you keep this up, one day people might believe we run an actual bookstore."

SEVEN

"MOM! HEY, MOM, I'M HOME!" Thomas shouted a greeting even though her car wasn't in the driveway, just in case she'd caught a ride share or a colleague had given her a lift. Silence. He pumped his fist, locked the door, and sprinted up the stairs. Exhilaration flooded his brain as his bedroom door slammed shut and he dove across the floor.

Everything else faded into the background as he swept the box out of its hiding place. It felt heavy, as if something larger than a book had crammed itself into the small wooden container. Maybe heavy was the wrong word. Weighty? Dense? The sensation was impossible to properly describe.

Thomas ran his fingers over the intricately carved pattern in the wood. The pseudo-hieroglyphic characters were still nearly invisible, as were the vines and flowers. He reached into the bedside drawer, still staring at the faint pattern in the light wood. His fingers met metal. An electrical jolt buzzed up his arm, strong enough that he almost let go.

"Ow! What the heck?"

Nobody answered. He shrugged his shoulders and inserted the key into the lock, excitement welling in his belly. The key went partway in and then stuck. Thomas rotated the prongs and tried again. The key slid smoothly into the clasp. He gave it a gentle turn and was rewarded with a soft but satisfying click. The lock released, and the lid began to rise, silently lifted by tiny inner springs.

Thomas didn't realize he was holding his breath until he laid eyes on the book and heard the air whoosh out of his lungs. The cover was disappointingly ordinary. Faded leather, worn and grooved, with the faintest outline of an illustration on the front. The picture may have once been clear, but the colors and lines had faded to near invisibility. It looked as if the book had been sitting in the sunshine for decades rather than preserved in a small wooden box.

Thomas ran his fingers over the leather, tracing the delicate lines of a thin vine before gently lifting the cover. The top page rose with it. He caught the edge with his fingertip and lowered it back down. The material was exceptionally thick and firm, with a crisp, almost brittle, feel to it. Not paper. Maybe papyrus or some kind of animal skin. Whatever it was, it felt as if a wrong touch might tear the page right in half. His eyes drifted to the elegant lettering.

The Book of Sorrows

The words were written in a beautifully flowing script, the lines clear and strong, the curves smooth and graceful. Below the text was a small hand-drawn picture. No author. No publisher. No subtitle. Just *The Book of Sorrows* and the little picture.

The picture was exquisite. In the foreground, a man stood, half of his face in view, his left hand reaching out to creatures that were partially hidden by foliage. The creatures were unlike any Thomas recognized, small and furry like lemurs, but with intelligent, humanoid faces. The man's fingers weren't touching anything, as if the garden were just out of reach.

Thomas peered closer and realized that the man wasn't actually in the garden. He was separated from the rest of the scene by an unknowable distance, his face etched with hope, longing, perhaps even a touch of despair. Thomas felt a wordless ache in his chest. He forced his attention away from the man's face and turned the page. The clock was ticking, after all, and he still hadn't gotten to the first chapter.

A star chart illuminated the left side page, a map the right. Both were as detailed and elaborate as the first illustration. The star chart looked at first like an ordinary diagram of the night sky, but the more Thomas looked, the more wrong it felt. There was no Big Dipper. Orion and his belt were nowhere to be seen. In fact, there was nothing on the page that made the sky recognizable.

Thomas might have assumed the differences were a matter of perspective, perhaps a view from south of the equator, except that the map on the adjacent page was every bit as foreign. The lone continent was a surprisingly symmetrical landmass in the center of an immense ocean. Thomas had seen artist's renderings of Pangaea in history class. This didn't look like at all like those drawings. The contours of the land were too smooth, the shape too unfamiliar.

He rotated the book in his hands, watching the shape and contours of the map as they shifted beneath his gaze. As the angle of the book reached a certain point, a squiggle of writing appeared just below the bottom edge of the landmass. The letters were so tiny he had to squint to make them out. *Elandria.*

One single word hidden in plain sight. He turned the book slightly, and the letters disappeared. Weird and weirder. He turned it again and the letters reappeared. *Elandria.* Whatever the trick, he didn't see how it had been done.

Thomas turned to the next page and found the heading for the first chapter. The handwriting was exquisite, with lettering that perfectly matched the inscription on the title page. The lines were smooth and entrancing. Each element on the page flowed seamlessly and beautifully into the next, creating an effect like water rippling through the text. Thomas felt drawn in, pulled almost, as if there were a subtle current sucking him downstream.

For a moment, the words themselves seemed unimportant, irrelevant. Thomas stared at the long, graceful lines with their intricate twirls, twists, and curls. He knew there were fancier words to describe these effects, but couldn't remember what they were, or if he'd ever known them at all. He forced his eyes to the top of the page.

The opening letter was shaped like a serpent with a cobra-like head forming the top line and a long slender body comprising the rest. The tail disappeared into a small rock formation at the mouth of a tiny cave. Something was hiding just inside the cave, but no matter how much he strained, Thomas couldn't make out what that something might be.

He had barely managed to pull his attention away from the picture when he heard the scrape of his mom's car pulling into the driveway. The garage door started rattling up the track. Thomas mentally kicked himself for lingering so long over the drawings and forced himself to tuck the book back into the wooden box.

"Thomas! I'm home!" His mom's voice carried up the stairs. "Thomas, are you here? Thomas. Hellloooo."

Thomas yelled down loudly enough to make sure his voice carried past the closed door. With the book and key safely hidden, he ran downstairs, taking the steps two at a time.

"Hey, Mom." He wrapped her in a hug, just like he always did. "How was your day?"

She returned the gesture with her usual enthusiasm, lifting him up until his toes were halfway off the floor. "Better now, sweet boy. Are you ready for dinner?"

"Always."

She ruffled his hair, and they walked together into the kitchen. As happy as Thomas was to spend time with his mom, his mind couldn't break free from the haunting power of the first sentence. "*This is the story of the first stories,*" it had read, "*the start of wonders, the beginning of sorrows.*"

EIGHT

THOMAS TURNED HIS BIKE up the narrow driveway to Enrique's house a little before nine the next morning. The buzz of activity inside was already at a level that could be heard halfway down the street. He smiled. The constant noise was jarring when he was first getting to know the Rodriguez family but now felt almost as normal as the quiet of his own house. He leaned his bike against the pillar on the front porch and knocked on the door.

"Hey, white boy!" Juan pulled Thomas into a half hug. Enrique's middle brother was as unique in appearance as the rest of the Rodriguez family—he had almond-colored skin, light brown eyes with yellow-green rings around the edges, and wavy black hair. The mix came courtesy of Spanish, Mayan, and European ancestors. "You come over to give me a game, *ese*? The table's set, and this time I ain't takin' it easy on you."

Juan was referring to the chess set on their coffee table, and the fact that Thomas had crushed him in their last meeting. They'd been battling back and forth for almost as long as he and Enrique had been fighting their doodle wars. Of Enrique's five siblings, Juan was Thomas's favorite. He smiled easily, joked often, and always made sure Thomas felt like part of the family. He'd be transferring from the local junior college to Stanford in a few months. Thomas was going to miss having him around.

"Hey, Juan. Not today. I was hoping to grab Enrique and head downtown. Is he up?"

"Yeah, he's up, but remember who said no to the game. I'm going to count that as a win for me."

"No way," said Thomas. "You've got to earn victory."

"Then don't go hiding from me, Tee-Dub. I'm ready, anytime, anywhere." Juan had at least a dozen nicknames for Thomas. Tee-Dub. Tommy Boy. TomTom. White Boy. Guero. The list was constantly shifting and expanding. "Come on in. You remember Marcus and Carlo?"

"Hi, guys. Hey, Maria." Thomas waved at two of Enrique's cousins who were sitting at the dining room table with Enrique's sister. Maria was the second youngest in the family, just a couple of years older than Enrique.

"Sup, Thomas." The boys nodded and lifted their hands.

"Hey, Thomas," said Maria.

"Have you met our Uncle Andre?" asked Juan.

A tall man in a flowing white shirt walked out of the kitchen with a plate in his hand. His skin was Caribbean brown, his shoulders wide and solid.

"I don't think so," said Thomas. "Not yet."

"For reals?" said Juan. "That's crazy. Thomas, this is Uncle Andre. He's cousin Lettie's dad. Uncle Andre, this is Thomas, my other little brother."

"It's great to meet you, Thomas." Uncle Andre's large hand swallowed Thomas's in a firm but gentle grip. His smile widened, brightening the whole room. Thomas smiled back.

"It's great to meet you, too, Mr—?" Thomas had met Lettie at least a few times, but he wasn't sure he'd ever heard her last name. If he had, it had been lost in the noise and distraction of a dozen other conversations. Rodriguez family events were enormous affairs, full of aunts, uncles, cousins, and friends. Keeping track was no easy task.

"Bishop. But you can call me Andre. Or Uncle Andre. Are you a friend of Enrique's?"

Thomas nodded. He and Enrique had been friends since the first day of first grade, when Enrique pummeled a bully for trying to steal Thomas's lunch. They'd been inseparable ever since. "He's my best friend."

"Very nice." Uncle Andre patted Thomas on the back with one hand and held up his plate with the other. "If you'll excuse me, I've got eggs and chorizo calling my name."

"Of course," said Thomas. "It was nice to meet you, Uncle Andre."

"Nice to meet you, too, Thomas."

"Is that my little *guerito*?" Mrs. Rodriguez came rumbling out of the kitchen, flour on her cheek and a smile on her face. She pulled Thomas into a hug with her well-muscled arms. For a relatively small woman, she carried an enormous amount of power. "Good morning, Thomas."

Thomas hugged her back. "Good morning, Mrs. Rodriguez. How are you?"

"Busy. Very, very busy. We've got a bunch of family coming into town later, so I'm making pozole and tamales. You'll come join us for dinner, okay?" She swatted Juan lightly on the back of his head. "Juan, where are your manners? Go get Enrique. We don't just leave our guest standing around."

"Not cool, Ma." Juan made a face and rubbed the back of his head. "Thomas isn't a guest. He's family."

"Get your brother, *mijo*." Mrs. Rodriquez squeezed Thomas's shoulder and bustled back toward the kitchen. "Thomas, come find me if you need anything."

"Enrique!" Juan's voice rose above the din, bringing a momentary quiet to the house. " 'Rique! Get off your lazy butt and come downstairs. Thomas is here!"

"Language, Juanito!" Mrs. Rodriguez yelled from the kitchen. "Don't make me come back out there!"

Juan winked at Thomas and disappeared down a hallway. "See you later, Tee-dub."

Enrique came bounding down the stairs, two at a time. His dad was out of the picture, too, like Thomas's, only still alive. According to Julio, Enrique's oldest brother, Gustavo Rodriguez had volunteered to be in some kind of research experiment the year before Enrique was born. Things were different after he came home. Constant arguing, weird stuff happening around the house, some kind of trouble with the law. He finally took off when Enrique was three and hadn't been back in half a decade.

"Hey, Thomas. What's happening?"

"Not much," said Thomas, sliding sideways to dodge Enrique's jab. "Want to go downtown?"

"What's downtown?"

"Only the coolest bookstore ever," said Thomas. If Huxley and Adelia met Enrique, maybe they'd decide it was okay to bring him in on the secret. "Plus, I thought maybe we could hit up Collectors' Universe. You know, grab some comics and a slushy or something."

"Collectors' would be cool but another bookstore? Seriously?" Enrique had been along for several of Thomas's attempts to find magic books, and the experiences hadn't been pretty. "Anyway, Jameel and Ming are heading down to San Clemente. We should cruise down and join them. It's going to be hot later. Prime beach weather."

As much as he wanted to take Enrique to the bookstore, it was hard to argue with volleyball and a dip in the Pacific. The Surfliner to the station at Pico took about forty-five minutes. It was a trek, but on a hot Saturday, the beach sounded pretty good. He looked at the clock. Unless the schedule had changed, the next train left in about an hour.

"All right. I'll head home and grab my stuff. I'll call if

my mom throws up a block, otherwise, I'll meet you at the station in time for the 10:35."

"Cool. Grab some snacks from your place. Other than what my mom is cooking, there's nothing here but carrots and celery and hummus and stuff like that," said Enrique. "Oh, and grab a couple Gatorades if you've got any. We're out. I'll bring water and sandwiches."

"Deal," said Thomas. "I'll see you in a little bit."

• • •

"Do you have your phone with you? And sunscreen?" Thomas's mom asked as he headed toward the door.

"In my bag." Thomas patted the front pocket to make double sure. Yup. All set. "Love you. See you later."

"Love you, too. Have fun and be careful. Call if you need me to come pick you up."

"I will." Thomas hoisted his beach bag onto his shoulders and climbed onto his bike. Purple-blue jacaranda blossoms lined the street, forming an almost perfect tunnel right in front of their house. Thomas loved the trees, especially this time of year, but they made for a lot of extra work. He'd just swept a few days ago and already the blossoms were piled three-deep on the sidewalk.

A gentle breeze swooshed through the trees as Thomas kicked the bike forward. A shower of bright petals fluttered through the air, falling like confetti to the ground. One landed on his nose, sticking for just a moment before sliding off.

The train station was a relatively short ride from home. They'd lived in the house on Magnolia Court since his mom took a faculty position at Chapman University. He was six at the time and had only a few scattered memories of life before Orange County. Of those, one was so vivid it might as well have happened yesterday. *Magic is real, Thomas. No matter what happens, always remember that.*

The words thundered in Thomas's head as he hung a left on Citrus. Three blocks later, he skidded to a stop in front of the bike rack where Enrique was waiting with printed tickets in hand. The clock at the top of the station tower showed 10:30. The train had already arrived, and passengers were lining up to climb on board.

"What took you so long? The train leaves in like five minutes."

"My bad. It took a couple minutes to convince my mom, and then I got stuck trying to find decent snacks. We're practically tapped out at my place, too." Thomas wiped sweat from his forehead and leaned over to lock up his bike and helmet. "Thanks for picking up my ticket. I owe you."

"No worries. You can get me on the ride back."

Enrique fired a surprise jab as Thomas stood up. On instinct, Thomas shifted his weight and rotated his body. Enrique's fist slid past, barely grazing Thomas's shirt. Thomas turned his hips and let his shoulder thud into the outside part of Enrique's arm. Enrique pinwheeled toward the ticket booth, catching himself on a bright red vending machine.

"Huh," grunted Enrique. "Not bad. Maybe that Kung Fu stuff isn't a total waste of time after all."

Thomas grinned. It was the best he'd ever done at deflecting a surprise attack, and it had happened on pure instinct. His training with Master Sifu was finally starting to pay off. Not bad indeed. "Come on, let's go."

Enrique stuck out his tongue and started toward the train. Thomas turned and felt a sudden shiver run up his spine. The man in the olive overcoat was on the other side of the platform, staring at him through the gap between passenger cars. The man's eyes were hidden by distance and a tangle of dark hair, but Thomas felt them anyway, boring into him like a drill.

"Hey, are you coming or what?" Enrique's voice sounded distant, though he was only a few feet away.

A family bustled past, their beach bags and boogie boards briefly cutting Thomas's line of sight. When the family cleared, the man was gone, the space between cars empty. Thomas turned to Enrique, an unsettled feeling in his gut. "Yeah. On my way."

NINE

"I'M HOME," CALLED THOMAS, stumbling through the front door and plopping his beach bag on the ground. The car was in the driveway but the house was silent. The place felt empty. He looked at the clock. Almost six. After spending the entire afternoon playing volleyball and splashing in the waves, he had optimistically dreamed that dinner would be waiting on the table. "Mom! Where are you?"

Silence. He kicked off his flip-flops and walked toward the kitchen, an unexpected prick of anxiety stabbing at his chest. It wasn't like her to go out on a Saturday night and never without advance warning. His eyes landed on the fridge, where a note dangled from a potato-shaped magnet with his kindergarten photo in the middle.

Dear Thomas,

Sorry I forgot to remind you, but tonight is the annual faculty dinner. There's lasagna and ice cream

*in the freezer. Please clean up after yourself, and
make sure to be in bed before ten. I'll be home late.*

Love,

Mom

The faculty dinner. A smile lit up Thomas's face. Not
only was his mom okay, but the faculty dinner meant
a night home alone. All hints of tiredness vanished. He
started toward his room at a near sprint, skidding to a stop
at the bottom of the stairs, then grabbed the banister and
launched himself up. A hollow growl issued from his stomach as he reached the landing. He paused, and his stomach
growled again, louder than the first time. *Fine. I'll eat first.*

Twenty-two minutes and three dozen lasagna-burned
taste buds later, Thomas finished his dinner and sprinted
upstairs. Excitement flooded his brain as the wooden box
slid into sight. The key delivered the predicted jolt, but this
time, he was ready for it. The buzzing disappeared as he
inserted the key into the lock. The lid lifted, and the faded
leather came into sight.

Thomas's heart skipped a beat. The picture on the cover
was more visible than he remembered, as if someone had
snuck in and traced the outline in faded pencil. The vine
around the edges framed a faint landscape of bulbous trees
and seaweed-like shrubs. He ran his hand over the image. A
soft tingle ran up his spine.

The picture was definitely clearer than it had been. There was no question about that. But how, and why? Maybe the oil on his hands had moisturized the leather and brought the ink to the surface. *Maybe. Or maybe it's something else.* The idea whispered through his thoughts, dangerously close to believable.

With an effort, he shifted his attention and lifted the cover, flipping past the curious illustrations to the start of the first chapter. He didn't waste time admiring the handwriting. His eyes went right to the cobra-shaped "T."

This is the story of the first stories, the start of wonders, the beginning of sorrows. Thinkest thyself worthy of curious instruction? Then read, fortunate seeker, and discover mysteries; true as day, dark as night, passed in secret from the dawn of time. Yea, proceed, following close all that hast been commanded; then, if resideth in thy breast the blessed spark, thy light shall be lit, and the beginning shall begin.

Thomas climbed into the shower, the fragmented remnants of a fitful dream running through his head. Most of the dream had been shadowy, confusing, but the last sequence was strikingly clear. He let the scene run through his mind while the warm water splashed on his face.

• • •

A man and woman standing side by side in a room full of glass display cases, their attention on something just out of sight. An enormous man looms in the background, bowling-ball hands dangling at his sides, staring in the same direction. The perspective shifts until the hidden item is in view. A glow radiates from something that bathes the scene in subtle crimson. The woman speaks, her hushed voice falling from lips as fiery as the crystal. "We will find the others. I have seen it."

• • •

"Thomas, honey! Breakfast is ready!" His mom's voice barely rose above the hum of the overhead fan. "Hurry, so your food doesn't get cold."

"Almost ready!" shouted Thomas. "I'll be down in two minutes."

Three minutes later, he was downstairs, fully dressed and ready to eat. There was a plate of bacon and eggs on the table, waiting next to a tall glass of orange juice.

"Good morning, sweet boy." His mom set down the newspaper and smiled.

"You cooked. Thanks!" Thomas grabbed a strip of thick-cut bacon and took a bite.

"You're very welcome. Sorry for leaving you alone last night. I completely forgot about the faculty dinner. Was everything okay around here?"

"Mmm hmm. How was it?"

"The faculty dinner? Oh, you know. Lots of chit chat, a guest speaker, people making nice with the department heads. The usual. How about you? Anything out of the ordinary?"

"Not really. We didn't get back from the beach until late. Jameel, Ming, Enrique, and I played volleyball all afternoon. I read a little and went to bed." Thomas chewed silently for a minute. He wasn't lying but wasn't thrilled with the sneaky redirect either.

"Very nice. How are Jameel and Ming? They haven't been over in forever."

"They're good. Busy with volleyball and school. They're both playing club this year, plus they're on the school team, so they've got practice or a game practically every day. Jameel's doing student government this year, too. Class Treasurer."

"That's a lot. No wonder I haven't seen them." She took a slow sip of tea. "You know, there was one interesting thing last night. Interesting and a little surprising. Want to hear about it?"

"Duh," said Thomas. "Of course."

"One of your father's old mentors is coming to teach at the University. Professor William Reilly. Bill. They announced it last night. He and I talked for a few minutes this morning, and he's graciously agreed to spend some time tutoring you."

"Tutoring? Really?" Thomas made a face.

"Yes, tutoring," she said. "It's not just for people who can't keep up. Smart people who want to accelerate their learning turn to tutors, too. Yours truly included. Besides, Professor Reilly's field is interdimensional physics. I thought you might find the subject intriguing."

"Interdimensional physics?" Thomas took another nibble of bacon and chewed on the concept. "I'm not sure what that means, but it sounds kind of cool."

"I thought you'd be interested. And Professor Reilly isn't just some guy with a hobby. He's a genuine pioneer in the field. He was the first to postulate the theorem now known as the Quantum Paradigm Paradox. It was that piece of work that led your dad to Berkeley and inspired him to split his research time between genetics and physics."

Thomas's eyes narrowed. He didn't know that his dad had split time between genetics and physics research, and he didn't know that because his mom *never talked about him*. He opened his mouth to let fly a zinger, but his mom continued before he had a chance.

"Professor Reilly was the person who most influenced your father's scientific career. When it comes to unraveling the mysteries of the physical universe, you'd be hard-pressed to find a better guide." She paused, an almost guilty expression on her face. "And, maybe, you know, maybe he'll have an easier time talking about your dad than I do."

Thomas took a breath and swallowed down the swell of resentment. He was being offered the possibility of learning about his dad from someone who also happened to be an expert in something that sounded really interesting, even if he didn't understand exactly what it was. Obviously, he couldn't pass that up. Besides, if this Professor Reilly guy was anything less than amazing, he could always bail out later. There was nothing to lose.

"All right. Sure, fine, I guess. When is this supposed to happen?"

"Great." She ruffled Thomas's hair. "The professor is scheduled to arrive in a couple of weeks. We'll work out the details once he's in town."

TEN

MONDAY CAME FAR TOO QUICKLY, the morning sun chasing away the last remnants of the weekend. The golden orb was just above the horizon, a fiery sphere rising into a clear blue sky. The closest thing to a cloud was the thin vapor trail left by a passing plane. Thomas rolled out of bed and wandered downstairs. A fresh note was stuck to the silver surface of the refrigerator. Thomas ignored the picture of his half-toothless younger self and read the note.

A smile spread across his face. *If mom left early for work, I've got time home alone.* He almost ran upstairs, but instead yanked opened the fridge and splashed milk over the bowl of cereal his mom had left on the table for him. He shoveled in the first bite, his thoughts turning to *The Book of Sorrows*.

The first chapter hadn't been what he was expecting at all. Instead of spells or magical instructions, he'd found himself reading a myth. A story. Literally "the story of the first stories," set in a time before people had the ability to make-believe. The idea had seemed silly at first, but there had been a time before writing, and before that, a time before language. If those things were true, and they were, then someone must have been the first to use their imagination and make things up. According to the book, that someone was a boy named Isham.

In Isham's day, every tribe had someone who memorized the stories of their ancestors and passed them down to future generations—a Keeper of Stories. Isham's father was the Keeper of Stories for the people of Asharia, and his father before him, for a dozen generations. Isham was next in line, but he was different. He was able to think beyond the limits of the physical world, to imagine people that didn't exist, events and adventures that had never happened. He could shape these imaginings into stories that seemed utterly real.

What would that be like? To be the very first to manifest a new ability? What if I could fly or use my eyes like laser beams? Would people freak out, like the villagers did when Isham told his first made-up story? Probably. On the positive, Isham hadn't been killed or exiled—at least not yet—but the chapter had ended there, after the telling of his first story.

Time to find out what happens next. Thomas dumped the rest of his cereal down the drain, sprinted upstairs, and belly-slid toward his bed. With the wooden box in his hands, he grabbed the key, ignored the shock as he grabbed the strange metal, and felt a second jolt as the lid popped open.

Adrenaline shocked through his system as he lifted the book out of the box. The picture was clear now, the lines and images unmistakable. The change was far beyond the level he could reasonably explain with dust or oily fingers.

Thomas tried to rationalize what he was seeing. Special ink? Some kind of chemical activated by changes in heat, light, or humidity? These might be plausible explanations, but his mind couldn't quell the sense of wonder. The picture had changed. There was no doubt about it.

He glanced at the clock. 7:12. Plenty of time to read, shower, and still make it to the bus on time. He opened the book, took a quick look at the perplexing map and star chart, and flipped forward to the start of the second chapter. The graceful script pulled his eyes down the page and through the chapter. He read it twice, then flipped back to the paragraph that sent his pulse spiking.

Then entereth into Asharia a stranger, black-clad and silent. Strange he, this hooded figure; wove of darkness, a shadow amongst the shadows. With glassy visage, the stranger waiteth, seeking he the eye of one man alone; and though Isham weaveth a wondrous tale to which all the people do listen in silence, the eye of the storyteller falleth upon the curious visitor.

When the tale draweth to an end, and the people depart unto their places, Isham then turneth to seek the dark stranger, for in some wise the creature didst call unto him. In shadow, the stranger waiteth, and in shadow, speaketh he unto Isham. In words and voice most curious, the stranger doth speak, whispering soft words of wisdom and power.

Then stretcheth he forth a hand, curious of shape, gloved in cloth that shineth even in the darkness. The eyes of Isham rest upon the misshapen palm, for thereon art three crystals, each a thing of immeasurable beauty.

The first shimmereth softly; clear as winter ice, yet thereupon the colors of earth and sky shine like the lingering rays of a distant sun. Isham coveteth the first crystal, yet his eyes are drawn to the second, a fiery spire of luminous red. Curious symbols adorn the red crystal, without and within, and each gathereth light that doth burn like unto the sacred flame. Desire riseth in the breast of Isham, for the symbols call unto the depths of his mind, whispering of the power whereof the stranger didst speak.

The stranger remaineth still, silent, as Isham looketh upon the third crystal. Darker than the black-gloved hand, it seemeth at first an ordinary stone; but behold! in the depths of the darkness a deeper light. And not one light, but many, and these unfolding like the vastness of stars in infinite space.

Isham reacheth out, for he must possess the crystals, but the gloved hand hath closed. Yea, the stranger doth speak; yet Isham listeneth not unto the instruction of the dark stranger, for his mind burneth with fire and

light, and his heart desireth the crystals above all things.
The gloved hand then opens, and unto himself
receiveth Isham the dark gifts. What expression lighteth
the shrouded face of the curious stranger? Isham
knoweth not, for the creature hath drifted like smoke
into the darkness of night and is gone.

Thomas's hands clenched and unclenched, aching to turn the page and keep reading. Who and what was the dark stranger? He took a breath, his promise to Huxley holding back the rising tide of curiosity. Bracing himself against temptation, Thomas tucked the book into the box. With a longing look at the inexplicably changing cover, he closed the lid and turned the key. It was time to get ready for school.

• • •

The rest of the day blurred past, quickly becoming Tuesday. In history class, Thomas avenged his doodle war loss, dealing Enrique a crushing defeat that nearly ended in disaster. His drawing of Principal Wainwright picking his nose in whitey-tighty underwear made Enrique laugh so hard the entire class came to a screeching halt. Thomas barely managed to hide the picture before Mr. Dilstrom arrived at Enrique's desk. It was a dangerously close call.

At lunchtime, he saw Peggy disappearing into the small auditorium next to the cafeteria. A sign in colorful bubble-letters read *Student Government Meeting, 12:15.* Thomas walked past, peering into the auditorium. Jameel was inside, munching on a sandwich. He flashed a peace sign. Thomas waved back as the door swung shut.

Thomas's thoughts turned incessantly to *The Book of Sorrows*. The possibility of getting home in time to read the next chapter didn't help his concentration in the slightest. He barely made it through the day with his head attached.

When the last bell rang, Thomas rushed straight out to the bus and took a seat in the first row. It was a risky move, but he hadn't seen Parker all day and the rest of the herd was pretty mellow when the moron in chief wasn't around to stir them up.

"Hey, Akhil." Thomas slid over as the wiry kid climbed on, hoping Akhil would join him.

Akhil flashed an uncertain half-smile and shuffled toward the back of the bus. The kid was proving harder to connect with than anticipated. Thomas made a mental note to step up his game and make friends with him. It wasn't right for anyone to be treated like an outcast just because of a couple stupid bullies, much less a new kid. Not right at all.

Peggy Epelson followed a minute later, leading a pair of her girlfriends. She smiled. "Hi, Thomas."

Thomas tried to answer, to smile back, but his face refused to react. Blood rushed to his cheeks. She was past before he could form a syllable, pressed forward by her friends to their customary seats. Thomas kicked himself and pulled out his laptop. Instead of getting his homework done, he stared blankly at the screen, his brain bouncing from Peggy to *The Book of Sorrows* and back again.

Before he knew it, the bus was pulling to a stop a few blocks from his house. He slid the laptop away and sprinted down the street. After unceremoniously dumping his book bag on the coffee table, he detoured through the kitchen to grab a snack. The newspaper on the table was opened to an article titled *Sinner or Saint*. He popped a cracker into his mouth and started reading.

The subject was Arius Strong, a billionaire who had purchased ten thousand acres of Amazon rainforest and multiple historic sites in Canada and the Western United States. The sites were to be set up as ecological preserves, but the acquisitions had been marked by controversy. The collapse of the Canadian cave was the most recent in a series of accidents on or near his new environmental preserves. Several of the incidents had been marked by violence and death.

Strong had declined to be interviewed for the piece, continuing a policy of public anonymity he'd maintained since the beginning of his meteoric rise through the business world. That policy, paired with the recurring accidents, led the author to speculate about the motives of the reclusive industrialist. Was Arius a hero for his environmental work or a villain playing at a game that only he understood?

Thomas's curiosity was piqued, but he was ready to dive into a mystery of his own. He put the newspaper down and hustled upstairs.

ELEVEN

AT FIRST GLANCE, the cover looked almost the same as it had last time. Almost. A creature hid in the bushes, its strangely shaped head hardly more than an outline. Thomas looked closer, wondering how he had missed it before. The creature looked back, one eye peering through the bushes.

Thomas shook his head. *Pictures don't look at people.* Of course not.

He looked away from the eye. Were there other differences, too? A shift in the position of the tree? A rotation in the angle of a vine? He stared, his eyes picking up dozens of tiny, almost invisible differences—but differences shouldn't be possible. Even invisible ink didn't change position. Nothing did. *Except magic.* Thomas quieted the whisper and rotated the book, trying to figure out the trick.

It would have been easy to keep staring, but his mom's timing was a wildcard. She could be home any minute or not for two hours. Thomas flipped forward with a grunt, skipping past the map and star chart to his place at the start of the third chapter.

He read the entire chapter in detail, then started again, skimming past Isham's prolonged withdrawal from village life and obsessive struggle to make the crystals work. All that stuff was a warmup.

And behold! the dark stranger appeareth in a dream, speaking softly of that which must be done; and in the dream light blazeth forth, shewing unto Isham the pattern whereby the power of the curious stones might be awakened.

Isham then riseth, his mind alight with strange fire, and gathereth unto himself the crystals. Hour upon hour his hands shape the pattern he hath seen, a pattern visible to his inner eye alone. At last the red crystal waketh, the symbols thereof burning with furious light, and a second pattern shineth suddenly forth. This, too, Isham traceth.

Then behold! the crystals lock together, red upon black, black upon clear, unmoving and unmovable. A sudden light burneth within the dark crystal, faint at first, growing ever greater in strength and power. The light increaseth, moment upon moment, then shineth forth with the brilliance of seven thousand suns.

The storyteller crieth out and shieldeth his eyes. The light burneth a moment longer, and though the crystals then return to their natural luster, sight returneth not to the eyes of Isham. Yea, scorched to the core are the eyes of the storyteller, never again to glimpse the light and color of this world.

And though his outer sight hath ceased to be, Isham rejoiceth with great joy, and laughter spilleth forth from his tent, for more hast changed than that which can be seen without. Yea, the greater work hath happened within, and the light thereof continueth to increase in measure.

Isham unlocked the power of the crystals but lost his sight. *Why would anyone rejoice about blindness? What could possibly be worth that price?*

Thomas flipped the book shut. He shook his head and put the book away, his mind spinning with questions and possibilities. Power versus eyesight? *No way it could be worth it.*

Could it?

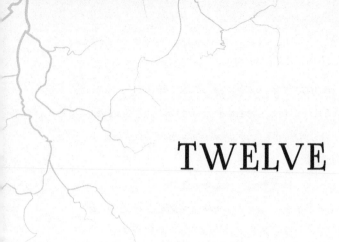

TWELVE

"OWWW." THOMAS'S PRE-CLASS STUPOR was broken by a surprise jab to the shoulder. The punch was solid enough to send a stab of pain dashing to his brain and break up his thoughts about *The Book of Sorrows*. "What was that for?"

"Just saying hi." Enrique's grin was even more mischievous than usual. "What's with the space face? You look like a zombie."

Thomas shrugged. They turned the corner and headed down the hall toward Mr. Dilstrom's classroom. "I don't know. Kind of a weird morning, I guess. What about you? Want to come over after school?"

"Can't. Volleyball tournament. How about tomorrow? The championship game is at 4:30. I could come over right after if we make it, or ride the bus with you if we don't."

"Works for me." Thomas followed Enrique into their classroom. Mr. Dilstrom ignored them and continued writing on the whiteboard. "Doodle war?"

"It's on." Enrique raised an eyebrow and flashed a look of mock ferocity.

Thomas summoned his energy and put on a matching expression. Enrique scrunched up his face and stuck out his tongue. Thomas extended his front teeth over his bottom lip and wrinkled his nose, answering the challenge. Enrique rolled his shoulders and eyebrows in unison, his lips forming a perfect "O." Thomas's game face collapsed, destroyed by an insuppressible smile.

Enrique mouthed "oh yeah!" and did a little dance move in his seat. Thomas grimaced and went to work, furiously sketching as Mr. Dilstrom launched into a painfully boring review of their reading assignment. Slowly, his idea materialized on the page. It was a classic, Enrique's sister Maria giving Sean Parker an atomic wedgie. Parker's slack-jawed expression and wide eyes were almost as perfect as Maria's transformer suit.

Enrique coughed. Thomas glanced sideways, his concentration broken. A big-lipped caricature of Peggy Epelson dressed like Wonder Woman stared back, her lips puckered, and a heart-shaped word bubble floated over her head, *I love you, big boy.*

Thomas felt his cheeks suddenly burning. He chortled, tried to cover it with a cough, and squawked instead.

"Is there something you would like to add to our discussion, Mr. Wildus?" asked Mr. Dilstrom.

"No, sir, Mr. Dilstrom," managed Thomas, his face burning. He forced another cough and tapped himself on the chest. "I'm fine, sir. Just had something catch in my throat."

"Bam!" whispered Enrique. "That's one for me."

Thomas tucked his doodle away, ignoring Enrique's victorious grin. *Next time. Next time he's going down for sure.*

After school Thomas stopped at the bookshop to finish out his commitment of five hours. He had a growing list of questions, but once again Huxley was gone on business. After chatting with Adelia for a few minutes and dusting another row of books, he headed home, hoping to get there in time for a crack at the next chapter.

He made it with time to spare. On his second pass through chapter four, Thomas skimmed past the material describing Isham's painful adjustment to blindness. After two days spent impatiently waiting for a chance to read about Isham's newly acquired powers, he wanted the good stuff—details about what the powers actually were. His eyes settled on the top of the last page, where things finally started to get interesting.

On the eve of the third moon, Isham returneth unto his place by the fire, guided thereto by Elara, the fairest of his wives. A gasp riseth from the people, and children cry out, for none hadst yet seen the white and marbled eyes of the storyteller; and yet the eyes are the least of the changes wrought in Isham.

Yea, the people fall silent, for the very earth trembleth at the presence of Isham, and with force like

unto the heavy drum do the words fall from his lips.
And behold! dust and air, smoke and fire, even they
respond to the sound of Isham's voice.

The storyteller speaketh, and images appear in
the light of the fire, called forth by the words thereof.
Strange characters and curious things take shape, born
of earth and sky, painted with color and light, moving
through flame and shadow as if they didst truly live.
Fear filleth the people, and awe, for in all the world
such wonder hast never been seen.

When the tale hath ended, a shout riseth from the
people, and upon their hands is Isham lifted up; yea,
borne unto his dwelling upon the hands of the people
is Isham, whilst the voices thereof lift him in song.
Isham rejoiceth also, for all he hath spoken liveth still
in the eye of his mind, the places and things therein
shimmering with the light and color of life.

When all have returned unto their places, the
storyteller layeth soft upon his bedcloth, giving thanks
for all he hast seen and all he hath yet to see.

Thomas reread the key sentence twice. *Strange char-*
acters and curious things take shape, born of earth and sky,
painted with color, moving through flame and shadow as if
they didst truly live. Isham's stories had become more than

make-believe. They'd become magic. His words created images, color, and light, like television, only thousands of years before electronics were invented.

The sound of a familiar voice pulled Thomas's attention away from the book. He peered out of his window. His mom was standing next to her car, cell phone in hand and an earpiece in her ear. Her posture was rigid, her expression serious. Thomas hadn't even heard her car pulling into the driveway. He pressed his cheek against the window and listened.

". . . not ready. I'm sorry, it will have to wait." She stared at her phone for a moment, then dropped it in her purse and headed for the front door. Thomas tucked the book away and hustled downstairs. "Understood. We'll talk about it later."

"Hi, Mom." Thomas wrapped her in a customary hug. The book and key were once again tucked away and hidden.

"Hey, sweetie," she replied, squeezing him right back and ruffling his hair. Whatever the phone conversation had been, she'd managed to shake it off. "I don't think we've got much to eat around here. How about we head over to the Circle and find some dinner?"

"Yeah, sure. Of course," said Thomas. She was referring to the enormous tree-lined traffic plaza at the center of downtown Orange. The Circle was a throwback to another era, a literal traffic circle ringed by historic buildings. There was an old Masonic lodge, a variety of shops, restaurants, and a couple of small office towers. "What did you have in mind?"

"How about we hop in the car and see what turns up?"

"Works for me," replied Thomas. A bunch of his favorite restaurants were near the Circle, not to mention Collectors' Universe. "I'm ready whenever you are."

"Oh, I'm ready," she said, squeezing him around the shoulders with one arm and messing his hair with the other. "Come on, slowpoke, let's get out of here already."

"Not my hair. Mom, seriously. Mom!" protested Thomas as he wriggled out of her grip. "Mom!"

"Okay, fine, but I'm definitely going to do it again if we see any girls at the restaurant. A little embarrassment is good for you. Helps you get over the fear of failure. It's very scientific, I promise."

"Mo-omm," said Thomas, as he smoothed his hair.

"Okay, fine," she said, laughing as she walked out the front door. "No embarrassment. Probably."

Thomas smoothed his hair while his mom unplugged their silver Chevy Volt, the backup car she used for driving locally. Their destination was settled the moment they turned onto the Circle and the Green China Palace came into sight. The dumplings had long been famous among the locals, and the sesame chicken was Thomas's absolute favorite. As usual, there was a wait. As far as Thomas was concerned, that was perfect.

"Hey, Mom, can I borrow twenty dollars?" he asked.

She raised an eyebrow. "Comics?"

"Mm-hmm," said Thomas. "Please. I'll only be a couple minutes. I promise."

She fished around in her purse and came up with a pair of tens. "Hurry back. I'm starving, and they won't give us a table until we're both ready to be seated."

"Me too, and I will." Thomas tucked the cash into his pocket and headed for the door. "Thanks, Mom!"

Thomas made the fastest pass through Collectors' Universe that he possibly could, grabbing the newest editions of *Teen Titans* and *Ghost World* without so much as a glance at anything else. The owner, Frank, looked from Thomas to something under his register and back again. Apparently satisfied, he pulled a glossy comic from under a pile of papers and tucked it into the bag with the others.

"A little gift for a loyal customer," said Frank. "Enjoy."

"Thanks!" Thomas smiled widely. He grabbed the bag and sprinted back to the restaurant, making it just in the nick of time.

"Wildus, table for two." The hostess's voice was just barely audible over the chatting and clatter that filled the little restaurant. She held up a pair of menus as Thomas skidded to a stop next to his mom.

"That's us," said Susan. She followed the hostess to a small round table by the window. "We don't need menus, do we? Perfect. We'd like sesame chicken and Mongolian beef for entrees. And can we get started with some egg rolls and two orders of pan-fried dumplings?"

"Of course. The appetizers will be up in just a few minutes."

"Perfect," said Susan. "Thank you."

"You're very welcome." The woman stepped away with a slight bow of her head.

"How's work?" Thomas was genuinely curious but also interested in keeping the attention off himself.

"Not bad. I just finished the proposal for a new project."

"Nice. What is it?"

She told him her idea, which had been inspired by a Harvard philosopher who suggested that dark matter might not exist. The idea had been mostly criticized and ignored, but she wanted to develop new models and theories for the "missing" parts of the universe and see if anything revolutionary turned up.

"Sounds pretty cool," said Thomas. "What are you going to—"

"Egg rolls and two orders of pan-fried dumplings." The waiter set the steaming trays down on their table. "The Mongolian beef, steamed rice, and sesame chicken will be coming out in just a few minutes. Would you like anything else?"

"This looks perfect," replied Susan. "Thank you."

"You're very welcome. It's always nice to see to you here, Professor." The waiter smiled and headed back toward the kitchen.

Between bites, Susan talked more about her idea and the challenges the project would face.

By the time they finished eating, Thomas had run out

of questions about the project. He did, however, have one more request. "Can we get funnel cake?"

"I'm stuffed." She looked skeptically from Thomas to the stack of empty plates on their table. "Are you sure you still have room?"

"For funnel cake? Yeah, of course. Can we mom? Please?"

"Sure, but you're on your own this time. I had two dumplings too many."

"I'll manage," said Thomas. Funnel Cake Kitchen was only a half block away, and he could always find room for funnel cake. Always.

By the time they pulled into the driveway, Thomas was stuffed beyond comfort and more than half asleep. He barely managed to drag himself upstairs to bed, slipping off his shoes before falling heavily onto his pillows. The door to his room creaked open as he started to drift off to sleep.

"My sweet, brilliant boy," whispered Susan, her voice dancing at the edge of Thomas's awareness. "Have I done enough to prepare you?"

"What?" Thomas's eyes fluttered open. "Did you say something?"

"I love you," said his mom. "Sleep well, my sweet boy."

Her words were as distant as yesterday's dreams, disappearing like vapor as Thomas drifted off to sleep.

THIRTEEN

THOMAS READ THE CLOCK through bleary eyes. 6:56. He opened the slats and peered through his window. The driveway was empty, his mom's car already gone. He yawned and burrowed back into the covers. A thought flashed through his mind and suddenly he was wide awake. The wooden box was in his hands so quickly he hardly noticed himself climbing out of bed. He pulled the key out of the drawer and slid it into the lock, the electrical jolt hardly registering above the excitement.

The lid popped open. Thomas's eyes nearly popped out of his head. The creature was peeking out through leaves that were tinted green. Green! Blood pounded into his ears, filling his head with a swift rushing sound.

"What the—?"

Thomas stared, thunderstruck. The other changes were subtle; shifts in the positioning of the vine, faint hints of color in other parts of the picture. He ran his hands over the cover, trying to wrap his head around what he was seeing. Color-changing technology? Maybe such a thing existed, but on an ancient leather book? And on top of the other changes?

Only one word seemed to fit. *Magic.* The thought echoed in the back of his head as he muddled his way through the next chapter. The pages swam and blurred as he grasped for an explanation for the changing cover. Near the end of his third read, his mind snapped into attention.

Then into the mind of Isham cometh a beast, terrible to behold, with the countenance of a lion, yet with body laden with snakelike scales. Unbidden hast the creature entered the mind of Isham, and unbidden do the words of his mouth describe the shape thereof, and behold! the creature appeareth in the sky, woven of smoke and dust.

Yet though the creature liveth not, the people cry out in fear, for the beast increaseth in size until the shadow thereof doth cover them all. Yea, greater than any creature born of land or sea is the beast wrought by the mouth of Isham, monstrous of countenance and dreadful to behold.

Fear riseth also in Isham, for the face of death filleth his thoughts and stirreth his heart; but the words of his mouth wilt not cease. Nay, Isham canst not cease, but rather speaketh of the vengeance wherewith the creature dost strike; and behold! the beast devoureth many whose forms the storyteller didst call forth in the telling of his tale.

And above Asharia, the beast seemeth to become a living thing, clothed in flesh, ready to spring forth from thought to being. The people then flee unto their dwellings, yet the beast entereth not into the village, but departeth into the deepening sky.

Why couldn't Isham stop speaking? Without thinking, Thomas nearly turned the page to the start of the next chapter. Instead, he closed the book and stared at the cover. The undeniable changes stared back, hinting at things he couldn't begin to understand. The red light on his digital clock caught the corner of his eye. 7:49. *What?* His heart jumped into his throat. Eleven minutes to get out the door and to the bus stop. Not good. Not good at all.

He swore at himself as he tucked *The Book of Sorrows* under his bed, pulled on yesterday's jeans, grabbed a fresh t-shirt, and splashed water in his hair. The scramble paid off. Ten minutes later he was climbing onto the bus, backpack in hand and tiny beads of sweat lining his forehead. Thomas slid down the aisle, sidestepping Parker's deliberately flung-out leg and grabbing the last empty seat. A wad of paper thumped him in the cheek as he sat down. He ignored it, along with the chorus of cruel chuckles, and looked around.

Peggy was a few rows up, chatting brightly with her friends. Across the aisle, Akhil sat with his forehead pressed into the window. There was a grass stain on his shoulder and a welt on the back of his neck. Thomas's blood boiled.

"Akhil. Hey, Akhil." If the older boy heard his name being called, he didn't show it. Thomas tried again, slightly louder. Akhil continued to stare out the window.

The bus pulled away from the curb, bouncing as the driver shifted gears. The brakes squeaked as they pulled up in front of the stop sign at the end of the street. As they slowed, Thomas felt a familiar shiver tickle the back of his neck.

He looked around, wondering who was looking at him. The other kids were either absorbed in their own conversations or working on laptops. Nobody on the bus was paying any attention to him at all. He glanced outside. His eyes landed on a beige van idling at the corner ahead. Somebody with unbelievably thick arms and massive shoulders was hunched over the steering wheel, face hidden behind the dark window. The entire van tilted toward the driver's side of the vehicle.

Thomas couldn't see the eyes of the enormous watcher, but he could feel them. The man was watching. A shiver ran down Thomas's scalp and raised goosebumps on his forearms.

The bus jolted forward and turned, a little too crisply, sending Thomas sliding sideways in his seat. He caught his balance and glanced through the window as the van disappeared from sight. It didn't follow, but a lingering uneasiness settled in Thomas's gut. He leaned back in his seat, the attempt to connect with Akhil temporarily forgotten.

. . .

After school, Thomas scrambled down the steps of the city bus, hopped to the sidewalk, and took a hard right. For the second time he plowed into the tiny woman with the dragon pendant. For the second time, she put a steadying hand on Thomas's arm and froze him in place. This time, her visor was tilted upward, revealing a face that was ageless, distinctly Chinese and entirely unsurprised by the apparent coincidence.

Thomas met her dark eyes, and something flashed in his mind, shapeless and powerful, a giant thing moving through his thoughts. She was speaking.

". . . be very careful."

Before he could think or ask questions, she was gone, moving briskly down the sidewalk. He stared after her, not at all certain what to think or how to react. *Careful of what?*

Deeply and inexplicably unsettled, Thomas jogged the last three blocks to the bookstore, hustling past everyone and everything until his thumb was pressing on the old-fashioned latch. He pulled on the door. It rattled, but the handle didn't budge.

He tried again, pulling harder. Nothing. His eyes shifted, settling on a beige envelope taped to the upper left corner of the door. His name was scrawled on the outside in large, thin letters. He pulled the envelope down and tore it open.

Dear Thomas,

Sorry we couldn't be here to meet you today, but Adelia and I had to attend to an urgent matter. By now, you've undoubtedly started reading the book, and perhaps have begun to realize how special it is. Instead of helping here, your assignment is to learn everything you can about the book and its history. We'll meet here next Monday at 4:30 to discuss your findings.

Sincerely yours,

Huxley

Thomas's heart dropped all the way down to his stomach. No Huxley. No Adelia. No answers. Not even a few minutes inside of the shop. He pounded the door hard enough to rattle the handle. He hit it again. A stab of pain ran up his arm. The only answer from inside was silence. He slumped forward, his forehead thumping into the door.

"Oww," grunted Thomas, as much from disappointment as pain.

A musical note cut suddenly through the silence,

hummed in the same tune that called him down 16th street in the first place. A shiver ran up Thomas's spine, spreading across his scalp like a dozen scuttling spiders. Olive caught his eye, a flash of movement just at the edge of his sight.

Thomas spun around, expecting to see the man with the tangled black hair. There was nobody there. The street was empty except for a woman sweeping the sidewalk in front of her shop at the corner of Main.

The musical note hung in the air for a long moment, and then was gone. Cars sped past as if nothing were out of the ordinary. Thomas felt eyes on the back of his head. He whirled around, but again, there was nobody there.

He turned and sped up the street, brushing past a stray pedestrian at the corner and turning onto Main at a near run. Cars and trucks rumbled past. A woman in neon spandex jogged in the bike lane, pushing a pair of yipping Chihuahuas in a modified stroller. Businessmen and women passed by, oblivious to everyone and everything that wasn't work.

Thomas glanced over his shoulder. Sixteenth Street was essentially empty, vacant except for the lone sweeper in front of her shop. There was no sign of the man in the olive overcoat, no hint of humming or music. *Just nerves. That's all. It was nothing but nerves.*

FOURTEEN

THOMAS STEPPED OUT of the Orange Public Library and into the fresh air, his mind spinning with the results of his research. The visit had turned up two history books, a *National Geographic* from the 1970s, and an old fiction book called *The Lost Treasure of Africa* by someone named Adelia Ehrlenthal. Adelia wasn't a particularly common name, and fiction or not, Thomas decided to give the book a shot.

The Internet, on the other hand, had been almost useless. An old Goth band had put out an album titled *The Book of Sorrows*, clogging the search results with videos, pictures, and articles strange enough to make Thomas shudder. After filtering out most of those results, Thomas found exactly one thread that seemed relevant. The summary in the search results had been just enough to warrant a click-through.

Jackman's proposal referenced a scroll of unknown origin, citing the document as evidence of an ancient treasure . . .

The article was about a British nobleman named James Jackman who acquired an ancient scroll and spent his fortune searching for the treasure it described—mystical crystals that would bestow their owner with unimaginable power. According to the article, Jackman died in 1632, penniless and alone, after multiple unsuccessful attempts to find the crystals. Fruitless expeditions by similarly ambitious treasure hunters led the scroll to pick up the nickname "the book of sorrows."

The reference to magical crystals was too intriguing to ignore. If the book and scroll were connected, and it seemed like they must be, then maybe the crystals Jackman searched for were the same ones the dark stranger gave to Isham. Thomas had a printed copy of the article in his now-bulging backpack and emailed himself the link for good measure.

If there were more non-Goth references to *The Book of Sorrows* on the Internet, Thomas didn't find them. The search for more information about Jackman was a little better. It led to the record for a book titled *Los Cristales Magicos: Un Tesoro Escondido*, published in Spain in 1634. The author's name was James Jackman.

Tesoro meant treasure. Thomas remembered that from Spanish class. The translate app on the terminal had brought back the English word for *escondido*. It meant "hidden." *The Magic Crystals: A Hidden Treasure*.

Thomas turned on Willow Street, puzzling through the details of that particular find. The publication date was two years after Jackman's alleged death. Had Jackman lived longer than the first article asserted? Had the book been submitted before his death and published later? Was the book written by a different person with the same name? There were no answers, and no known copies of the book left in existence.

Prolonged honking and a shouted obscenity pulled Thomas's attention back to the present, cutting through the web of thoughts and questions. He glanced over his shoulder. A beige van with a heavily tinted windshield was half a block away, approaching so slowly traffic had to veer around it.

The front of the vehicle slanted toward the massive figure behind the steering wheel. Thomas felt a rush of fear. It was the same van he'd seen on the way to school, he was sure of it, only this time, there was a second person in the passenger seat. Just like the giant, the smaller figure was obscured by the dark windshield. Thomas angled to the far edge of the sidewalk, putting as much distance between himself and the van as possible. It crept closer until it was almost parallel, tracking his speed precisely.

Thomas sped up. The vehicle matched his pace. He glanced sideways. The face in the window was hidden behind heavy tinting and long hair, but he could feel eyes on him. He stopped walking and tightened his grip on the backpack. The van continued at a crawl, the eyes of the passenger never leaving Thomas's face.

"Drive, you freaking moron!" The furious shout was accompanied by a fresh round of honking. A bright red beemer veered around the van, the front passenger leaning out of his window and shouting obscenities. He flipped the bird with one hand and aimed a smartphone at the front of the van with the other.

The van accelerated, leaving Thomas squeezing his backpack so tightly his knuckles were pure white. He stared long after the van disappeared around the corner, profound uneasiness squeezing his chest. The people in the van had been watching him. Both of them. He was sure of it. And he was pretty sure he knew why. They were after *The Book of Sorrows*.

FIFTEEN

"THOMAS? THOMAS, HONEY! DINNER'S HERE."

"I'll be right down!" Thomas set down *The Lost Treasure of Africa* and took the stairs two at a time, hopping down to the landing and sliding into the kitchen on his socks.

"Hey, sweetheart."

"Hey, Mom." Thomas returned her hug and looked at the bag of takeout on the table. The logo was unfamiliar. "What's that?"

"A new place just opened near campus. I thought we'd give it a try." She opened the bag and pulled out a pair of cardboard containers. "These are for you. Tacos. One chicken, one steak, no lettuce, onions or cheese. Guacamole on the side, with homemade chips."

"It smells really good." Thomas's mouth watered. He unwrapped the first taco and chomped in. Carne asada. His taste buds smiled.

"How is it?" she asked.

"Delicious," said Thomas, his mouth still half full. "What's the place called?"

"Pacos Tacos," she said. "It's only a couple blocks from the comic shop. Maybe we'll eat there next time we head to the Circle. How was the library?"

"It was good. Quiet. Full of books. The usual." The library had been good. The creepy van, not so much. He imagined the side door sliding open and a giant jumping out to grab him. The thought sucked some of the flavor from his food.

"And what were you working on over there?"

"Just a little research project," said Thomas. The memory of tires squealing as the van sped away sent a fresh burst of adrenaline pumping through his veins.

"You know I love research. What's the project?"

"A book report, I guess." His mouth was still full, so the words sounded more like "ook port, ah gesh."

"What's that?"

"Sorry. Just a book report." It wasn't the whole story, but it wasn't a lie either. Not exactly.

"Sounds interesting. On what book?"

"Aww, come on, Mom. It's just an assignment." Thomas took another bite to keep himself from squirming. Keeping secrets wasn't his thing, and his mom was tenacious. She was going to keep asking questions until she got satisfactory answers. The only way out was to escape. He forced a cough. "Anyway, would it be all right to take this up and eat in my room? I've got some reading to do."

Susan looked disappointed. "I suppose that would be okay."

"Awesome. Thanks, Mom." Thomas forced a smile and grabbed his food, not waiting for any further discussion. He felt guilty bailing on his mom, but there was no way he'd hold up under any amount of questioning. The safer play was to lay low. He started toward the stairs and froze. *Later.* He smacked himself on the forehead. "Oh, hey, I almost forgot. Enrique's supposed to come over in a little bit. Is that all right?"

"Enrique? Sure, of course. Do you want me to just send him up when he gets here?"

"Yes, please."

"Okay. I love you, sweet boy."

"Love you, too, Mom."

"Come down if you want to hang out a little. I don't have any grading tonight. We could play a quick game of chess or Scrabble if you have time."

"Deal." Any other night, Thomas would have been thrilled to hang out and play a game with his mom, but the events of the day were too fresh for an unintentional inter-rogation. He flashed a thumbs up and started for the stairs.

After two tacos and a long stretch spent staring at the top bunk, Thomas grabbed the bag from Collectors' Universe. *Teen Titans* and *Ghost World* slid onto the bed, with a third comic tucked underneath. Thomas gave a quick tug and the full cover came into view. The image was of a scar-faced man holding a glowing staff over a battlefield littered with warriors. A dark crevasse split the battlefield in half and lightning crackled above the wizard's head.

Zantar, Wizard of Sumeria.

Sumeria? The *National Geographic* article and both the history books he'd picked up at the library had connected *The Book of Sorrows* to ancient Sumeria. According to the Internet article, Sumeria also happened to be the origin of James Jackman's treasure scroll. There were way too many coincidences for any of it to feel coincidental.

"Yo yo!" Enrique's voice accompanied a familiar pattern of knocks on Thomas's bedroom door. "Thomas, you in there?"

Thomas sat up so fast he hit his head on the top bunk. He winced, rubbed the spot, and opened the door. "Hey, 'Rique. I didn't even hear you come in."

"Hey, yourself." Enrique slid a jab at Thomas's shoulder. Thomas barely dodged. "You didn't hear me 'cause I'm superstealth."

"Superstealth? That's not even a thing," said Thomas. "Anyway, I was distracted. An elephant could have climbed the stairs and I wouldn't have noticed."

"Distracted by what?" asked Enrique.

"Tacos, mostly," said Thomas. The whole telling-partial-truths thing was getting easier, but he wasn't sure that was a good development in his life. It would have felt a whole lot better to tell Enrique the whole story. "So, what's up with you?"

"I dunno. Just the usual, I guess." Enrique tried to look nonchalant, but every inch of his expression spoiled the effect.

"What?" Thomas knew he didn't have to ask but couldn't help himself.

"Nothing. Well, a couple things I guess. First, we won the tournament." Enrique paused, his smile stretching his cheeks until it looked like his face might split in half. "And afterward, Celeste kissed me. On the lips."

"Wait, what?" Celeste was the captain of the girls' volleyball team and Enrique's current crush. A kiss of any kind was a big deal. On the lips was completely next level. "What happened?"

"We were playing that team from Placentia. You remember the one with the tall guy who used to shave his head to look like a volleyball? Anyway, it's his team, and we're down 12-7 in the third game. Jameel drills an ace, and then I have an epic stuff right in that tall guy's face. They scored one more point—it was kind of a lucky shot, right on the line, you know—and then we got it back. I take the serve and hold for six straight points and the trophy. It was beautiful."

"Not the volleyball, dingleface. Celeste. What happened with Celeste?"

"Oh, right. That." Enrique pretended to be surprised.

"The girl's team had already finished their last game, so they were watching us. They took third, which is pretty good, but I didn't get to see any of it. Anyway, after we win, everyone is celebrating, giving high fives and hugs and all that, right? Except instead of a high five, Celeste grabs my face and kisses me. Right here, on the lips."

"Just like that?" asked Thomas. *What if Peggy did that? What if she just walked up and kissed me?* His heart raced at the thought. "That's crazy. A championship and then that? That's a solid day."

"Solid? It was a little better than solid. Awesome. Spectacular. Maybe epic. What about you? Anything interesting happen after lunch?"

"My afternoon was nothing like yours," answered Thomas. It was true. Their experiences had been night and day different. He toyed with the idea of telling Enrique about the creepy van, but he didn't know how to go there without also talking about *The Book of Sorrows*. He decided to shift topics. "I guess I did sit next to Peggy in English again. That was cool."

"Did you at least talk to her?"

Thomas shook his head. "Not really. But she said hi and smiled at me a couple times. That's got to count for something, right?"

"Nope. Definitely not." Enrique shook his head. "I know she's cute and smart and all, but why don't you grow a pair and ask her out? She might actually say yes, you know."

"I don't know," said Thomas. Connecting with girls had always come naturally to Enrique, but it wasn't like that for him. Girls made him nervous, and Peggy wasn't just a girl. She was the cutest and most interesting girl in their class. And what if she said no? Or worse, what if she laughed? The idea was more terrifying than the giant and his creepy van. "Maybe next time."

"Fine, you big wuss. Let's see the goods."

"Deal," said Thomas, relieved to change the subject.

Enrique unzipped his backpack and tossed the newest editions of *Guardians of the Galaxy* and *X-Men* onto the bed. Thomas spread his comics out next to them. It was part of a longstanding routine. They'd each buy a couple of their favorite comics, read them, and then swap for a couple hours. That way, they both got double mileage for their comic-book bucks.

Enrique picked up *Ghost World*. "Is this one any good? Last episode was kinda weak."

"Don't know. I haven't read it yet."

"What?" Enrique looked at Thomas as if he was crazy. "Since when do you buy comics and wait two days to read them? I feel like I should call a doctor or something. There's something seriously wrong with you."

Thomas made the most ridiculous face he could manage, scrunching up his eyes, wrinkling his nose, and forcing his lips into a weird shape that made him look buck-toothed. "Whadya mean?"

Enrique laughed. "Chum muncher."

"Takes one to know one." Thomas made a face and picked up the Zantar comic. Enrique flopped into the bean bag chair, still laughing.

Thomas read *Zantar* front to back, then held it up and stared at the cover. A mysterious visitor, a magical gift, an uncomfortable transition into power. Zantar was a wizard rather than a storyteller, but the first part of the storyline was decidedly familiar. If you switched the staff for crystals and Zantar for Isham, it was practically the same start.

"Zantar? What's that?" asked Enrique. "Is it any good?"

"It's kind of weird," said Thomas. "Frank gave it to me, but I've never seen it before. It's about a guy who turns into a wizard and fights a bunch of battles, then kind of just disappears. Not a very satisfying ending, if you ask me."

"Wait a second. Frank? As in the owner of Collectors' Universe? Well, that's gratitude for you! I'm the one who introduced you to the stinking place, and he's never given me a free comic. Not cool, Frank. Not cool at all." Enrique scowled, but there wasn't any real energy behind it. "Whatever. Pfft. Zantar. What kind of name is that anyway? Toss me *Titans*, all right?"

Thomas slid *Teen Titans* across the floor, took a last look at the picture of the gnarled wizard and his magical staff, and picked up *Guardians of the Galaxy*. His head whirled with questions, none of which he knew how to answer.

By the time Enrique loaded his backpack and headed

out the front door, Thomas was completely fried. He hugged his mom, stumbled upstairs, and tumbled into bed. Comics, crystals, kidnappers, and coincidences slid out of his awareness, only to cycle back and dance through his dreams like so many mysterious strangers.

SIXTEEN

THOMAS WATCHED from the kitchen window as his mom unplugged her car and climbed into the driver's seat. The sleek little vehicle backed into the street and pulled away, moving silently beneath the canopy of purple blossoms. Matching petals swirled in her wake, making the street dance with splotches of color as the car whooshed toward the supermarket.

As soon as the car turned onto Bristol Street, Thomas dashed upstairs. Although the joy that normally accompanied the start of a long weekend was diminished by Enrique's absence—the Rodriguez family was camping in the mountains all weekend—there was a silver lining: *The Book of Sorrows.*

Excitement flooded Thomas's body as his fingers wrapped around the box, breaking a chain of monotony that had started Wednesday morning. The second half of the school week had been test-filled and unconscionably dull, almost like the teachers were punishing them for getting a day off. The only highlights had been pulling a laugh out of Enrique during their doodle war and a hurried read of the fourth chapter of *The Book of Sorrows*.

As far as Thomas was concerned, the lack of excitement wasn't so bad. There had been no van sightings, no sign of the man in the olive overcoat, and no run-ins with Sean Parker. All in all, that was a win. He settled into his bean bag chair and reached for the key. The usual shock rippled up his arm, stronger this time than before. Thomas shook out the tingling in his hand and unlocked the clasp.

The breath caught in his throat. Eyes stared at him from *above* the bushes. Not between them. Above them!

And the rest of the picture? It was dotted with splotches of purple, red, orange, and green, the colors faint but unmistakable. He ran his fingertips softly over the confounding image and shivered. There was no plausible explanation for what he was seeing, leaving only implausible explanations he hardly dared consider. He forced himself to lift the cover and turn the page.

The previous chapter had confirmed Isham's deepest fear. The giant lion-monster had come to life for real, destroying a neighboring village and killing a bunch of villagers. Now the people of Asharia had to find a way to destroy the monster, but was that possible? And if they did, would they discover a hidden treasure like the people in Isham's story had?

There was only one way to find out. He opened the book and—

Thump thump.

A knock on the front door interrupted his musings. He looked up, confused. His mom hadn't mentioned any visitors, and Enrique was out of town. Maybe it was a delivery of some kind, a package from Amazon or something. If so, they'd leave it on the porch. He flipped forward to the bookmarked page.

The doorbell rang.

"Hello!" A loud male voice echoed through the house. Thomas peered through his window. A run-down sedan was parked on the sidewalk, the back seat completely covered with boxes and junk. He gritted his teeth and tried to ignore the intrusion. The doorbell rang again, followed by another round of heavy knocks. "Hello! Is anybody in there?"

"Just a second!" yelled Thomas. The annoyance in his voice was clear even to his own ears. *This better not be a salesman.* "I'll be right there!"

He tucked the book away and jogged downstairs. Thomas pulled the front door open, revealing a shaggy-bearded bear of a man with piercing brown eyes partially hidden by heavy eyebrows.

"Thomas? I'm William Reilly. Professor Reilly. Your mum said you'd be expecting me."

The man had a deep booming voice and a slight but noticeable accent. Australian? Maybe British? Wherever he was from, the accent had been thinned out by his time in

America. He wore a wide smile and stood with his right hand extended. Thomas gathered his composure and reached for the large hand.

"Hi. It's, uh, it's nice to meet you, Professor Reilly."

The professor pumped his hand with so much energy that Thomas's entire body wobbled. "And you, Thomas. Let me take a look at you." The professor looked intently at Thomas and laughed. "Ha! You're exactly what I would have expected. A bit of your mum and a great deal more of your dad."

"Uhh, thanks, I guess." Thomas paused, not sure what to say next. "I—I wasn't expecting you for another couple weeks."

"I wasn't expecting to be here for another couple of weeks. As it happened, my apartment opened early and the movers were available." He shrugged in a way that seemed to suggest he was perfectly happy things hadn't gone as planned. "And voila! Here I stand."

"My mom says you teach interdimensional physics. That sounds pretty cool."

"Ha! Only the son of John and Susan Wildus would think so. But yes, it is cool. Far cooler than most people could ever imagine. She says you have a knack for the sciences, but we'll put that to the test, won't we? By the time we're through, you won't know which way is up, down, left, or right. Or better said, you'll know there's no such thing as up, down, left, or right." Professor Reilly laughed again, apparently amused at the expression on Thomas's face. "How old are you?"

"I'll be thirteen in a couple months," said Thomas.

"Almost thirteen, eh?" Reilly studied at him from behind the beard and bushy eyebrows. "You're a bit smaller than I would have expected, being your dad's son and all. Well, I reckon it's the engine that matters, not the accessories. And not to worry. Time and testing will toughen you up."

Thomas was saved from responding by a car pulling into the driveway.

"Bill! You're here sooner than I expected. Welcome!" Susan climbed out of the car, smiling brightly.

"Susan, my girl! How are you?"

They hugged. Thomas looked at his mom sideways. She'd hardly been gone five minutes. Had she found out that the professor was coming?

"I see you've already met Thomas. I hope the two of you have been getting along?"

"We have indeed." Professor Reilly winked at Thomas. "We were just starting to get acquainted."

"Wonderful! Please come in," said Susan. "Thomas, you're going to laugh, but I got halfway to the store and realized I'd left my purse in the kitchen again. We'll have to go out again later and stock up for the weekend."

Thomas laughed. It wasn't the first time she'd done that. "No worries, Mom. If you go later, maybe I'll come with you."

"That would be perfect." She walked into the living room and gestured toward the couch. "Bill, can I offer you something to drink?"

"A short glass of Scotch would be wonderful," said Professor Reilly. "If you have any, that is."

"We do. On the rocks okay? Great. I'll be back in a jiffy." She sped through double doors and into the next room, leaving Thomas alone with the professor.

"Almost thirteen, you said. I suppose that would put you in seventh grade, give or take a year. An interesting age for a young man." Professor Reilly's eyes twinkled and one of his heavy eyebrows lifted knowingly. "Yes, an interesting age indeed. Especially for a Wildus. Tell me, Thomas, has anything unusual happened in your life lately?"

"That's kind of a complicated question, Professor."

"Complicated. Ha!" Professor Reilly slapped Thomas on the back and let out a belly laugh. "I imagine that is quite the understatement, my boy."

"Here you are, Bill." Susan handed over a glass of amber liquid.

"Thank you, dear." Professor Reilly smiled and took a sip. "Ahh. Just what an old man needs to put himself at ease."

"You're very welcome," said Susan. "I thought you were still a few weeks out. Have you managed to move in already?"

"More or less." Professor Reilly took another sip of his

drink and sighed contentedly. "Less, really. It feels like my entire life is in boxes. Between home and the office, I'll be unpacking until the start of summer."

"It was like that when Thomas and I moved, too. I didn't see the bottom of the last box until we'd been here the better part of a year."

Professor Reilly's eyes widened. "That long?"

"I'm sure you'll do much better than we did." Susan ruffled Thomas's hair. "Thomas was only five at the time. Getting things done while he was awake was impossible, and I was exhausted by the time he went to bed. Now he helps around here more than I do."

Professor Reilly nodded appreciatively. "I'd expect nothing less. How about you, Susan? I feel like we barely scratched the surface when we talked by phone. Besides raising this fine young man, what have you been up to lately?"

Thomas listened as his mom and Professor Reilly shared the details of their recent projects, his attention fading in and out as they dug into the technical details of their work. The conversation was full of enough jargon that he only understood some of what they were saying. Then, almost without warning, the conversation shifted to a topic he found intensely interesting.

"John was the one who originally came up with the solution." Professor Reilly had been talking about a research paper that was almost nine years in the making. "His idea was so simple and clever that it took the rest of us five years just to understand what he was getting at. After we finally figured it out, the rest of the project was easy. Remarkable, that man's mind. Truly remarkable."

Thomas sat up straighter. It felt strange to hear about his dad after so many years of silence, but now there was an opening, a chance to ask questions. His cheeks flushed, and his palms went sweaty, but he couldn't let the opportunity slip away. "Hey, uh, how did you meet?" he interrupted. "You and my dad, I mean."

"Ah, now that's a great story." Professor Reilly sat back in his chair and ran a hand through his beard. He smiled and shook his head. "It was up at Stanford, and I was giving a guest lecture for a friend. Afterward, as I was packing up my things, this blue-eyed tornado comes charging to the front of the lecture hall. He had questions. Good, insightful questions, mind you. Not like the normal drivel I usually hear. Well, we get into it so deep that the professor for the next class has to kick us out so she could start her own lecture. It must have been an hour, maybe longer.

"Anyway, your dad and I weren't anywhere near done, so he offered to buy dinner. Ha! If I'd known he wouldn't let me escape until after two in the morning, I'm not sure I'd have agreed, but I did, and thank the great maker for that. Before the night was over, I'd promised to take him on as a postdoc. One of a kind, John Wildus. One of a kind."

The conversation shifted back into other topics, but Thomas wandered through the rest of the afternoon on a cloud. He didn't even argue when his mom picked out healthy snacks at the supermarket. A window had opened into a part of his life he'd almost given up on, and it felt really, really good.

SEVENTEEN

MONDAY ROLLED AROUND SWIFTLY, following a quiet Sunday. Thomas took advantage of the day off by sleeping until almost eleven, when the grumbling of his stomach finally compelled him to get out of bed. Food was forgotten almost as quickly as his brain kicked into gear. Today was a teacher training at school, not a holiday. The thought hit like lightning: *Mom left for work!*

Thomas forced himself to ignore the key shock and disengaged the lock. The cover came into sight and once again the breath caught in his throat. A solitary flower had blossomed into bright, beautiful purple, highlighting a cascade of changes that continued to ripple through the picture. The creature stared out at him, its head now tilted slightly above the increasingly colorful bushes, its eyes curious and intelligent.

Theories flashed through Thomas's head one after another. Special ink? Three-dimensional imaging technology? Multiple copies of *The Book of Sorrows,* each with a slightly different cover? Each theory was discarded as soon as it surfaced, leaving the lone illogical answer whispering in his inner ear. He opened the book and didn't look up again until he'd read the last word. His eyes flitted to the top of the final page.

> *Then turneth the chief of the warriors of Asharia unto his men and commandeth that they remove from the litters the leaves wherewith they art covered. The leaves art removed, and behold! the air shimmereth with the gleam of metal and gemstones. Yea, not only the lion-beast didst Isham speak into being, but the treasure also; and this have the men brought forth from the lair of their fallen foe.*
>
> *The voice of all Asharia then riseth up in triumph, for all the men thereof didst return unharmed, and the treasure borne unto the people is truly vast. The destruction of Kala is forgotten by the people of Asharia, but Isham canst not forget; his thoughts o'erflow with innocent blood, and creatures ever more terrible claw at the corners of his mind. Yea, the world without remaineth dark, but the world within becometh darker still.*

Thomas read the section again and again. Not only had the lion-beast come into existence, but so had the treasure. Isham's words literally had the power to create things, to call them into being from nothing but thin air. People had dreamed and written about such abilities since the beginning of time, but nobody had actually achieved them. *Had they?*

The shrill ring of his flip phone jarred Thomas out of his thoughts. The inbound number was blocked, ruling out his mom and Enrique. He picked up just in time to keep the call from going to voicemail.

"This is Thomas."

A quiet voice whispered into the other side of the receiver.

"I'm sorry," said Thomas. "What was that?"

"You have the book," came the soft reply. The voice sounded muffled, almost disguised. "Is it waking for you?"

The words shocked Thomas's system, sent a flood of adrenaline coursing through his body. "Who is this?"

"You don't deny it," whispered the man. He sounded almost gleeful. "The Sumerian speaks the truth."

"What? Who are you? What are you talking about?"

"Don't play the fool, boy. You are part of the game now. There is no turning back after entering the arena." The tone was harsh but the voice strangely resonant. "Tell the alchemist to stay out of my affairs or his time will be ended. Him, or anyone else who stands in my way."

"Who is this?"

"I'm watching you, Thomas Wildus. We all are."

The line clicked dead. Thomas's heart pounded into his throat, which had tightened so much he could hardly breathe. Fear froze his body. Clear thought became temporarily impossible. The caller didn't just know his name and phone number. He knew about *The Book of Sorrows*, too, and other things Thomas didn't remotely understand.

A sharp rapping on the front door sent a fresh burst of adrenaline surging through Thomas's body. *What if he knows my address? What if he's here right now?* The thought sent a fresh wave of terror through Thomas. Fighting wasn't an option. Not against an unknown enemy. If the person at the door was the same one who had just called, he was going to have to run. He tucked the wooden box into his backpack and tiptoed toward the stairs.

"Thomas? Thomas, my boy, are you there?" The rapping repeated and a deep voice called from the front porch. Professor Reilly.

The air exploded from Thomas's lungs. The relief was so profound that he nearly sank to the floor. "Just a minute, Professor," he shouted, trying to compose himself. "I'll be right down."

Thomas took deep breaths as he walked down the stairs. He paused in front of the door and closed his eyes for a moment.

"Thomas, my boy! How are you?" boomed the Professor, his bushy beard bouncing slightly.

"Hi, Professor Reilly." Thomas smiled thinly, sidestepping the question. "How are you?"

"Splendid, as always." Professor Reilly took a long look

at Thomas. "You look terrible, my boy. Are you feeling all right?"

"I'm okay," Thomas replied. "I, uh, I've just been upstairs reading all morning. I guess I could probably use a little fresh air."

"Ha! Well, there's nothing to stop us from doing our work outside," boomed the professor. "A little sunshine would do me good as well. That's assuming you're ready to dive into the mysteries of life, enlightenment, and the multi-dimensional universe, of course. Are you?"

"Yeah, sure. That sounds good." Thomas hadn't expected to start so quickly, but his appointment with Huxley and Adelia wasn't for a few hours. "I've got to be downtown at four o'clock. That gives us about two hours. Is that enough time?"

"For physics or enlightenment?" The professor looked at Thomas, his expression deadpan.

"Uhhh . . ."

"Ha!" Professor Reilly laughed loudly and clapped Thomas on the back. "If I could offer either in two hours, I'd be the richest man alive. Come on. A couple of hours should be plenty for an introductory session. To the great outdoors, my boy. Lead the way."

Thomas managed a laugh as he led the Professor through the house and down the back steps. Thomas brushed purple petals from the picnic table under the jacaranda tree while the professor pulled out a thick textbook. "What's that?"

"Physics," replied Professor Reilly. "Your mom says you're familiar with a few basic concepts. That's great, but I'd like to start at the beginning and work our way forward. The advanced stuff won't make any sense if you aren't comfortable with the basics, and believe me, my boy, one day you're going to need the advanced stuff."

Thomas started to nod and caught himself. He tilted his head and looked at the professor curiously. "Need it for what?"

The big man answered with a deep laugh. "All in good time, my boy. All in good time."

EIGHTEEN

"THANKS, PROFESSOR REILLY."

"You're very welcome. I'll see you next week, Thomas. Same time, same place. Try to do some reading between now and then. We'll cover more ground that way."

"I will." Thomas watched the professor pull away. The time had flown by. The material was complicated, but the professor made it interesting and accessible. In spite of the terrifying phone call, the session had been genuinely enjoyable.

Thomas gathered everything he'd managed to find about *The Book of Sorrows* and headed toward the bus stop. The afternoon was bright and pleasant, the tree-lined street covered in purple blossoms.

I'm watching you, Thomas Wildus. We all are. The memory of the sinister voice instantly put Thomas on edge. Anger and fear mingled in his gut. He glanced over his shoulder, afraid he might find the creepy van coming at him. Instead, he saw Ms. Teflaw walking her dog on the other side of the street. The little thing yipped and yapped, straining at its leash like it always did. Thomas offered a half-hearted wave, but if his neighbor saw him, she didn't show it. Thomas didn't care. His head was a mess.

I'm watching you. The voice played over and over as he headed downtown. The threatening words were like a song set on a permanent loop in his head, repeating to the sound of the tires and the hum of the engine. It wasn't just the caller messing with Thomas's head. There was the van, too, and the man in the olive overcoat. The old woman with the dragon pendant had said something similar. There were things happening that he didn't understand, loose threads that didn't quite connect.

He stepped into the bookshop, head still spinning, and saw Huxley standing between aisles near the back of the shop. The feeling of relief was palpable. In the back of his head, he'd been afraid Huxley and Adelia would be gone again, or worse, that he'd run into the beige van.

"Thomas! Welcome back," said Huxley, eyes twinkling. The little man rushed forward to greet Thomas with an awkward handshake and lopsided smile. A pair of reading glasses dangled from the front of his apron. "I trust you've had an interesting week?"

Thomas nodded, but Huxley was already moving toward the back of the shop. Interesting was a massive understatement. He followed as Huxley turned right and stopped at a table covered with books, notes, and printed articles.

"Thomas!" said Adelia. Her voice was cheery, her smile

genuine. She slid a large leather-bound book between a pair of similarly ancient-looking texts. "Welcome back."

Thomas tried to smile but his face felt awkward, rubbery. Beads of sweat trickled past his ears and onto his neck. He waved weakly. "Hi, Adelia."

"Are you okay?" Huxley stared at Thomas intently, his gold-flecked eyes curious but unwavering. "You look . . . shaken."

"I, uh . . ." Thomas took a deep breath. His voice quavered. "Honestly, I'm a little freaked out right now."

"Why? Did something happen?" asked Huxley.

"A bunch of things, and then a man called my cell phone and asked about the book. He said he was watching me. Something about an alchemist, too."

Adelia set down her duster and came closer. "Who was it? What did he want?"

Huxley's brow furrowed, and his eyes narrowed. "What happened? Tell us everything."

Thomas glanced at Adelia.

"It's okay," said Huxley. "Adelia is part of this."

Thomas set his backpack on the table and slid into a chair. His body felt limp, exhausted. He told them everything, starting from the day he got the book, describing what happened the first time he opened the box, the old woman and her jade pendant, the beige van, and finally the terrifying phone call just a few hours earlier.

Huxley and Adelia listened intently, only occasionally

interrupting to clarify details. After taking it all in, they stared silently at each other for a long minute.

Huxley finally said, "That is quite a lot, and not all of it can be readily explained."

Adelia nodded. "The experiences you had when touching the key and opening the book are to be expected. Everybody reacts to the material differently, but most people feel something. The woman with the dragon pendant we can explain as well. Her name is Ling Sun, and she is part of our inner circle. We've asked her to keep an eye on you."

"We considered introducing you properly, but at the time, it seemed like a better idea to have her watch over you quietly," said Huxley. "Perhaps that was a mistake. We certainly didn't intend for her to frighten you."

Thomas nodded. He hoped the good news would continue.

"Some of the other items are more concerning," Huxley continued. "Very few know that *The Book of Sorrows* exists, much less where to find a genuine copy. The idea that someone tracked it down so quickly after we gave it to you is almost beyond imagining. As much as I'd like to put your mind at ease, I can't. Not yet. But you have my word that we will give the matter our full attention."

Thomas's stomach and chest tightened. The fear must have shown on his face.

"Don't worry." Adelia smiled gently. "We're not going to let anything happen to you."

"No," echoed Huxley. "We most certainly are not. It may be that these incidents were simply intended to frighten you. To turn you away from your destiny. I hope they didn't succeed?"

"At frightening me? Yeah, actually, that part definitely worked," said Thomas. *Turn away from my destiny? What's that supposed to mean?*

"Fear is a natural response." Adelia put a hand on his arm and squeezed. "I hope you will trust yourself—and us—enough to see this through."

The fear was real, but so was the book. And if the book was real, there was at least a chance at discovering real magic. Thomas let out a sharp breath and nodded.

"Good." Huxley smiled widely, his eyes twinkling in the light. "Now, when did you first notice the cover changing?"

"I don't know. The second time it looked different, but I thought it might be my imagination. The third time it was different for sure. Now I'm not sure what to think."

"It wasn't your imagination," said Huxley. "We'll talk more about what it all means when you've finished reading. In the meantime, let's talk about your research. What have you learned about *The Book of Sorrows*?"

Thomas unzipped his backpack and pulled out two pages of typed notes and a couple of printouts. Huxley set them down and sat in one of the chairs. Thomas's eyes shifted to the material on the table. There were dozens of magazine articles and newspaper clippings, many of them yellow and faded, a couple of opened books, and a Mac laptop opened to a web browser. The article on the screen was the one he'd found about James Jackman. They had everything he'd found and ten times more. His two pages of notes felt suddenly and woefully inadequate.

"Ah! You found the Mubarrack expedition." Huxley was referring to an article Thomas had extracted from one of the magazines. "Excellent work. Most people miss this reference. Mubarrack did find the complete third scroll, but the footnote is incorrect. He and his team weren't lost in a sandstorm."

"Not all his team, anyway," Adelia interjected. "Akbar Mubarrack survived, along with one of his guides. They made it to a nearby village shortly after the storm and sent the discovery to their financier. After that, Mubarrack and the guide were never heard from again. Any guesses about who financed their expedition?"

Thomas thought for a moment and shook his head.

"No? Would you believe me if I said it was James Jackman?"

"The article said Jackman was dead by then, but he wasn't, though, was he? He wrote the book about the crystals. The one in Spanish."

"That's right," said Adelia. "*Los Cristales Magicos.* In England, Jackman was disgraced, but the rumors of his death were exactly that—rumors, many of them fabricated by Jackman himself. He disappeared for a while, then resurfaced in Spain. The book and scrolls were part of his campaign to find new backers for a final expedition."

"How come the scrolls and the book you gave me have the same name?" asked Thomas. It was a question that had tickled at the back of his mind since his trip to the library. "They're not the same, but it seems like maybe they're connected."

"Excellent question," said Huxley. "Are you familiar with the idea of misinformation? The idea that when a person wants to hide the truth, they sprinkle bits of untruth into a story that sounds like it could be real? Add a detail here, tweak a detail there, make it impossible to figure out what's real and what's made up."

"What was the truth?"

Huxley ignored the question and squinted through his glasses. "I must say that I'm impressed, Thomas. This was a very thorough first pass."

"Thanks," said Thomas. "But what about—?"

"Ah! I see that you found the Ehrlenthal book as well," said Huxley. "What did you think?"

"I've only made it about halfway through, but so far sounds a lot like the stuff I found about James Jackman."

"Very good," said Huxley. "Along with *The Book of Sorrows*, that little novel should be at the very top of your reading list."

"But it's fiction," said Thomas. "How important can it possibly be?"

"Fiction is a matter of perspective." Adelia looked away, her eyes suddenly distant.

"Don't worry about true or false for now," said Huxley. "Pay attention to the characters in that book and the lessons they learn. We can discuss the details when we reconvene next Monday."

"Next Monday?" said Thomas, hardly believing his ears. "I have to wait a whole week to come back?"

"The time will pass faster than you can imagine," answered Adelia. "Besides, you have quite a bit of reading to do, and today's conversation has left us with important questions to investigate. A week will give us all time to get done the things that need doing. In the meantime, perhaps you could help by dusting a few books for us. This row is uncommonly messy."

• • •

"Hey, Mom," said Thomas. "What're you doing home so early?"

"I shipped the grant proposal off for review and thought I'd squeeze in some extra time with my boy," she said. "You've got a birthday coming up, and other than a new phone, we haven't talked about a party or presents or anything."

It was true. Thomas's birthday was less than six weeks away, and something as big as a birthday was impossible to forget—even with all the craziness in his life. He'd thought plenty about what he wanted to do.

"I don't want a party this year. Can we do a trip to Magic

Mountain instead? Just a couple people. You, me, Enrique, Jameel, and Ming, maybe one other friend." Maybe Akhil.

"Magic Mountain, huh?" his mom replied, one eyebrow raised a bit higher than the other. "I don't do well with roller coasters, but I'd be happy to take you and your friends for the day. I could drop you off and head over to the outlets for some shopping. I've been meaning to get you new gear for summer anyway."

"Awesome!" shouted Thomas. "Enrique is going to be so fired up. Can I tell him right now?"

"Of course. Dial away." She paused, an almost wistful expression on her face. "Thomas?"

"Yeah?"

"Never mind. It can wait until after your birthday."

NINETEEN

FRAGMENTED DREAMS EVAPORATED as Thomas opened his eyes and looked at the clock. 6:13. Too early to get ready for school and too late to go back to sleep. Besides, his head was already spinning with thoughts and ideas. He stretched and rolled out of bed.

His mom was at the kitchen table with a bowl of yogurt and granola. Thomas put his hands on her shoulders and gave them a gentle squeeze. "Morning, Mom."

"Good morning, sweetheart," she said, squeezing his hand and leaning her head into his chest. "Are you hungry?"

"A little. I'm going to practice my form for a couple minutes. I'll eat after I'm done."

"Sounds like a great way to start the morning. Sifu will be happy to hear that you're keeping up your practice."

Thomas kicked off his shoes and walked to the center of the Ba Gua circle he'd laid out with small stones. He picked a single jacaranda blossom as a point of focus, letting everything around it blur into his peripheral vision. His toes gripped grass as he adjusted his posture. When his body felt right, he took a deep breath and dropped into the Ba Gua low form. After fifteen minutes of work, his muscles were on fire and small beads of sweat trickled down his face. His legs wobbled as he made his way up the back steps.

"Feel better?" asked his mom.

"Much," said Thomas. "And hungrier, too."

"Great. There's a bowl of cereal on the table and milk in the fridge. Do you need anything else before I head out?"

"Nah. I'm okay."

"All right. I love you, bubba. Have a great day." She squeezed his sweaty cheeks and planted a kiss on the top of his head. "Blech. Sweat. Make sure you shower before school. Girls aren't so big on the stinky guys."

Thomas laughed. "Love you, too. See you tonight."

"I should be home around normal time. Call if you need me earlier."

"I will."

It was barely seven, leaving Thomas with plenty of time for a session with *The Book of Sorrows*. He quickly circled the downstairs, making sure all the doors and windows were properly shut, then went upstairs and did the same.

Thomas pulled the box out from under the bed and leaned back into the pile of pillows. He glanced briefly at the cover. The strange creature had tilted its head sideways and was looking at him curiously. A second purple flower had taken bloom among the vines, and other colors had started to fill in the rest of the picture, complementing the multiple shades of green that now enriched the cover. Thomas ran his hand over the leather. Amazing.

The chapter was short and dissatisfying—basically nothing happened other than the villagers enjoying their wealth and Isham refusing to tell more stories—but he read it twice anyway. Disappointed, he turned to the map and star chart at the front of the book. He'd hardly looked at either since the first time he opened it. The star chart still looked wrong, but this time he felt like he could see patterns in the strange configuration. Constellations, shapes. A few stars that were brighter than the others. None of it held any meaning, though. Not to him, anyway.

He looked at the opposing page. The smooth, rounded contours of the lone continent felt as wrong as the star chart, but still, the map seemed to just be a map. He rotated the book this way and that. *Elandria*. The tiny letters appeared and disappeared as his perspective shifted. He still had no idea how the effect was achieved or what Elandria was supposed to mean, but it was interesting.

Thomas looked from the book to the clock. Fifteen minutes until he had to leave, and he still hadn't showered or eaten breakfast. Time to get moving. He locked the book away and stood up, tilting the blinds so he could peek outside and check the weather.

His heart leaped into his throat.

A beige van was parked across the street, half-hidden by the boughs of a nearby tree. The front window was heavily tinted, but it looked like someone was behind the wheel. Someone exceptionally large. Thomas dropped below the line of sight, adrenaline pumping through his body. There was no time to think or react. He had to get to school, but there was no way he was leaving *The Book of Sorrows* behind. Not with the van and giant nearby.

He grabbed his backpack, tucked the box inside, and pulled on a fresh shirt. Stinky or not, it was time to move. He grabbed the key and tucked it in his back pocket, just for good measure.

Thomas crept down the stairs, thankful he'd shut the windows. Somewhere nearby, a dog yipped and barked. He pressed his eye against the peephole on the front door. The lens distorted his view, but the van was still there. He stared, struggling to make out the details. The front seat looked empty now, but it was impossible to be sure. He slipped into the kitchen and tilted the window shade just enough to peek outside.

The backyard looked clear. Thomas stared out through the small window long enough to be sure there wasn't anyone back there. It was possible for someone to be hidden in the side yard, but if he ran, he should be able to get clear anyway. He turned the handle as quietly as he could and let the door swing a tiny bit open. With an adrenaline-fueled burst, he leaped outside, slamming the door and speeding toward the narrow opening in the back fence.

Thomas didn't look back to see if he was being followed,

didn't slow down until the cluster of students was in plain sight in front of him. He slumped down with his back against a tree, gasping for breath. Nobody seemed to notice.

By the time the bus arrived, he'd stopped sweating and his heart rate had dropped to only double its normal pace. A leg whipped out as he passed Sean Parker. He saw it coming and stepped over. Wadded-up pieces of paper whacked him in the head. A chorus of mean-spirited laughter rose and then faded. Thomas didn't give them the benefit of a reaction.

Peggy looked up from her conversation. She smiled and waved, her lower lip clenched gently between her teeth. Thomas blushed and lifted his hand into a feeble wave. Her friends giggled as Thomas moved past.

Once again, Akhil was sitting alone in the hump seat, staring out the window. His hair was tousled, and his eyes downcast. Thomas had a feeling Parker and his crew had made his morning unpleasant as well. On a whim, he sat down next to him. Akhil turned his direction, eyes wide with fear and surprise.

Thomas smiled and extended his hand, hoping to put him at ease. "Hey, I'm Thomas. You're Akhil, right?"

Akhil looked at him, his eyes suspicious. A thin brown hand tentatively reached out in return.

"Yes, I am Akhil. Akhil Nagarajan," he said in a voice barely louder than a whisper. His accent was slight but noticeable. "And you should be careful talking to me. Sean

Parker and his friends may pick on you if they see us sitting together."

"I've been on the receiving end of their picking before," Thomas replied. "I can handle Parker. How about you? Are you all right?"

"I'm okay," Akhil replied, brown eyes averted to the floor. "They're just common bullies. I'm lucky none of them has any real creativity."

"No doubt," said Thomas. "But even an idiot can make life unpleasant."

"They can push me around, but at the end of term, I'll be the one laughing."

"Because you've shown them up academically? I'm not sure that's a message they'd receive."

"A trained monkey could show them up academically." The hint of an amused smile lifted Akhil's lips. "No, I have a much better plan for Sean Parker and his bullying friends."

"You do? What is it?"

Akhil leaned closer and looked around to make sure nobody else was listening. "I'm going to change their grades and add negative comments to their end-of-year report cards. The issue will eventually be sorted out, but the summer will not start on a pleasant note for any of them. Especially not for Sean Parker."

"How—?" Thomas started. The light bulb went off in his head. He let out a soft whistle. "Oh. Oh, I get it. You're a hacker."

It was a statement rather than a question. Other than getting the teachers involved, the only way to do what Akhil had just suggested was to hack into the school grading system. It probably wasn't as tough as breaking into the computer at a bank, but it couldn't be an easy task either.

"Let's just say I'm good with computers," said Akhil. "My dad started teaching me about systems and programming when I was four. He wants me to be the next Satya Nadella."

"Nice!" said Thomas. "Maybe you can teach me some of your tricks one of these days."

"Computer systems are built on logic and math." Akhil offered an almost apologetic smile. "Since you test well in both, learning to break them should be relatively easy for you."

It was a small enough school that information about the students was bound to circulate among staff, but Thomas was surprised to hear that his skill with numbers had been noted by an older student. The confusion must have shown on Thomas's face.

"I read your charts and test scores," whispered Akhil. "I've read everyone's charts and test scores. Yours are impressive."

The statement revealed the extent to which Akhil had penetrated the school's computer defenses. The answer was "all the way." Thomas burst out laughing, taking the timid boy completely off guard.

"I'm sorry, but you have to be one of the coolest and scariest people I've met lately," said Thomas. "That's saying a lot, by the way. It's been an interesting month."

A blush showed behind Akhil's brown skin. His lips turned up at the corners, then stretched farther. The smile on Akhil's face expanded until Thomas thought it might just break in half. He wondered if anyone had ever called Akhil cool before, or scary. Probably not. He laughed again, and this time Akhil joined in.

They talked about math and computers, and how Akhil's dad built technology solutions for military and industrial use. The two were having such a good time that they didn't notice the bigger kids waiting outside as they exited the bus.

Without warning, legs swept out from either side and hands shoved them forward. Thomas fell roughly onto the sidewalk. He rolled to the side and saw exactly who he had expected to see. Sean Parker and his tag-along friends. Thomas climbed to his feet.

"Look what we've got here, boys. A pair of nerd birds." The beefy eighth-grader laughed, and his entourage of feeble-minded followers chuckled in response. Thomas liked to think they followed him out of fear more than respect, but it was possible they actually enjoyed his company. It was a scary thought. "Hey, nerds, my friends forgot their lunch money today. I think you should give them yours."

Akhil reached for the front pouch of his backpack.

Thomas caught his hand and moved between the thin boy and Parker. "Don't."

"You'd better give." Parker reached out to grab the strap of Thomas's backpack.

"I wouldn't do that if I were you." Thomas took a half step back, moving just out of Parker's reach. Akhil hid behind him, trying to make himself look even smaller than normal. Thomas pulled his backpack off and handed it to Akhil. Even on a normal day, he'd refuse to hand his things to Parker. Today wasn't normal. He was carrying *The Book of Sorrows* and had a new friend to protect.

"I'll do what I want, Wildus, and there's nothing you can do to stop me. Hand it over."

"Not today," said Thomas. Anger smoldered in his chest and belly. Parker had gotten away with far too much. It was time to set things right. He locked eyes with the bully, half wanting him to make a move. "And not ever."

"That wasn't a request, idiot. Give my friends your money, or I'll rearrange your face and take it anyway. *Now!*" He raised his voice, but there was the hint of a crack on the final syllable. Thomas could see the splinter of fear working its way into Parker's head. Obviously, the bully hadn't expected any resistance. A circle formed around them, a cluster of kids drawn to the action like magnets.

"No," Thomas replied with a hard grin and harder eyes. This time, he slid his front foot forward and shifted his weight, deliberately invading Parker's space. It was a technique Sifu had taught him, drawn from an art called Xing Yi. "No, I don't think we'll give you or your friends anything."

Parker's face turned from red to purple. He raised his fist as if to strike. Thomas inched forward another fraction, eyes flashing and hands ready to fly. Sifu forbid him to fight except in self-defense or the defense of others. This was both. Thomas watched as the fear that had prickled through the bully a moment earlier drove all the way into his heart. Parker's bluff and bluster collapsed like an empty shopping bag. His clenched fist dropped as quickly as the blood left his face. He looked like he might cry.

"You s-stupid nerds aren't worth it," sputtered Parker. "Besides, I don't want my friends to catch nerditis from touching your stupid money. I've got enough to buy everyone lunch anyway. Come on, guys, let's get out of here."

Some of his friends managed to chuckle at Parker's attempt to save face but most stared wide-eyed at Thomas. Thomas stared back, watching carefully as Parker and his herd turned and walked toward school. The first morning bell rang, shrill and jarring.

Akhil looked at Thomas with mouth agape. "H-how did you do that?"

"It's one thing if he wants to pick on me," said Thomas, "but nobody messes with my friends. Parker's a big, dumb bully, but he made a good choice walking away."

"That was amazing," said Akhil. "Thank you."

"Any time," replied Thomas. "Come on, classes are about to start."

"I'm that way." Akhil pointed in the opposite direction of Thomas's homeroom.

"Oh, right," said Thomas. "Well, thanks for hanging out. I'll catch you later, Akhil."

"See you later." Akhil waved goodbye, a wide and genuine smile on his face.

As Thomas walked toward his class, he noticed Peggy going in the other direction. Her auburn hair reflected the morning light as she walked into school. The thought that she might have seen him stand up to Parker brought a smile to his face.

"TW!" Jameel materialized and draped his arm around Thomas's shoulders. In his deep voice, Thomas's initials sounded like tee-dubya. "What was that about?"

"With Parker?" asked Thomas. "Just the usual. Parker being Parker. No big deal."

"Looked to me like you put that fool in his place. Well played."

"Thanks." Thomas pushed down an unexpected flush of pride, hearing an echo of Sifu's voice in the back of his head, cautioning humility. "What are you up to?"

"The usual," said Jameel. "Volleyball, student government, trying to keep my mom off my back. She's crazier about grades than ever. *How you do now will set the tone for high school, and high school determines where you go to college.*"

You know how it is. It's too bad you couldn't come out for the team. It'd be cool having you out there."

"I know," said Thomas. Volleyball practices had conflicted with Kung Fu for the past two years, and his mom was adamant that he keep up his martial arts training. "It sounds like you guys are doing all right without me."

"We'd be better with you. And it'd be a lot more fun."

"It would for me, for sure." Thomas would genuinely love to be on the team, if he could make the logistics work. "Maybe next year."

"I hope so." Jameel veered left toward Mrs. Majersczak's classroom, the home of AP English. "This is my stop. See you later, TW."

"See you later, Jameel."

• • •

After the second-period bell, Thomas found himself nose to nose with Peggy. Well, almost nose to nose. She was right in front of him. Inches away. Smiling. At him. His heart rate accelerated faster than a rollercoaster.

"Hey, Thomas." Peggy looked shy and cute and wonderful all at the same time.

Thomas tried to answer, but the speech connections in his brain had shorted out. He managed to force his lips to do something, but he couldn't tell quite what. He hoped it resembled a smile. If Peggy noticed his struggle, she kept it to herself.

"So, the Spring Dance is coming up next month, and I'm in charge of the planning committee. I was wondering if you'd like to join me." She blushed and looked down. "The committee, I mean. It should be a lot of fun."

Thomas was floored. She had never asked him to be part of a project before. And a dance, no less. What did that mean?

"Uhhh, ahhh," he stammered, trying to come up with an appropriate response but finding the connections between his brain and lips still lacking in effectiveness. He took a breath and tried again. "Um, sure, yeah," he managed.

"Amazing!" Peggy clasped her hands together and beamed like a ray of sunshine. "I'm hoping to do something special this year. You know, a DJ who's under 100, music people actually want to hear, something other than those awful veggie platters for snacks. We need a theme, decorations, all kinds of stuff. Our first meeting is next Monday at lunchtime. We'll be in the admin room next to the cafeteria. Start thinking of ideas, okay?"

Thomas nodded, not trusting himself to organize a coherent sentence.

"Okay, I've gotta run. See you later, Thomas."

Thomas watched Peggy melt into a sea of students. *Did I seriously agree to join the dance committee?* The idea was madness, and yet it had just happened. But how? *Because Peggy asked.* The memory of her smile was shattered by the shrill ringing of the tardy bell. He sprinted to class and managed to slide into his seat while the teacher was scribbling on the whiteboard.

Peggy Epelson filled his brain for the rest of the day. He didn't even mind when Enrique beat him at their doodle war. The sketch of Principal Wainwright done up like Captain Underpants was worthy of a laugh.

Before he knew it, the last bell had rung. Thomas debated heading straight home, then decided to swing by the library instead. Carrying the book around in his backpack made him nervous, but there was a chance he'd be able to turn up more information before heading home to read the next chapter. Assuming his mom finished work at her normal time, there would be plenty of opportunity to do both.

TWENTY

THE LIBRARY WAS A BUST. Thomas stepped out the front door without a single shred of new or useful information. The afternoon was warm and sunny, with hardly a cloud in the sky. The street, on the other hand, was completely clogged with traffic. He grimaced. The smell of exhaust fumes blended with distant sirens and the closer-by sound of a motorcycle revving its engine at the stoplight.

Sensory overload was putting it lightly. On the positive, it was still early enough to get home and take a crack at *The Book of Sorrows*. He hung a right and headed for the bus stop.

At the corner of Oak and Main, the familiar prickling tickled at the back of his neck. He glanced over his shoulder. The beige van was back, five cars behind and edging closer. The shape of the hulking driver lurked behind the tinted window. Thomas's footsteps and heartrate accelerated in unison. The light changed, and traffic surged forward, rushing toward the next set of bumpers half a block away.

Thomas glanced sideways. The van was next to him,

the side door sliding open. A slight figure crouched inside, her features hidden by shapeless clothes and long black hair. Light illuminated her right hand, a crackling reddish-white that flickered in the shadows. A taser?

Adrenaline flooded Thomas's body. He started to run. The engine roared and the van shot forward, veering into the bike lane just a few feet away. Thomas cut right, dodging under the awning of a bakery. A sudden flash of purple lit up the air. Tires squealed and the van sped around the corner and out of sight.

Thomas stopped running and put a hand on the brick wall to steady himself. The breath whooshed from his lungs. *Did that just happen? There's no way that just happened.*

The flash of purple triggered something in the back of his mind, but more urgent thoughts thundered through his brain. *I almost just got kidnapped. Holy shipwreck! I almost just got kidnapped!*

He looked around, his breath ragged and legs like jelly. The people walking on the street kept going like nothing had happened. The guests sitting in front of the bakery either had their faces buried in cell phones or were looking at menus. Nobody seemed to have noticed or cared.

A scrap of olive caught at the corner of his eye. He looked down the street. Half-hidden by a lamppost, the overcoat man stared after the van, his scruffy face obscured by concrete and locks of tangled black hair. The man turned and swept into an adjacent alley without so much as a sideways glance, the tail of his jacket trailing behind him like a cape.

Thomas stood frozen, unsure which way to go or what to do. The guy in the overcoat was that way. The giant and taser-lady could be just about anywhere else. He slumped to the sidewalk, his back pressed into the warm brick wall, and reached into his backpack. A sigh of relief escaped as his fingers closed on the crinkled twenty tucked in the zipper pocket. The stash would cover a cab ride home, which was good, because there was no way he was walking anywhere. He pulled out his phone and dialed, wishing for the thousandth time he had a smartphone and ride-sharing app.

• • •

The taxi took almost half an hour to arrive, but eventually it came and got him home. Thomas gave the driver the whole twenty, even though the fare was less than fifteen bucks, and felt like it was totally worth it. The house was still empty, so he ran upstairs, pulled the box out of his backpack, and dropped into his beanbag chair.

The cover had continued to change, but the differences weren't dramatic. Knowing his mom could be home any minute, he flipped to the start of the next chapter. It picked up with Isham still unwilling to tell stories and hounded by people who would never understand the impossibility of the choice he faced. The elders tried to make him take his place by the fire, but he refused every request until his most beloved wife became deathly ill and asked to hear one last story. Isham couldn't refuse.

The people then carry Elaria unto the fire and set her beside Isham, that she may lay her head upon his breast. The very body of Elaria burneth with fever, and the eyes thereof grow dim. With heart exceeding heavy, Isham holdeth her close and beginneth to speak, that his wife may know wonder once more and mayhap be healed.

Long into the night continueth Isham, and long into the night do the words of his mouth take shape in the night sky. The people behold in wonder as all that he speaketh doth appear in the sky, for the magic of his words hast not failed.

But alas! Elaria passeth over the threshold of darkness unto death. Grief and fury filleth the heart of the storyteller, at himself above all, for he didst not possess the power to stay the steady hand of death.

A terrible thing then entereth into his mind, a beast greater and more terrible than the destroyer of Kala. Unbidden, the words of his mouth give unto the creature form and shape until it filleth the sky, blacker than night, greater than the dwelling places of the chief men; with scorpion tail the beast striketh the hero of

Isham's tale. The man falleth, and from the people of Asharia ariseth a groan.

Yet the tale endeth not, for in the eye of Isham's mind, the beast emergeth, like unto life, and yet the words of his mouth wilt not cease. Fear o'ercomes fury in the heart of Isham, and the people cry out, for behold! earth and air and ether gather together, and in the night sky, the creature taketh shape and form most real.

Yea, in flesh the creature descendeth upon Asharia, and upon the people thereof. The living flee, whilst the sounds of dying follow Isham unto the tent whereto he beareth the lifeless Elaria.

Thomas and his mom were wrapping up a quiet but pleasant dinner of microwave meat loaf when the doorbell rang.

"That's Enrique!" Thomas had weighed the possibility of breaking his promise to Huxley against his willingness to continue on the adventure without a friend in his corner. The choice wasn't easy, but he'd made up his mind and called while waiting for the cab. Enrique was in. "Love you, Mom. See you later."

Thomas dashed down the hallway and used his sock-covered feet to slide the last ten feet to the front door.

" 'Rique! What's happening?" Thomas said as the two bumped knuckles.

"Same old," Enrique answered, walking in. "What's happening with you?"

"Tell you in a minute," Thomas replied.

"Hi, Mrs. Wildus," called Enrique, kicking his shoes off by the front door. "Thanks for having me over."

"You're very welcome, Enrique. Help yourself to anything you can find in the kitchen if you need a snack," she replied.

"We've got fudgecicles and ice cream," Thomas offered.

"Nah, I'm cool. Just finished eating at my place a couple minutes ago," Enrique replied. "Maybe later."

"We'll be upstairs, Mom. Yell up if you need me," Thomas called out.

"Mmm-kay. Will do," came her reply as the boys barreled up the stairs and into his room.

"All right," said Enrique. "What's such a big deal you've got to call an emergency meeting of the Jedi council? Did you finally talk to Peggy or something?"

"Well, yeah, kind of. She asked me to be on the dance committee. But that's not it. I've got something way bigger."

"Wait, what?" Enrique said incredulously. "Peggy asked you to be on the dance committee, and that's not your big news?"

"Right," replied Thomas. "But you've got to promise that what we talk about stays in this room. Swear it?"

"Yeah, of course," said Enrique. "When have I ever blabbed one of your secrets?"

"I know, I know. You never have. But this is serious. Just

you and me, no matter what. Swear it." Thomas stared at Enrique, his eyes unwavering.

"All right, all right. Take it easy," Enrique replied. "I'll double dog swear if that makes you feel any better."

"It does." Thomas smiled. "A lot better, actually."

"Okay, great. I double dog swear. Now, what's this big secret?"

Thomas started with his discovery of the bookstore.

Enrique rolled his eyes. "Seriously? Man, you've got to get yourself a real life."

Enrique's tone changed quite a bit when he heard about the kidnapper van with the giant and taser-lady. "Are you serious?"

"Dead serious," said Thomas. "It was in front of my house this morning. I'm ninety-nine percent sure it was the same one that chased me yesterday. No joke."

"That's messed up. How come you haven't gone to the cops?"

"With what? I don't have a name or license plate or anything. I don't have any idea who they are," said Thomas. "But I know what they want."

"What?"

"This." Thomas pulled the wooden box out from under the bed and handed it to Enrique. The key was already in the clasp. "When I got this, the cover was plain leather with just the outline of a picture on the front. Now check it out."

"Ow! What the heck?"

"Oh, right. Sorry. The shock will go away in a second. Go ahead and open it."

Enrique pulled his sleeve down over his fingers and turned the key without touching the metal. The lid popped open.

How come I didn't think of that? "None of this was here at first."

"Maybe they used invisible ink or some kind of crazy color-changing chemicals or something."

"I thought of that, too, but Huxley and Adelia said that's not it. Besides, have you ever heard of chemicals or ink that can make the entire picture change?" said Thomas. "I mean, check this out. When I first got this, the vine was over here. These flowers didn't exist. This weird-looking thing was hiding behind the bushes."

Thomas's eyes lingered on the creature whose face had previously hidden in the bushes. The creature stared back at him with its mouth partially opened and eyes that no longer seemed shy or curious. He couldn't help but notice that the thing had surprisingly sharp teeth.

"And you're sure no one swapped out the book? You know, snuck in here and traded out the old one for this?"

"I thought of that, but no one knows I have it except the people who gave it to me and the creeps who want to take it away. Besides, it's changed just since morning. If someone wanted to swap it out, they'd have had to do it while I had the backpack with me. Not likely."

Enrique whistled. "What are you going to do?"

"I don't know, and there's no way I can handle all this on my own. I need a partner," Thomas said. "A wing man. So how about it? Are you in?"

"Of course I'm in," said Enrique. "You think I'd let you take on an adventure like this without me? No chance."

"I hoped you'd say that." Thomas's relief was tangible and profound.

"So, what's next?"

"That's what we've got to figure out. I figure a thing like this is going to take brains and muscle. I've got the brains. I thought you could help me find some muscle. Any ideas?"

Thomas stuck out his tongue as Enrique's fist shot out in search of his shoulder. This time, Thomas anticipated the attack. He caught Enrique's arm and sent his friend tumbling into the beanbag chair.

Enrique sprawled out on the chair, a big smile on his face. "All right, Brainiac. What's the plan?"

"I have no idea," replied Thomas. "I'm sure we'll think of something."

They talked for a long time before Thomas's mom called up the stairs, letting them know it was time to wrap things up and get to bed. Thomas walked Enrique to the door.

"See you tomorrow." Enrique slapped Thomas a high five and fastened his helmet. "Goodnight, Mrs. Wildus!"

"Goodnight, Enrique. Are you sure we can't give you a ride home?"

"Positive, but thanks for the offer," said Enrique. "Oh, hey, Mrs. Wildus. Is it okay if Thomas comes over on Saturday? It's Maria's quinceañera, and my mom says I can invite a couple of friends."

"Of course," said Susan. "Your sister is turning fifteen? Already? That's hard to believe."

Enrique grimaced. "Mm-hmm. And all her friends are coming over. *All* of them."

"Good luck with that," said Susan. "Ride safe. It's dark out there."

"I will," said Enrique. "Thomas, no flaking out on Saturday. Seriously, I'm not sure I'd survive on my own."

"I'll be there. See you tomorrow." Thomas waved as Enrique glided toward the street. He felt guilty about breaking his promise to Huxley, but it was worth it to have Enrique on board. Did it matter that their best idea so far was to build an Iron Man suit? Not in the slightest. He wasn't alone anymore. Sleep came easier than it had in days.

TWENTY-ONE

THOMAS TURNED ONTO ACORN STREET and pedaled toward the Rodriguez house. Both sides of the street were packed with cars, from new and shiny to rusted out and nearly falling apart. Latin pop filtered out of the backyard, giving the whole block a party vibe. Thomas rolled up the sidewalk, climbed off his bike, and flipped down the kickstand. Voices filled the air, coming from inside and out, blending with a variety of rich aromas.

Above the open front door hung a giant pink banner. *Feliz Cumpleaños, Maria!!!* The letters were huge and glittery gold. An SUV with dark-tinted windows pulled up alongside the curb. The doors opened, and a pair of familiar faces materialized.

"Tee Dubya!" hollered Jameel.

"Thomas," said Meng. "Good timing."

"Hey, guys. What's happening?"

The front window rolled down. Jameel's mom materialized, a giant smile on her face. "Thomas! Come say hello."

"Hi, Mrs. Johnson," said Thomas. "It's been a long time. How are you?"

"I'm doing great, sugar. How are you?"

"I'm doing great," said Thomas. "Just—"

"Bye, Mom," interrupted Jameel. He waved impatiently for her to go. "See you later."

"Oh, come on now, Jameel. You're not embarrassed by your momma, are you? Maybe I should take you inside, make sure you've been properly introduced to all of Maria's friends?" She made a motion to open her door and climb out. "Just hold on a sec. I'll be right there."

Jameel's eyes widened in horror. "No, Mom. Seriously, no. Mom!"

Mrs. Johnson leaned back and laughed. "I'm just teasing, baby. You boys behave for Mrs. Rodriguez, okay? And be nice to Maria. Jameel, Meng, I'll be back to pick you up at 7:30."

"Nice to see you, Mrs. Johnson." Thomas waved goodbye. Mrs. Johnson had been his second-grade teacher and was still one of his favorite people on the planet. Her sense of humor was as legendary as her ability to make her students feel special and make learning a game everyone could win. *Progress, not perfection*, was her motto, and she celebrated every step forward.

"Thanks for the ride, Mrs. Johnson," called Meng.

"Yeah, thanks, Mom." Jameel looked relieved as the car

rolled down the street. "That was too close. I thought she was actually going to come in."

"She'd have been fine," said Thomas. "Everyone loves your mom."

"Unh-uh," said Jameel. "No way. She's been finding all kinds of ways to embarrass me lately. She thinks it's good for me or something. But it's not. At all."

"It's good for me, I'll tell you that much," laughed Meng. "You should have seen her at the mall the other day. Went right up to a group of the eighth-grade girls and told Carla Flores that Jameel has a crush on her. I didn't know brothers could blush like that."

"Man, shut up," said Jameel. "That was *not* funny."

"Oh, it was funny," said Meng. "Very, very funny."

Thomas laughed. "Come on, let's head in. I'm starving."

"Ditto," said Jameel. He slapped Thomas a high five. "Do you smell that? Enrique said his mom was making twenty pounds of carnitas and old-school tacos al pastor. Not the pan-cooked junk. The kind they carve right off the spit."

Thomas's mouth watered. "Ooh, I love that stuff."

"What's not to love?" asked Jameel. "Seasoned pork seared to perfection. It's magic."

The house was full to overflowing. Maria and her girl-friends had overtaken the living room. A handful of boys from her school lounged on the couch, trying to act cool and disinterested, but looking up every few seconds as the girls laughed and danced. Two of Enrique's older cousins slid past with plates loaded with meat and tortillas. Thomas waved as they walked past.

"Enrique!" shouted Meng.

"'Rique," said Jameel. "What's happening?"

"Hey, guys." Enrique came down the stairs looking beleaguered and relieved all at the same time. "Man, I'm glad you're here. It's been estrogen central all afternoon. My mom was on fire. *Don't eat the cookies. Don't touch the meat. Save the guacamole until everyone gets here.* And don't even get me started on Maria. She was wound so tight I just about—ah, forget it. Come on, there's food and drinks in the backyard."

Thomas followed the group into the backyard. The place was full of Enrique's aunts and uncles and cousins. The next-door neighbors were hanging out, their cups full of colorful drinks. Margaritas, probably. Younger kids and older adults danced under a canopy draped with twinkle lights. Others gathered around the fold-up tables, eating and laughing. The music put everything into rhythm, made the gathering feel like a real party.

"Hey, Uncle Timo," said Thomas. Enrique's uncle shook Thomas's hand, his thick mustache twitching at the ends. "Hi, Aunt Fabi. How are you?"

"*Hola,* Tomasito," said Uncle Timo. "*Mucho gusto en verte.*"

"*Igualmente*," said Thomas, wincing at his own awkward accent. "How are you?"

"Doing great," said Timo. "Grab yourselves some food."

"Come on," said Enrique, ushering them toward the food. "You guys get food. I'm going to snag that last table before Maria and her friends come out here."

"You don't have to tell me twice," said Jameel. "Look at that. It's beautiful."

Thomas had to agree. The al pastor rotated on a vertical spit with a flame running up the side, crisping the outer layer of the meat and putting off a smell that literally made his mouth water. He grabbed tortillas, smothered them with guacamole, and held out his plate. Enrique's cousin Tommy ran a long knife down the spitted meat, sending a shower of seasoned happiness onto the tortillas. "Thanks, Tommy."

"Aren't you going to have some?" asked Jameel.

"Me? Nah. I'm going to stick with carnitas," said Meng. "That stuff kind of freaks me out."

"What are you talking about?" asked Jameel. "Pork is pork. Other than tasting less good, how is carnitas different from al pastor?"

"I don't know," said Meng. "That thing just looks weird, you know? Like it's still part of an animal or something."

"It is part of an animal," said Jameel. "A pig. So is that."

"Whatever." Meng scooped a mound of carnitas onto his plate. "You eat your pig, I'll eat mine."

"Oink, oink, ooweeee." Jameel's pig sounds were

surprisingly accurate, drawing looks from a number of the nearby adults.

Thomas laughed and headed to the back table. "You're up," he told Enrique.

Enrique hopped out of his seat. "Make sure Maria and her friends don't steal the rest of the table. I can't handle one more minute. All morning, I listened to them talk about this boy, and that boy, and this class, and that teacher. It's too much."

"What'd you say?" said Jameel. "Make sure all the cute high school girls sit at our table? Got it."

"Yup, that's what he said." Meng looked at the door and made a come-over gesture. "Over here! There's seats available!"

Enrique pulled Meng's hand down, his eyes wide with fear. Thomas looked toward the house. Maria and her friends were nowhere in sight.

"Not cool," said Enrique. "Not cool at all."

Meng raised his eyebrows and grinned. "Sucka."

Thomas and Jameel laughed. Enrique ran to the serving table at a jog, looking at the house every few steps. By the time he came back, Thomas had already eaten two tacos and was starting on a third. Jameel's plate was empty, his mouth completely full. Meng was picking daintily at his plate with a plastic fork, eating one nibble at a time.

"You guys wanna head upstairs and play some NBA360 after this?" asked Enrique.

"Nah," said Jameel. "How about we go to the park and play for real? It's Saturday. There'll be some ballers out there for sure."

"Works for me," said Meng. "You guys in?"

Thomas nodded. "Yeah, sure. Of course."

"Not yet, you don't." Firm hands gripped Thomas's shoulders. "The *guerito* owes me a game. Come on Tee Dub. The board is set. Are you ready?"

"I'm always ready," said Thomas. "Are you guys okay waiting a couple minutes?"

"Don't worry about them," said Juan. "Worry about me and my mad chess skills. These chumps can watch and learn."

Thomas followed Juan to the porch, where the chess table was set up between a pair of wooden deck chairs. They played with a thirty-second timer, snapping moves back and forth with speed and intensity. The first game ended in a draw, with Thomas barely escaping an early checkmate. Juan took the second game with a clever knight trade. Thomas squeaked out a win in the third, pinning Juan's king with a rook and his queen.

"And that's mate," said Meng. "Time for some hoops. Let's go."

"No, no, no. One more," said Juan. "For the tie-breaker. Come on."

"No way," said Enrique. "I'm not watching any more chess. Let's head to the park. Juan, you want to come?

That'd give us five, enough to jump into the pickups with our own crew."

"Yeah, sure," said Juan. "Let me put on my kicks."

. . .

Thomas didn't say his goodbyes until the sun was hovering just over the edge of the horizon. The party was still in full swing, but after three hours of basketball and another half-dozen tacos, he was tired, happy, and ready to get home. Besides, his mom had a rule about riding his bike on the streets after dark. Don't do it. It wasn't a terrible rule. Drivers with cell phones were dangerous enough in the daytime.

Thomas cruised down the street, full and happy. He passed the supermarket and cut through an office complex. Suddenly, there was a flash of olive, a glimpse of dark hair, a sense of strange movement. The world blurred, came back into focus. His bike clattered to the ground as strong hands gripped his shirt and yanked him into the shadowed space between buildings.

He tried to resist, to fight back, but his arms and legs were noodles, powerless to react. His body thudded into the wall. Wild green eyes stared between strands of tangled black hair. Eyes lit with a spark that burned even in the dim light. Thomas tried to look away. He couldn't. Time froze. *You broke the rules!*

The voice was a whisper in Thomas's mind, disconnected from the man's unmoving lips.

Thomas tried to answer but panic sealed his mouth

shut. He struggled, but the hands pressing into his chest were strong, unrelenting, the wild eyes blazing from a face streaked with dirt and grime. Thomas heard a soft clicking sound. A stream of memories flashed through his mind, snippets of the past few days played back and forth as if his brain were being used as a DVR.

The panic swelled. He tried to launch a kick. His legs refused to move. He let his body go limp, his full weight falling toward the ground. The sudden shift pulled the man off-balance. The hands pressed him harder into the wall. The eyes blazed.

Good. Now fight back!

Formless energy slapped against Thomas's mind, a wave of darkness that threatened to carry him into unconsciousness. Something moved inside of him, fierce and unshapen. A fire sparked in his belly, burning a trail of liquid lava through his veins. He thrust upward, his hands slamming into the ribs of his attacker. Faint blue light shimmered in the shadows as the man shot back, his olive overcoat billowing around him.

Blazing purple light flashed, blinding Thomas for a fraction of a second. He flinched, bracing himself for another attack.

It never came. The man was gone.

Thomas jumped on his bike, panic-stricken, a single phrase hanging in the space between his synapses. *Not bad. Learn a few things, and you might have a chance after all.*

The words were a whisper, the voice the same he'd heard in his head a moment earlier. He covered the remaining mile to his house at warp speed, nearly tumbling over as he skidded to a stop at the front steps. He looked up the street, his heart hammering and entire body wracked with shakes. There was no sign of the man.

Thomas sat on the bottom step and stared at his shaking hands. Even as he tried to piece things together, the details blurred and swam together. The voice, the eyes, the feel of the man attacking his mind, the fact that he and his bike had wound up between buildings two blocks away from where he had first turned.

Attacking my mind? What does that even mean? What the hell is happening? Thomas clenched and unclenched his fists, forcing himself to breath.

Slowly the sun dropped below the horizon, melting the blue sky with golden fire. Thomas sat still, watching a solitary cloud light up, its fluffy white folds tinted with purple, pink, and red. He closed his eyes, trying to calm his thinking before stepping inside. Soft music filtered from inside the house, the resonant voice intimately familiar. Andrea Bocelli, his mom's favorite. An old sedan cruised past, a heavier beat thumping through its open windows.

Time passed. Minutes, maybe hours. Thomas's phone vibrated. He pulled it out of his pocket and looked at the text. *It's getting late. Do you need me to come pick you up?* He put the phone away and looked up. It was almost completely dark out. He took another breath, stood up, and headed inside. The door swung open with a gentle creak.

"Thomas, honey, is that you?"

"Hey, Mom." He stepped into the living room.

She was sitting on the couch with her laptop. "I was afraid you were going to ride home in the dark. How was the party?"

"Great."

"Just great? No details?"

Thomas shrugged and cleared his throat, not fully trusting his own voice. "I don't know. There were a ton of people there. Maria seemed happy. Me and the guys played basketball. I ate like fifteen tacos. Mrs. Rodriguez told me to tell you hello. It was great."

"All right, almost-teenager, I guess great will have to do." His mom ruffled his hair. "Ugh. Sweaty again. Why don't you run up and take a quick shower? When you come down, we can have a popcorn and movie night. Okay?"

"Can we watch the new *Transformers*?"

"Sure," said his mom. "Now go on. Get freshened up. There's no snuggling when you're stinky. House rules."

TWENTY-TWO

THOMAS WHISTLED AS HE PULLED *The Book of Sorrows* out of the box. In the two days since showing the book to Enrique, the cover had become spectacularly illuminated. The colors were rich and full, the creature so realistic it almost seemed alive. And hungry? Yes, that seemed like the right word. The thing looked out with narrowed eyes and a half-open mouth, as if contemplating a meal. The expression made Thomas uncomfortable.

He opened to the bookmark almost reluctantly. There were only a few pages left, not more than a single chapter, and the thought of returning the book made him so sad he almost closed and put it away. Almost. Instead, he took a breath and started reading.

A few minutes later, Thomas stared at the last handwritten sentence. The one-line postscript stared back. *Caution, curious seeker, else thou shalt suffer likewise.* He looked at the empty space on the back of the last page, hoping it had magically filled with a fresh set of words.

It hadn't.

That was it. The end. Asharia destroyed, the crystals separated, and Isham killed by one of his own creations. The title of the book was right on-target. At least for Isham, the story had been full of sorrows. Thomas flipped back to the previous page to reread the ending.

Isham then taketh from hiding the three crystals and gathereth to himself the three scrolls whereon his story hast been writ. Upon the back of each scroll, he now draweth in secret, that each might possess instruction of which only he might know. The sons of Isham then return, and with them, the brave and strong of Asharia; yea, all they who might step forth into battle with the beast.

But Isham wisheth not that the warriors be sent unto the creature, for he hath seen in a vision how his dark creation mightest be undone. He calleth unto himself Esham, the eldest of his sons, and showeth to him the instruction writ in secret upon the first scroll. The dark crystal also he entrusteth unto him, and that sewn in a pouch of leather, that Esham might not look upon the crystal and find temptation therein.

Thus, instructed in all he must do, Esham selecteth three warriors and gathereth the wives and children thereof, that all might go in secret to the place where the crystal must be hid. There also shall they remain;

they and their children, and their children's children, until the end of time; for they shalt be guardians of the crystal, that no man mightest unite the three and awaken again the terrible power thereof.

Like instruction Isham giveth unto Issam, and also unto Alai; and lo, they take also unto themselves three warriors each, and the wives and children thereof, and depart unto far corners, each bearing a crystal hid in leather.

When all has been accomplished, Isham riseth to his feet, for the sun also rises. Sorrow filleth the heart of Isham, and fear also, for he knoweth what must be done. Yea, the great scorpion dost stir, and the sounds thereof resound through all Asharia. Yet without pause, he proceedeth to the place where the creature now stirs, that he might meet his dark creation.

The ground trembleth beneath the feet of Isham, and great claws carry the beast closer with each scuttling step. In the eye of his mind, Isham seeth the creature; mighty pincers slash the air, whilst the ponderous stinger riseth into the softening sky. The storyteller knoweth what must come but shrinketh not from his fate.

Silence descendeth upon Asharia, swift as the stinger's strike. And behold! on the very earth where Isham spake wondrous words, his body doth lie, and

162

upon the selfsame earth lieth also the form of a great beast, the body thereof fashioned of fine ash and sand, for like unto Isham, the creature hath returned to the dust from which he was fashioned.

* * *

Caution, curious seeker, else thou shalt suffer likewise.

The postscript stood alone, poking at Thomas like a needle. He had always wanted power like Isham's, but the seeds of doubt had been sown. What would he do if he were given the opportunity to achieve extraordinary abilities? Would he be willing to risk blindness? Death? Or infinitely worse, the possibility of hurting the people he loved? What if he wasn't capable of mastering the gift? What if, like Isham, he gained power but lost control?

He flipped the book shut and set it in the wooden box. Sunlight filtered through the blinds, stray beams lighting up the nearly glowing cover. Huxley's voice spoke from a memory. *The moment you finish reading the book, please bring it back.* Thomas sighed. The little man had said that, or something like it, and he had agreed.

A sudden buzzing cut through the quiet. Thomas jumped up from his bed. The buzzing paused, then started again. The air whooshed out of his lungs. He half-laughed as the cell phone vibrated again. He pulled it out of his backpack and looked at the tiny display.

"Enrique! What's happening?"

"Not much. What about you?"

"I was just getting ready to run downtown and take back the book I showed you. Wanna come with me?"

"Not unless you can wait a couple hours. Aunt Tanya and Uncle Marco are about to leave, and then I've got to help clean up. My mom won't let anyone go anywhere until our house is spotless. I'll be lucky if we finish before dark."

"That's a bust. Can you hang out after?"

"Yeah, probably. Depends when we finish cleaning." Enrique paused. "Hey, I didn't get a chance to ask yesterday. Has anything else happened? Anything weird?"

Thomas thought about the man in the olive overcoat and the bizarre attack on his bike ride home. "Weirder than I can possibly describe. Come over when you're done cleaning up and I'll tell you about it."

"All right. And just so you know, I'm still down to build the Iron Man suit. I'm pretty sure we're going to want one of those no matter what."

Thomas laughed. "For sure."

A voice yelled in the background. Mrs. Rodriguez.

"What? All right, Mom, I'll be right down!" called Enrique. Thomas winced. "Sorry, I've gotta go. Cleanup patrol."

"No worries. I'll see you later then, right?"

"Yeah, I'll figure something out."

"Good," said Thomas. "Try to hurry."

TWENTY-THREE

THOMAS SPRINTED the last hundred yards to the red door and gave it a yank. It didn't budge. He looked over his shoulder and yanked again. The van wasn't in sight. Not yet. But he'd seen it, lurking on the corner of Main and 14th. *Did the giant see me?* He wasn't sure. It didn't matter. He wanted to get inside as fast as possible. He pounded his fist against the heavy wood, not wanting to find out. "Huxley! Adelia! Are you in there? It's me, Thomas!"

Thomas pounded again. No response. He glanced nervously at Main Street. The van had been waiting for him, almost as if the giant had known he would be coming downtown. *Maybe he didn't see me.* Thomas thumped his head and fist against the wooden door, less energetically this time. Small drops of sweat splattered on the red paint.

Thomas heard shuffling inside, followed by a faint metallic click, and nearly tumbled into Adelia as the door swung open from the inside.

"Thomas! What a pleasant surprise. Please come in."

Thomas stepped into the cool sanctuary, his heart still hammering.

"I'm really glad you're here," said Adelia. "What inspired the surprise visit? We weren't expecting you until tomorrow."

"I promised Huxley I'd bring the book back as soon as I finished reading it," said Thomas. He pulled the box out of his backpack. The words felt choppy, labored, but Adelia didn't seem to notice.

"You finished? That's wonderful! May I take a look?"

Thomas fished the key out of his pocket and turned the box toward Adelia. Her eyes went wide.

"It's fully illuminated! How much of this happened since Monday?"

"A lot." Thomas looked at the door. The panic was subsiding, but he half expected the giant to walk in. "More than half, I guess."

"Amazing. Huxley is going to be very excited to see this." Adelia looked at Thomas for a moment, then reached behind the front desk and grabbed a purple placard. She hung the placard, then pulled the door shut and threw the bolt. Thomas couldn't help noticing the lines around her eyes. She looked tired. "Follow me."

Adelia started toward the back of the shop. Thomas followed. He didn't see Huxley anywhere, but Adelia continued directly toward the last set of shelves. She glanced back at Thomas, flashed a smile, and put her pointer finger on top of a large leather book. Thomas heard a faint click and whir. The bookshelves slid silently sideways into the wall, revealing a hidden passageway. He stared, mouth wide open.

"Come on," said Adelia, beckoning him forward. "In here."

Thomas followed Adelia into the darkness, a prickle of uneasiness tickling his brain. Narrow stone stairs angled into the earth below the bookstore. He counted thirty-three dimly lit steps before coming to a concrete landing. A passage branched off to the left. Adelia followed until the passage ended at a heavy steel door with a high-tech security panel on the outside. *What is this place?*

Adelia smiled reassuringly, then punched a series of numbers into the touchpad and pressed her palm flat against the screen. The peculiarity of biometric scanning and a seven-digit numerical combination wasn't lost on him. Why on earth would a bookstore need such a cutting-edge security system?

The scanner gave a short beep and flashed green. There was a subtle whir followed by a loud click, and slowly the big metal door swung open. A flood of white light spilled out of the room on the other side, bright enough that Thomas flinched and squeezed his eyes shut. He opened his eyes slowly to let them adjust.

The space was as bright and sterile as a hospital operating room. High-end computers sat atop glass tables along one wall, while the rest of the space was filled with an assortment of sophisticated but unfamiliar equipment. Yellow-orange flames flickered inside a white furnace behind a thick glass panel. He looked at Adelia, wide-eyed. "What is this place?"

"This is where we do our most interesting work. Come in."

Thomas wanted to ask more questions, but just then, a side door opened and Huxley came bustling in. In place of his normal apron, he had on a long white lab coat and was carrying a tray with an old book and an assortment of tiny instruments. Adelia coughed gently. Huxley looked up with a start. He flashed a quizzical look at Adelia, then smiled at Thomas.

"Hello, Thomas," said Huxley. "Welcome to our lab. I hadn't planned for you to see this quite yet, but I'm glad you're here. What do you think?"

"I-I don't know. It's amazing, I think. But what is it?" he asked, repeating his question from a moment before and hoping that perhaps Huxley would give more details.

"An excellent question, to be sure, but a bigger one than I'm able to fully answer right now," Huxley responded. "Let it suffice to say that this is where we house our most precious items and conduct our most important experiments. I'd ask what brings you in here today, but I see that you've brought *The Book of Sorrows*. Does that mean you've finished reading it?"

Thomas nodded. Adelia took the box from his hands and tilted it so Huxley could see.

"Look," said Adelia, her voice awed. "Given the recent developments, I thought you'd want to see this right away."

Huxley's eyes widened as he took in the colors and images that covered the book jacket. "Remarkable! Thomas, when did the book reach this level of illumination?"

"Just in the past day or two," said Thomas.

"You were right to bring this to us immediately," said Huxley. "We've just received some alarming news. It seems the book is signaling a readiness for action that we simply can't ignore. Adelia, did you alert our new friend?"

"I did."

"Excellent." He glanced over her shoulder at the dark hallway. "Ah, yes, I see that you have. Thomas, I'm sure you have a great many questions. We'll explain everything as soon as we can. I hope you'll understand."

"Understand what?" asked Thomas. Movement caught the corner of his eye. He turned toward the exit and found a hand inches from his face. A grimy finger touched his forehead. Something exploded, and the bright room faded to darkness.

TWENTY-FOUR

A DULL HEADACHE and dreamlike disorientation accompanied Thomas's return to consciousness. His mouth tasted like he'd licked a bowl of dog food, and his neck had a horrible kink in it. He rolled over, wanting to go back to sleep. His elbow bumped into a large and unfamiliar cushion. His eyes opened groggily to a large room bathed in shadow.

Everything was unfamiliar. The soft cushion under his body, the slim pillow under his head, the shape of the objects around him. He rubbed his face, flexed his arms and legs. Every part of him seemed intact except for his brain. *Where am I? Why can't I think straight?*

A fragmented memory flitted past. Then another. And another. More images danced into awareness, each partial, incomplete. He puzzled with the disjointed shards until suddenly the pieces snapped into place.

He sat bolt upright, adrenaline pumping through his veins. The hidden passage and secret lab had been real. So had the blurry hand and grimy finger. A sick feeling gripped Thomas's stomach. It didn't make sense. Huxley and Adelia had set him up, turned him over to the man in the olive overcoat. But why? What did that mean?

Thomas's thoughts were interrupted by the metallic jingling of keys. His eyes swung to the door. It swung open and a thin, backlit figure with long hair appeared in the doorway. The lights clicked on, leaving him temporarily blind. Before his eyes could adjust, the door thudded shut, and keys jingled again.

Thomas ran to the door, yanking on the handle. It was locked from the outside. Anger cut through the fog and ache, clearing his head. He banged on the door. "Hey! Hey, come back here! Let me out!"

Silence.

He banged again. "Hey! Whoever you are, get back here and let me out!"

Nothing. He slumped forward, thumping his head into the door. "Owwww."

When the pain passed, he flipped the light switch and turned around. The breath whistled through his lips. The room was nice. Really nice. Every inch looked expensive, from the leather couch to the fancy bookcases and wall coverings. Even the floor was impressive, carved marble covered with thick decorative rugs. The paintings looked like the ones he'd seen in the ancient China exhibit at the Museum of Art, dangling scrolls covered in symbols and scenes of nature.

The awe wore off and the reality of being trapped sank

back in. Anger pierced the last remnants of mental fog, bringing his mind into focus. There were no windows in the room, no doors other than the one that had just been locked from the outside. The keyhole taunted him. Thomas added lock picking to the top of the list of things to learn. *I've got to get out of here, but how?*

His eyes fell on a pair of air vents. One was at floor level, the other right up near the ceiling. He crouched next to the lower grate. The inside of the shaft was surprisingly wide, maybe even big enough to crawl through, but the grate was far too small. He looked around the room for a blunt instrument, something he could use to bash through the plaster and widen the opening. There were books on the bookshelves, but the only things heavy enough to do any damage were the chair and desk. Not exactly practical instruments.

Thomas walked to the wooden desk that stood in front of the bookcases and opened the top drawer. Empty. So were the rest. His eyes fell on a large piece of parchment spread open on top of the desk.

It was a map, larger and more detailed than the one in *The Book of Sorrows* but familiar all the same. Tiny illustrations dotted the surface of the lone circular continent. Forests and hills, a smattering of spread-out cities. *Elandria.* The name that appeared at the bottom of the illustration in the book was on this version as well. This time, he didn't have to rotate the picture to see it. He ran a finger over a forest of strangely-shaped trees. The material was thick and brittle, just like the pages of the book.

Thomas gently lifted one corner of the map and peeked at the other side. The star chart looked back, the strange constellations mocking him with their familiar unfamiliarity. He closed his eyes and tried to remember what the charts in the book had looked like. A picture began to take shape in his mind. It was the same chart, maybe even identical.

The image was shattered by the jingle of keys. Thomas looked up sharply. For the second time, the door swung open. This time, a tray with a domed metal lid slid into the room. A thin arm draped in emerald cloth disappeared as soon as the platter was clear of the door.

"Hey! Hey! Wait!" shouted Thomas. He rushed forward as the door swung shut. The lock clicked just as his fingers reached the doorknob. He pounded on the door, fiery anger flooding his body. "HEY!!!! Let me out of here!"

Nothing. He hammered more and met with the same result. He hit the door with his fist. Pain shot through his hand and up his arm. He hit it again, harder than the first time. The jolt ached all the way to his shoulder. A trickle of blood escaped from a thin cut on the knuckle of his second finger. He leaned against the door, hurt and frustrated.

His stomach growled, loudly. He looked down, suddenly aware of the smells wafting into his nostrils. The domed lid lifted easily, revealing a plate of grilled chicken, mashed potatoes, and seasoned green beans. A piece of chocolate cake with white frosting was resting on a side platter. The cake was loaded with chocolate chips and layers of fudge, just the way he liked it.

For a brief moment, Thomas forgot his surroundings. He had a drumstick in his hand and was about to take a bite when it hit him. Aside from the silver platter, it was the exact meal his mom cooked on special occasions. How was that possible? He stared suspiciously at the chicken. Was it laced with poison? A sleeping potion? Something even worse?

Torn between hunger, fear, and confusion, Thomas lifted the tray and nearly threw it across the room. Instead, he leaned forward and took a tentative nibble of the chicken. It was well-seasoned and juicy. He waited a moment and didn't keel over. Promising. He took a second bite as he walked to the heavy sofa. Still not dead. He sat down and picked up the second drumstick.

Grease dribbled down his chin. He wiped it with his sleeve and shoveled a spoonful of mashed potatoes into his already stuffed mouth. Within minutes, the dinner plate was empty except for the green beans. He ignored those and moved on to the chocolate cake. When the last bite had been wolfed down, he tilted the plate and knocked the last few crumbs into his mouth.

Thomas sat back, his stomach protesting the sudden onslaught of food, and let out a satisfying belch. He chuckled as a second and significantly larger burp echoed through the room. *Enrique would have appreciated that one.*

Thinking about Enrique sent Thomas's mind in a less pleasant direction. The great meal and comfortable room did nothing to erase the fact that he'd been knocked out and locked away without a shred of explanation. That he hadn't been seriously hurt was encouraging, but he felt betrayed and confused. Huxley and Adelia had set him up. Why?

Thomas wiped his face and hands with the napkin, then picked up the map and wandered to the leather couch. He stared at the shapes and patterns of the foreign stars until his eyes grew heavy and the dots began to swim together. His last thoughts were of escape. One way or another, he was going to get out of this place. All he needed was the right tool, and then he'd be gone. His eyes drooped, and he slipped into a world of shadowy dreams.

TWENTY-FIVE

THE ROOM WAS DARK, nearly pitch black, and Thomas wasn't alone. A creature was with him, clothed in shadow, filled with deadly intent. It stalked toward him. Raspy breathing echoed in the vast room. Long, razor-sharp claws scratched the marbled floor. Click-scratch, click-scratch, click-scraaaatch.

Thomas scrambled around the edge of the room, frantically searching for a way to escape. The creature stalked, slowly, deliberately. Thomas shouted for help. He was answered with a hiss. A claw dragged across the marble, scrrrreeeatch. The monster closed in, still hidden in shadow, a faceless beast preparing to pounce. Thomas turned and forced himself onto the desk. The bookcase! He grabbed a shelf and pulled himself up. The shelf wobbled, nearly pitching him backward.

He gripped harder, climbed faster. The beast was closing in. His fingers gripped the top ledge. One more pull and he'd be out of reach. A hissing roar shattered the silence. Thomas felt the creature hurtling through the air toward him. Sharp claws sank into his back, cutting through flesh, yanking him backward.

He fell, screaming in pain and fear.

Into nothing. His eyes snapped open, the echo of his own scream lingering in the quiet room. His hands reached for the gaping wound. The spot on his back where the claws had sunk in was tender but uninjured, kinked from sleeping on a couch. He gasped, falling back onto the cushions. There was no monster. *It was a dream.* A ridiculously vivid dream.

Thomas ran an arm over the thin line of drool at the side of his mouth, his heart still hammering in his chest. His surroundings came into focus, bringing with them a fresh wave of fear. The monster may have been a dream, but the kidnapping wasn't. He was alone in the big room, curled up on a soft leather couch. There was a blanket bunched up at his feet, as if it had been draped over him while he slept, then kicked down during the dream.

The map had been returned to the wooden desk. Next to it was a tray with an assortment of snacks and a pitcher of water. He rubbed his face, trying to shake off the lingering effects of the dream. The uneasiness persisted. He got up, poured a glass of water, and chugged it down in one long guzzle.

Munching on a wheat cracker, his eyes landed on a small cast iron replica of Rodin's *The Thinker.* There was one just like it on the mantle of their fireplace back home.

It was his mom's favorite sculpture. Thomas picked it up. It felt just like the one at home. Solid. Sturdy. He passed it from his left hand to his right and back again and looked at the vent. *How did I not notice this earlier? Was I so stressed I couldn't see straight? Or is this new?*

Whatever the case, he was now capable of bashing his way into the crawlspace. As he stepped toward the metal grate, something caught the corner of his eye. A tiny green light just above one of the tapestries. He froze. A hidden camera!

On impulse, he ducked below the range of the tiny lens. Still holding the Rodin, he slid the big wooden chair until he was close enough to stand and reach the camera. Pressing himself against the wall, he climbed onto the chair, gripped *The Thinker* and slammed it into the fragile unit. Twice. The green light disappeared as fragments of metal, glass, and plastic tumbled to the floor.

Thomas looked around to see if there might be any other cameras hidden in the room. At first glance, he didn't see anything, but then a small black shape on the wall above the couch caught his attention. He slid along the wall, reached up, and slammed the sculpture into the tiny lens. Bam! Done. Thomas allowed himself a brief moment of satisfaction.

The surveillance problem was handled, but he'd have to work fast if anyone was monitoring the video feed. He dragged the leather chair forward and wedged the top edge under the doorknob. It took significant effort, but he managed to slide the heavy couch across the floor. He tried to push the desk, but the thing wouldn't budge. The couch and chair would have to work. It was time to create an escape route.

He ran to the floor-level vent, sculpture in hand, and crouched down to look more closely. There weren't any screws securing the grate to the wall, so it was either form-fitted or fastened on the inside. He wedged the tips of his fingers between the metal slats and gave a tug. It didn't budge.

He tried again. There was an almost imperceptible movement. He strengthened his grip and pulled harder. The grate held, and held. He put his back and shoulders into it and tugged again. The grate slipped, just a little. The metal edges dug into his fingers, nearly breaking the skin. Thomas ignored the pain, pressed his feet into the wall, and yanked with all his might.

The grate popped free with enough force that he tumbled backward in an awkward half summersault. He crawled forward and stuck his head into the opening.

A narrow passage stretched in both directions, plaster at first, and then stone. Thin rays of light filtered through vents farther down the shaft, but most of the airway was dark. He stuck his head in deeper, wishing he had a flashlight. It looked as though there was just enough room for him to crawl in there, but it was impossible to know if the vent narrowed around the corner.

Voices in the hallway put him on high alert. A woman was talking, her voice soft, her words indecipherable. The doorknob jiggled, and then there was thumping on the door. Thomas grabbed *The Thinker* and started smashing it into the drywall around the vent. The opening widened with each blow, and soon the sculpture struck stone.

Another voice joined the first, this one louder. Thomas heard his name as he slammed the sculpture into the wall. A final pile of rock and drywall crumbled to the ground. He wedged himself through the opening and twisted his body to fit in the air shaft. The space was just wide enough to pull himself forward.

"Thomas! Thomas! Let us in!" More voices joined the first two. There were bodies slamming into the door now, the shouts growing louder and more frantic.

Thomas army-crawled down the rock-lined passageway, hoping to get out of sight before anyone could figure out which direction he'd gone. A loud screech and thud were followed by more shouting and clearer voices. The barrier had been breached. He pulled himself around a tight corner and out of sight.

He'd been right about the surveillance being monitored, which meant the rest of the house could be wired as well. Breaking out of the room had been the easy part. Escaping completely would require a plan. The voices came closer. A light flashed on the crawlspace wall just behind him.

Thomas kept moving, pulling himself toward thin slits

of light from the next grate. The opening was not only a possible path out, but also a window into the rest of the building. He peered into a dark room of indeterminate size. Not helpful, but if he wanted to get away cleanly, it would be key to know his choices.

The rocks pressed into his palms and battered his knees. He slipped his shoes off his feet and onto his hands, then pulled his pants up until there was an extra layer of cloth on his knees. Not perfect, but better. He kept moving, as quickly and quietly as he could manage.

He came to a T-intersection. He turned right, toward the streaks of light filtering through another grate. Voices stopped him in his tracks just a few feet from the opening. Shadows passed across the grate. The conversation stopped. A beam of condensed light entered the passage, separating around the metal slats and reflecting from the stones. Thomas shimmied backward.

A metallic scraping sound nearly froze the blood in his veins. They were pulling the grate out! *Did they see me?* He didn't know, but if they got in before he turned the corner, he'd be spotted for sure. The passage opened beside him. He bent himself around the rocks, struggling to go back the way he had come.

His shirt caught on a sharp edge. He yanked, desperate to get out of sight. The fabric caught. He pulled again, harder. His arm came free and the shoe slipped out of his hand. Thomas watched in agonizing slow motion as the shoe flew toward the opposite wall. They'd hear, and then it would only be a matter of time before he was trapped.

Scrape-thump. The grate came free just as his shoe slapped against the stone. The sounds were close enough together that nobody outside could possibly have known what just happened. Thomas snatched the shoe and pulled himself farther from the line of sight. The beam of the flashlight bounced right past the place where his shoe had rested only seconds earlier. Thomas leaned his head back and took a deep breath.

The light retreated, but the voices continued. Women, one old and one young, both speaking in another language. It wasn't Spanish, the only non-English language he could understand at all. The tone and inflection were decidedly foreign. Chinese maybe? The only thing he clearly understood was "Thomas." One of the women said his name in near-perfect English before continuing in the foreign dialect.

The light swept back in his direction and paused at the corner where he was hiding. He held his breath, wondering if he had left a telltale sign at the edge of the shaft. A lump formed in his throat as he looked down and noticed a tear in the fabric of his shirt. Had some of the material come off on the rocks? Is that why they were pausing?

The voices intensified in tone, rising almost to an argument pitch. A drop of sweat rolled down Thomas's nose and dripped onto a smooth gray stone in front of him. The soft splash was hardly audible even to him, but Thomas felt certain his pursuers would hear. He stayed stock-still. Ages passed, one second at a time. The older woman spoke again. The beam swept elsewhere, and then disappeared. The voices faded, then disappeared as well.

Thomas listened carefully for the sound of the grate being replaced. It didn't come. Had his pursuers inadvertently created a way for him to escape? He waited a few minutes, then heard the voices coming from around the next corner. He crawled toward the open vent, quickly and cautiously, all senses on high alert.

Another set of voices echoed into the ventilation system. He froze and listened. The sounds were coming from behind him. Light splashed against the stones. Picking up the pace, he pulled himself to the open grate.

Staying in the shadows, Thomas peered into a room that was large, white, and full of square machines that rattled and hummed. A pair of draped sheets dangled from strings. Mounds of towels and clothes were piled against an adjacent wall. *A laundry room?* He pulled himself a fraction of an inch closer. Yes, a laundry room, and a very large one at that. There were three washing machines, just as many dryers, and an oversized sink.

The door leading into the room was cracked open enough to see a warmly lit hallway. There was no way of telling if anyone was out there. He turned to a mountain of dirty sheets and towels piled high enough that a person could easily hide under them without being noticed. There was also a thin door adjacent to the main entrance, probably a closet, and a series of small cupboards lining the wall. Most were too small to climb into, but at least two had hiding-spot potential.

He closed his eyes and took a deep breath, wondering if there was anything else that he might have missed. He opened them and saw something he could hardly believe.

A window! He'd been so focused on what was in the room that he almost overlooked the window above the last washing machine. And it wasn't just any old window. It was cracked open and easily big enough to climb through. Thomas's heart leaped. An open window wouldn't trigger any alarms. He'd just found a viable way out of the building.

Thomas poked his head through the open grate but realized he'd never be able to get the rest of his body through without widening the opening. He'd left the Rodin back in the office, and that meant he'd have to improvise. He wrapped his fingers around the drywall and started to pull. The edges broke away easily in his hands.

Footsteps and voices in the hall sent him scrambling back into the shadows. The people passed without stopping, and soon the voices disappeared. Thomas took a deep breath and pulled himself into the room. Once inside, he dumped a pile of sheets in front of the hole, hoping to delay the discovery of his escape long enough to put some distance between himself and his captors.

Thomas tiptoed forward and looked out the window

and felt his heart drop. It was at least twenty feet down to the cobblestone courtyard, with nothing but air between the window and the rocks below. Even more shocking—there were snow-capped mountains rising above the building on the other side. Huge mountains. Thomas's mouth went dry. *Where the heck am I?*

He leaned forward to see if there was any way to climb down to the courtyard. Movement caught his eye. A woman wandered into the courtyard, her dark hair streaked with gray, a long visor covering her face. *The woman with the dragon pendant?* Thomas's pulse raced. He jerked his head back into the laundry room.

The precariousness of his situation sunk in. If anyone came into the laundry room, he was caught. If he climbed out the window, he was caught. If he tried escaping down the hallway, he was almost certainly going to be caught.

Approaching footsteps told him he might be caught soon anyway. Acting on instinct, he jumped behind the largest mound of laundry and pulled a pile of sheets over his head. No sooner had he covered himself than the door swung open and slammed shut. There were two people, one male and one female, both speaking the same foreign dialect he'd heard earlier. The voices sounded vaguely familiar, but he couldn't risk moving enough to see who it was.

The conversation went back and forth for a seeming eternity, slowly rising in pitch and intensity. The man made a quiet but definitive statement, which was followed by the sound of an open hand slapping the wall. Switching to English, the woman spoke softly. "We shouldn't have brought him here without explaining first. He isn't ready for all of this."

"I know," the man answered as he opened the door. "I wish we could have given him more time, but we both know that wasn't possible. Ready or not, we have to find a way to stop Arius before he recovers the crystals. Even if Thomas awakens his powers, our world is at risk. If he doesn't . . ."

The door creaked shut, cutting off the end of the sentence. Thomas's head spun. The voices had belonged to Huxley and Adelia, and there was no longer any question about whether they were responsible for his abduction. They were. The question now was why.

Footsteps and voices came and went. Thomas stayed hidden under the stack of sheets, torn between courses of action. The idea of staying in a place he'd been brought against his will was almost as repellant as leaving without answers. He needed to think of something, and fast.

An idea flashed into his mind. Staying hidden, he pulled the corners of two sheets together and tied them into a knot. He grabbed a third sheet and repeated the exercise, and then a fourth. He sat still and listened. The hallway was silent again. He jumped up from his hiding place and peered out the window. The courtyard was empty.

Finding the way clear, Thomas tied the end of the last sheet to the base of the nearest washing machine, pulled the window the rest of the way open, and tossed the makeshift ladder to the ground below. He moved the last pile of sheets away from the air vent, scattered broken bits of drywall on the floor around the grate, and climbed back into the air shaft.

• • •

It didn't take long for the sound of shouting to fill the building. Whereas the noise had been sporadic while Thomas was known to still be inside, it now bubbled into a frenzy that remained constant for hours. He caught shouts of "out the window," "floodlights," "grab the Jeeps," and "hurry!"

Although he found a sort of savage pleasure in having caused so much chaos, he mostly ignored the activity and focused on exploring the building. He needed to figure out where the important people gathered to talk. Without more information, there was no way to make a smart decision about what to do next.

Thomas wriggled past room after room, pausing at each to take in the details. There were more offices like the one where he'd been trapped, well-appointed bedrooms, at least two rooms that looked like labs, and more than a dozen areas too dark to see clearly or with vents obstructed by furniture. On two separate occasions, he put his hand into an open airshaft and nearly tumbled down to the lower levels of the building. After the second narrowly averted disaster, he made sure to keep a close eye on the path ahead.

He heard voices here and there, but they were distant

and only sporadically audible. As hoped, the search had moved outside. He circled back to a hidden spot adjacent to the two largest offices and leaned against the stone wall. His knees were raw, his body fatigued, and of all the rooms he'd seen, the big offices seemed the most promising venues for eavesdropping. He tucked his shoes under his head and closed his eyes, waiting for the searchers to return.

TWENTY-SIX

THE WHOOSHING OF AIR WOKE Thomas from a nap he never intended to take. His body was achy, his thoughts disoriented. He yawned and lifted a hand to rub his face. Instead, his elbow thumped into the edge a jagged stone. "Ow!"

The sound was louder than he intended, rebounding down the dark shaft before disappearing into the swirl of frigid air. He shivered. Jeans and a T-shirt weren't adequate cover in the cool air shaft. He grabbed his shoes and started moving, hoping to find a less chilly listening post. He rounded a corner and stopped.

Distant voices carried down the narrow vent, riding the current of swooshing air. He crawled forward on knees so sore he could hardly move, listening to make sure he was heading in the right direction. He paused. The voices were coming from the big office to the left.

Thomas hit a "T" and turned left. Light filtered through a grate in the passage wall. He quietly slid past the grate, carefully skirted one of the shafts leading downward, and bent his body silently around another corner. The voices grew suddenly clearer. He inched closer until he could make out at least three distinct speakers. Two of the voices belonged to Huxley and Adelia. The third was raspy and unfamiliar.

"He's got to be somewhere we can find him," Adelia said, her voice cracking with emotion. "He has to be okay. He just has to."

"All of the vehicles are accounted for," said the unknown speaker. "Given thirty minutes of silence, I should be able to get a read on his location. It's only been a couple of hours. He can't have gotten far."

"On his own, he can't have gone far," corrected Huxley. "If our enemies tracked him here and helped him escape, there's no telling where he might be."

"Nonsense. There's only one person with the motivation and resources to get to us here, and if he manages to take the boy, we'd know exactly where to look."

"That can't have happened." Adelia's voice was anguished. "If Arius has gotten to him, I-I'll—"

"If Arius has gotten to him, then our worst fears have been realized," interrupted the third speaker. "A rescue would be all but impossible, and Thomas doesn't yet know enough about his own powers to escape. And worse, he might believe that they were the ones doing the rescuing. If Arius were to convince Thomas that we were the bad guys and he was the savior, I have no doubt that he could bend the boy to his will."

Adelia made a sound that Thomas could only interpret as an audible shiver.

"Thomas is too smart for that," said Huxley. "Arius might fool him for a while, but eventually, he would see through the lies."

"Time is our enemy," said the man. "We can't afford to wait for eventually. That's not good enough. Not even close. We have to get to the crystals before Arius, but with our friend out of reach and Thomas missing, our chances for that are between slim and none. Even if I manage to find one of the locations, we lack the resources to recover them. We need someone with —"

"We have to find him," said Adelia. "And not just because we need his help. He deserves the chance to learn the truth, and an opportunity to grow into his true potential. My god! What am I going to tell his mother?"

"We'll find him," said the man, his tone brooking no room for argument or doubt. "And as soon as we do, the two of you will explain everything. No more secrets."

"Agreed," said Huxley. "No more secrets."

Thomas pulled himself silently forward, hoping to get a glimpse of the unknown speaker. Through the tiny slats, he could see Huxley pacing and Adelia sitting with her elbows on the desk, cradling her head in her hands. The third person was hidden behind a large leather office chair. From his angle, Thomas could see faded jeans, scuffed-up boots, and not much else. There was no sign of the man in the olive overcoat.

"And what about our new friend?" asked the third speaker. "He disappeared surprisingly quickly. Are you sure he hasn't betrayed us?"

"Yes," said Huxley. "If there's one thing I'm certain of, it's that he isn't helping Arius."

"Yes, but are you certain he's not helping himself? Pursuing his own agenda? Perhaps hoping to take the crystals for himself?" There was a long pause.

"What should we do?" asked Huxley.

"Continue to search the grounds and surrounding areas," said the man. "I'm going into the cavern. Perhaps I'll be able to get a quick read on his location."

"Okay." Adelia looked up. There were tear stains on her cheeks. "Okay. We'll do that, and I'll try to reach—"

The office door swung open and a large bearded man burst into the room. "You've already managed to lose the boy. Ha! He's every bit as resourceful as his father, that one."

"Professor, so good of you to join us," replied the unseen man. There was a hint of sarcasm in his rough voice. "Tell me, why is it that you're in such good spirits while the rest of us are panicking?"

Thomas couldn't believe what he was seeing. Professor Reilly? How was the professor connected to any of this?

"I haven't known the boy long, but I've known him long enough. If he's anything like his father, and I'm certain he is, Thomas will figure out for himself which way is up and which way is down. Ha!" Professor Reilly let out another booming laugh. "It took him no time at all to escape from you lot. I'd say that's pretty remarkable."

"And you aren't concerned that Arius might have taken him?" asked Huxley.

"Not in the slightest," answered the professor. "Not even Arius can work that fast, and I trust everyone here as completely as I trust myself. No, Thomas escaped on his own, and he'll turn up on his own as well."

"There's evidence that you might be right, Professor. Take a look at this." The unseen man extended a thick arm in a checkered flannel shirt. He held *The Thinker* in a heavily scarred hand. "The boy lay down to take a nap, and by the time he woke up, this was on the bookshelf. He used it to bash his way into the ventilation system."

Professor Reilly reached out, taking the sculpture in one hand and stroking his beard with the other. "Manifesting without instruction? It would be unusual, but not totally unheard-of. How certain are you that's what happened?"

"Completely," answered the man. "Aside from the map and a few small books, the shelves were empty when he arrived. We can go over the footage and find the exact moment the sculpture appeared, but I don't think that's necessary."

Manifesting? Appeared? What are they talking about?

"In all of our years, Adelia and I have met only a handful

of others who showed so much natural ability." Huxley gestured toward the desk. "Have you seen the book yet?"

"Of course not," said Professor Reilly. "I didn't have the luxury of skipping air travel like the rest of you. It took more than twenty hours to get here, and it was only that fast because your jet met my commercial flight in Singapore. Let's have a look."

Twenty hours? Singapore? Thomas's head spun.

Adelia reached under the desk and lifted a familiar wooden box. Huxley produced the whitish key and inserted it into the lock. Bright colors spilled out as the lid lifted, adding to the afternoon light like a prism. Thomas bit his tongue. If such a thing were possible, the cover was even more brightly illuminated than it had been earlier. The book literally seemed to be glowing.

"So, this is why you moved things along so quickly," said Professor Reilly. "I wondered about that."

"Yes, but it wasn't just that," said Huxley. "It was also the news from Africa. If Arius has really found one of the crystals, our time is running short. His people have been watching the boy as well, and we couldn't risk him falling into their hands. Without Thomas, our situation would be all but hopeless."

"Not hopeless, you old curmudgeon. Never hopeless," said Professor Reilly. "But bad. Exceptionally bad. That much is for sure. Has there been any word from the wizard?"

"I'm afraid not," answered Huxley. "If he were here, I'd

feel much more confident. As it is, we have to hope Thomas can harness his abilities in time."

"Well? What are we waiting for?" boomed Reilly. "Let's get out there and find him!"

The others exclaimed in agreement. The man behind the desk wheeled his chair backward, blocking the room from Thomas's view. Silence returned, but the racket in Thomas's head was deafening. He felt a sense of vertigo, as though everything in the world had somehow changed from solid to squishy.

The echoing questions threatened to drown his ability to form a clear thought. Through the thundering mess in his mind, the memory of Sifu's voice rang out like a lifeline. *Relax. Breathe. Answers will come.*

Thomas closed his eyes and took in a slow breath, counting to six as he inhaled and nine as he breathed out. He did it again and again until his heart stopped pounding and the knots in his head began to untangle. His hands unclenched. The series of recent events and conversations took shape in front of him, forming into little disks of sound and color. Like threads in the hands of a seamstress, the images began to link up and connect. A pattern began to form in front of him and suddenly Thomas knew what he had to do.

No longer worried about being heard or captured, he laced on his shoes, kicked the grate out into the room, and used his heels to punch holes in the drywall. When the opening was sufficiently large, he climbed out of hiding and into the room. He walked to the big desk, picked up the telephone receiver, and dialed "0."

"Mr. Garibaldi? I thought you had left." The voice was heavily accented, but Thomas could understand her well enough. *That's the name of the unseen speaker. Garibaldi.* Thomas made a mental note to find out exactly who that was.

"No, this is Thomas. Your boss is looking for me. You can let him know I'll be waiting in his office." He hung up, not waiting for a response.

TWENTY-SEVEN

IT TOOK A FEW MINUTES for the sounds of running feet to reach him, and when faces finally did appear, neither Garibaldi nor the man with the olive overcoat was among them. Professor Reilly, Huxley, and Adelia burst into the room, all three attempting to squeeze through the door at exactly the same time. Adelia wisely dropped back while the two men wedged themselves into the room, and then all three were rushing toward him.

Thomas found the sight of the professor's sizable belly pressing Huxley into the doorframe immensely comical, but he forced his face into a deep scowl and sat with arms crossed behind the big wooden desk. The onrush screeched to a halt.

"Thomas! You're okay! I was so worried." Adelia looked equal parts relieved and uncomfortable. "I'm so, so sorry. It's awful how this all happened, but you have to know that we would never do anything to hurt you. Not in a thousand years."

"Well, my boy," said Professor Reilly. "I guess the secret is out. You've got every right to be angry, but once you hear the whole story I think you'll understand why we've brought you here."

Thomas continued to glower, outwardly sullen but inwardly relishing the momentary reversal of power. After what they'd put him through, it only seemed right that they squirm a little.

"It's true, Thomas," added Huxley. "I was hoping we'd have time to explain everything back home, but circumstances forced us to act more quickly than anticipated. You have our most sincere apologies. I hope you'll forgive us the cloak and dagger tactics."

Thomas remained silent, wondering what else might come out if he left them on the hook a little bit longer. Professor Reilly took the bait.

"Out with it, boy. I know you have questions, and you have my word that there will be no more secrets. Scout's honor." The big man was clearly uncomfortable. The hint of a scowl hid behind the bushy beard as he shifted his weight from one foot to the other. It was like watching the reaction of a six-year-old who had forgotten his homework for the eleventh time. "Whatever you ask, we'll answer, and probably a lot more besides."

Thomas raised an eyebrow. "Whatever I ask?"

"Anything," said Huxley.

"Fine. Where are we?"

"On the edge of Snow Mountain in the Yunnan province of China," said Huxley.

China? Seriously? "What? How did we get here?"

"If it's okay with you, we'll explain the transportation a little bit later. There are a few other things we should talk about first," said Huxley. "If we go out of order, some of what we tell you isn't going to make sense."

Now we're getting somewhere. A growing sense of anticipation welled up in his belly. He uncrossed his arms and leaned forward. "Fine. Start at the beginning."

"You're not mad at us?" asked Adelia.

Thomas realized he was smiling. He mentally kicked himself. So much for the reversal of power. "I was. Really mad. But I heard you talking earlier and decided it was worth hearing you out. Plus, I was starting to get hungry again. Sooner or later someone was going to hear my stomach growling and realize I was still in the vents."

"So, that's how you did it," exclaimed Professor Reilly. "Left the rope ladder as a decoy and climbed back into the air duct. Brilliant!" He looked proudly at the other two. "Resourceful, just like his old man. John will be proud, I can tell you that much."

Thomas's expression darkened. "Why do you keep talking about my dad like that?"

"Like what?"

"Like he's still alive," said Thomas. "He's been dead since I was little."

"Dead? John Wildus? Not bloody likely!" Professor Reilly looked astounded. "What has your mother been telling you all these years?"

"That he's not on this earth anymore!" Thomas shouted, tears of anger and confusion forming in his eyes. "Why would she say that if he's not dead?"

The professor stared dumbstruck for a long moment, his mouth opening and closing. "Because it's true, I suppose. Your dad isn't on this earth anymore. The rest is complicated."

"Complicated?" Thomas was back to angry, maybe even furious. His voice echoed above the blood pounding in his ears. "I've thought my dad was dead since I was five years old. Is it more complicated than that?"

"No, it isn't," Professor Reilly replied. "But I have every reason to believe John Wildus is alive. That's one of the many reasons we've brought you here. When you're ready, we want you to help us find him and bring him back."

"Back from where?" Thomas yelled. "Where is my dad?"

"The last time I heard your dad's voice, it was on my voicemail," said Professor Reilly. "He said he had uncovered a clue that would help him unravel a mystery we'd spent nearly a decade investigating. He said he was leaving immediately to find out if it was real. Nobody has heard from him since."

"What mystery?"

"Your dad discovered a doorway to another world, Thomas," the professor said quietly. "An ancient portal."

"*What?*" Thomas's mind reeled. He stared from face to face in stunned silence. They looked at him without the faintest hint of uncertainty or deception. *Another world?* "How am I supposed to help find my dad if he's not on earth?"

"You can't," replied the Professor. "Not yet anyway. That's why we've started on the physics, but it's only one piece of the puzzle."

"What do you mean?" Thomas was more confused now than angry.

"Now we're getting to the good stuff." Huxley held up *The Book of Sorrows*. The cover was literally glowing. "Thomas, do you know what this is?"

"It's *The Book of Sorrows*."

"Yes, of course," said Huxley. "But do you know why the cover looks like this?"

Thomas thought of the underground lab and complex equipment he'd seen at the bookshop. "I don't know. I want it to be magic, but it's probably some sort of trick. Some combination of special ink and chemicals or something like that."

"It's not a trick, Thomas," said Adelia. "And as far as I know, no ink or chemicals in the world can do anything like this."

"Then what is it?"

"Magic!" boomed Professor Reilly, slapping his hands on the big desk. "Real magic, my boy."

Thomas's heart rate accelerated. Blood pounded in his ears. The memory of his dad flashed into his mind—John Wildus leaning down, his rough hand on Thomas's cheek, his blue eyes full of hope and mystery. *Magic is real, Thomas.*

"Are you familiar with the concept of a litmus test?" asked Adelia.

Thomas nodded. His face felt oddly numb.

"Among other things, *The Book of Sorrows* is like a litmus test," said Huxley. "Only instead of responding to levels of acidity, the book responds to the level of innate magical ability. The stronger the magic, the more the cover comes to life."

"What are you saying?" Thomas managed to form words, but they sounded strange in his ears, as if his own voice was coming from the end of a long tunnel. He felt lightheaded, almost dizzy. "Why did the cover change like that? Use small words."

"Because of you, Thomas." Adelia's voice was soft, a gentle smile crinkling the corners of her eyes. "The book came to life because of you."

"Me?" Thomas's voice reached a substantially higher pitch than normal. He thought for a moment that he might pass out.

"That's right," said Huxley. "And it's been some time since a copy of *The Book of Sorrows* was this fully illuminated. Almost thirty years, to be precise. You can see it, can't you? The book is literally glowing."

"Okay, back up for just a second. What are you saying? That I'm some kind of magician?"

"Yes, Thomas, that's exactly what we're saying," answered Adelia. "It will take time to discover the extent of your power, but we're here to help you with the process."

"I'm sorry to disappoint you," said Thomas, "but I can't do magic. Believe me, I've tried. Ever since I first heard the word, I've wanted to have magical powers. But I don't. I can't even do a proper card trick. I think your book has gone haywire."

The others looked at each other and burst out laughing.

"He doesn't know," said Professor Reilly, as the laughter subsided.

"Know what?" asked Thomas sharply. It felt like he was being laughed at.

Huxley held up the Rodin sculpture. "What can you tell us about this statue, Thomas?"

"It's called *The Thinker*. My mom has one just like it back at our house."

"Had one," Huxley corrected. "She used to have one just like it at her house. Past tense."

"What do you mean?" Thomas asked.

"I mean it's not there anymore," replied Huxley.

"Why not?"

"Because it's in your hands, Thomas," said Huxley. "You brought it here. Summoned it. With magic."

"That's right!" said Professor Reilly. "The statue you're

holding isn't just like the one from your house. It's the very same one. I remembered seeing it in your living room. We called your mom and confirmed. Look at the bottom."

Thomas turned the statue upside down. There was an inscription: *To SAW, my eternal Thinker.* Susan Alexandria Wildus.

"I'm not following. I brought this here by magic?" Thomas's voice was fully into the alto-soprano range now.

The adults laughed again, but this time, Thomas didn't feel like he was quite so far on the outside.

"That's right, my boy," chuckled Professor Reilly. "I'm guessing you wished for a way to escape, and for some reason, your mind settled on the sculpture. One second it was at your house, the next it was here. We call that summoning."

Thomas was stunned into silence. He sat for a moment with wide eyes and a slack jaw, staring at the bronze statue. "You guys aren't messing with me, are you? You know that would be seriously uncool, right?"

"No," replied Adelia. Her laugh was bell-like, her smile genuine. "We are most certainly *not* messing with you."

Thomas pointed his index finger to the sky and broke into a happy dance. Not the subdued schoolyard version. The big dance. The one usually reserved for the privacy of his own room, with jumping and rock star arms. The adults laughed. "Hey, thinking of magic, can we summon up some food? I'm starving."

This time everyone laughed, Thomas included.

TWENTY-EIGHT

AFTER STUFFING HIMSELF with chicken and pan-fried noodles, Thomas joined the others in a library-sized room with a giant fireplace and an assortment of couches, chairs, and tables. He parked himself in a wide leather chair next to the fire and sipped on a creamy mango drink. Professor Reilly sprawled next to him in a large recliner, feet up, sipping on a glass of amber liquid. Adelia and Huxley sat side by side on the long couch across from them.

"Thank you, Ling Sun," said Huxley. "Dinner was delicious, as always."

"Very welcome." Ling Sun bobbed her head and looked at Thomas. "How our new guest like?"

"Me? I loved it," said Thomas. "Thank you."

Ling Sun smiled. The skin around her eyes crinkled, showing an age defied by her energy and dark hair. "Good. Sticky bun?"

"Oh, none for me, thanks," said Adelia.

"I'd love one," said Huxley. "Thank you."

"Yes, please," said Thomas. "That sounds great."

"Two for me, please," said Professor Reilly. Adelia shot him a look. He shrugged his shoulders and grinned. "What? I'm a big man. It takes a lot to fill me up."

"That's what I'm afraid of," said Adelia. "One of these days, I'm going to get you on a proper diet."

"Diet? What? How can you use such language in front of the child? Thomas, cover your ears!" Professor Reilly shook his head, his eyes wide. "Diet? Why, that's the foulest of the four-letter words! Take it back. Hurry."

"Not a chance," said Adelia. "Not until you start taking better care of yourself."

"I bring sticky buns, you figure out how many go in belly." Ling Sun pointed at the professor's round middle and raised an eyebrow. "But maybe diet not such a bad idea."

Professor Reilly's mouth hung open, his jaw working as he tried to find the proper words to express his horror. Thomas laughed, as did Huxley and Adelia. Ling Sun disappeared through a side door, a half-smile crinkling the skin around her eyes. When she reappeared with the plate of sticky buns, Professor Reilly took two. He chomped into the first, glowering at Adelia. His face softened, and he lifted the remaining half in a complimentary gesture. "Mmm. Very nice."

Ling Sun bowed slightly. "Thank you."

The sticky buns weren't the kind Thomas was expecting. Instead of a cinnamon roll, it looked like a dumpling. He took one and nibbled on the corner. It was sweet, but not overwhelmingly so. He took a bigger bite. "Oh, wow. Wow. That's really good. Thank you."

"Very welcome," said Ling Sun. "You want one more?"

"Yes, please." Thomas grabbed another and popped the rest of the first one in his mouth. When both had been finished, he sat back, rubbed his tummy, and let out a quiet burp. His belly was full, and he was feeling a whole lot better when suddenly a thought occurred to him. He hadn't had a chance to talk to his mom. He looked around and noticed a phone on the long dining room table.

The professor must have seen him staring in that direction and picked up on his thoughts. "Would you like to make a call?"

"Would that be okay?" Thomas asked, almost timidly. He didn't want to get his hopes up, but suddenly, he really wanted to hear his mom's voice.

"You're not a prisoner, Thomas," Professor Reilly replied. "Everything you see here is yours. I think your mom will be incredibly happy to hear from you."

Thomas leaped out of the chair, accidentally knocking his drink onto the floor. The glass shattered, sending shards in all directions. He looked down, abashed, and started to apologize.

"Not to worry, my boy," said Professor Reilly. "Help is on the way. Go, make your phone call."

The professor was right. By the time Thomas picked up the telephone, Ling Sun was back with a young helper. The girl looked like she might be about his own age, but it was hard to tell because locks of long hair hid most of her face.

"It's an international call, so you'll need to dial 001 before the number," said Adelia.

Thomas punched the numbers into the phone, hit the green button, and heard the unfamiliar "boop" of an international ringtone. After the third boop, the line clicked, and he heard his mom's voice. "Hello." She sounded tired, stressed.

"Mom." His voice was hardly more than a whisper, emotion tearing at his throat and making it hard to get the sounds out. He fought back a flood of emotion and cleared his throat. "Mom, it's me."

"Thomas! Thomas, my brave, beautiful boy! Are you okay?"

"I, uh, I'm . . ." He started to choke up but forced himself to stand tall. "I'm okay."

"Oh, my baby boy. I'm so sorry you had to find out about things this way. There's so much I've wanted to tell you but couldn't. I know this all must seem crazy right now, but everything will make sense soon enough. Can you please forgive me?"

"Why? Why couldn't you tell me?"

"Because I promised not to," said Susan.

"Why not?"

"Your dad wanted you to have a proper childhood. To go to school, make friends, be a kid. He was afraid you'd lose all of that if he didn't make it home and you learned the truth about why. Selfishly, I agreed."

Thomas wanted to argue, but aside from growing up without a dad, his childhood had been pretty good. Factoring in Enrique, maybe even great. Would it have been different if he'd known his dad was missing and why? Probably.

"I get to come home though, right? I get to come back soon, right?" There was silence on the other end, and a sinking feeling crept into the pit of his stomach. "Right?"

"I hope so, sweet boy," his mom managed, though he could hear the tears in her voice. "I really hope so."

Matching tears welled up in his own eyes. "B-but I don't want to be away. I w-want to come home."

"I want that, too," she finally managed, her voice raw with emotion. "I want that more than anything in the world. But it's not safe for you here, and you can't come home until it is. I need you to trust in the people around you, sweet boy. They'll protect and teach you. Right now, that's the most important thing. You're part of something bigger now, Thomas, and that has to come first, before anything you or I might want for ourselves."

"I don't understand," he said, hot tears spilling down his cheeks. "What am I part of? Why can't I learn what I need to at home?"

"I'm going to leave it to Huxley, Adelia, and Professor Reilly to explain. It's a long story, and you need to hear it from the beginning. Just know that you're in good hands, and that everything will work out just the way it's supposed to." She paused. "Thomas?"

"Yes, Mom."

"I love you."

"I love you, too." Thomas's voice cracked. He let himself cry for a moment before setting down the phone, squaring up his shoulders and turning around. Adelia was right behind him, gathering him into a hug before he had time to protest. He gave in without a fight, burying his face in her shoulder. The tears started again, warm against the soft cloth of her shirt.

Professor Reilly patted Thomas on the shoulder. "I know it's a lot to take in, my boy, and I can't begin to imagine how you might be feeling right now, but we're going to have some fun. I can promise you that. By the time we're done, you'll be doing things you can't even imagine right now. The blighters on the other side won't know what hit them."

"The ones with Arius?" Thomas wiped a sleeve across his face and rubbed his eyes. "Arius Strong?"

Professor Reilly nodded. "The very same."

"How do you know that name?" Huxley looked at Thomas, a curious expression on his face. "We haven't talked to you about him yet. Have we?"

"I heard you talking about someone named Arius while I was hiding, and a couple weeks ago, I read an article about a billionaire with the same name. Who is he?"

"That's part of a very long story." Huxley put a gentle hand on Thomas's shoulder and steered him toward the living room. "How about we gather around the fire and start at the beginning?"

TWENTY-NINE

"THE FIRST THING YOU HAVE TO KNOW is that the story is a lot longer and more complicated than we can hope to describe in one night. The beginning goes back farther than anyone can remember, and some have much longer memories than you might imagine."

Adelia looked at Huxley, who nodded and jumped in. "Do you remember your research on *The Book of Sorrows*?" asked Huxley.

"Yes, of course."

"Good. Then you already know that *The Book of Sorrows* is distinct from the scrolls Isham created," said Huxley. "What you may not have guessed is that our *Book of Sorrows* isn't an original either. All three known copies were themselves copied from an even earlier text."

"The very first *Book of Sorrows*, the one ours was copied from, was created over a thousand years ago," said Adelia. "We don't know who created it, but he or she must have been very powerful. Over the centuries, only a handful of people have had the talent and will to replicate the complex magic that went into the original book. The most recent person to successfully do so was a British magician named Aldus Alpheus. When he took on the work, he also translated the text from Latin into English."

"What about the scrolls Isham wrote?" asked Thomas.

"Isham's scrolls weren't called *The Book of Sorrows* until much later, and even then, not for the reason people assumed. It was misinformation, not the misfortune of treasure hunters, that afforded them that moniker." Huxley grinned. "The original scrolls were intended to serve two purposes—to remind Isham's descendants of what they were protecting, and to guide them to the places where the crystals were to be hidden."

"Over the centuries, several copies of the scrolls turned up," continued Adelia. "Some were counterfeit, deliberate misrepresentations designed to hide the true location of the crystals. At least one copy was authentic, a genuine replica that revealed the location of a missing crystal. It was that scroll that inspired James Jackman's journey."

"You remember the Ehrlenthal book, right? *The Lost Treasure of Africa?*" Huxley asked. Thomas nodded, and he continued, "Did you finish reading it?"

"Mm-hmm. Yeah." *And now it's sitting in my room collecting late fees.*

"That book is a more-or-less true account of Jackman's adventures, first in search of the scrolls, and later in pursuit of the crystals," said Adelia. "The story was disguised as fiction, with a few of the key details changed. Jackman wanted the story captured, but with enough doubt and misrepresentation sprinkled in to keep the accuracy in doubt. He knew that sooner or later, others would pursue the crystals, and he didn't want them falling into the wrong hands."

"How do you know all of this?" Thomas asked. "I couldn't find anything like it in my research."

Huxley and Adelia exchanged a look.

"No more secrets," said Professor Reilly. "The whole truth."

Adelia let out a long sigh. "Because it was me, Thomas. I am Adelia Ehrlenthal. Or I was before Huxley and I got married. I'm the one who wrote the book."

"But that's impossible. The book was written over three hundred years ago."

"It's not impossible," said Huxley. "Adelia's longevity is a product of my craft. Our shared craft, really."

"Selling books?"

"Alchemy," said Huxley without missing a beat. "I am an alchemist, Thomas, part of an ancient sect that set out to unravel the mysteries of physical and spiritual transformation. Books are an extension of my craft, but buying and selling them is a hobby. In reality, *H&A Booksellers* was an excuse to stay close to you. We opened it shortly after you and your mom moved to Orange County, so that she could send you to us when the time was right."

"You expect me to believe that both of you were alive three hundred years ago? You've got to be kidding me." The words came out with an edge. A sharp edge. The joke had gone too far.

Huxley continued, unshaken. "I was born in 1402, in the Alsace-Loraine region of France, near the border of modern Germany. Adelia was born in England 142 years later. I am one of the few to have survived the experimentation that led to true alchemy. Adelia was my first and last successful apprentice. We have been together ever since."

Either he was an exceptionally gifted liar, or there was an element of truth to his story. Thomas looked imploringly at Professor Reilly, hoping the big man would put an end to the charade and let him in on the joke. He found no such relief.

"It's true, Thomas. I can't vouch for their birthdays, but I met these two almost forty years ago and neither of them has aged a day. As for me, well, you can see what the time has done to my figure. I used to be the belle of the ball, but now just look at me. Ha!" He slapped both hands on his belly and let out a laugh. "I look more like I swallowed the belle."

Thomas couldn't help smiling at the last part. "All right. So just for fun, let's pretend all of that is true and you were alive at the same time as James Jackman. What happened next?"

"James and I found the scrolls. He and I were . . ." Adelia

paused for a long moment before continuing, as though lost in a memory. "Well, I suppose you could say we were close.

"Finding the scrolls changed James, drove him to obsession. He never doubted that he would find the crystals, but I don't think he ever thought about what he would do afterward. Or what finding them would do to him. By the time we recovered the first crystal, our party had suffered horrible losses. Most people would have quit, but James was more determined than ever. He would do anything to succeed. People and money meant nothing unless they could help him in his mission.

"The hunt led us through some of the most hostile terrain in the world. Each time we got close to one of the crystals, we had to fight their protectors. The Asharians were fierce and creative warriors, but we had guns and numbers. By the time we recovered the third crystal, the last of Isham's descendants had been killed, along with most of our party. In the end, it was just me, James, and a handful of hired men."

Adelia paused again. This time, the silence was of a heavier variety, as though the weight of the memories threatened to squeeze the breath from her lungs. She let out a long sigh and continued.

"As power-hungry and relentless as he was, James was equally protective of his daughters. He knew the risks associated with awakening the crystals and didn't want to accidentally harm them or their families. He thought about staying where he found the last crystal, outside of modern-day Baghdad, but ultimately decided to take them farther away.

"James assumed an ocean would be enough to keep his children safe, but I wasn't convinced. I told him the crystals should be destroyed before any more harm could be done. He refused to consider the idea. Eventually I went home to England, unable to face the possibility that more people would die. That's when I met Huxley and began my study of the alchemical arts."

Thomas looked at her, trying to sense deception. He found none. His head spun. "The book said he ended up in Asia. Is that why we're in China? Because the crystals are here somewhere?"

"An excellent guess," said Huxley. "But no. As it turns out, we are a very long way from the crystals."

A pleased smile lit up Adelia's face. "James's final destination was the most important detail I changed in the book. The reference threw off power-seekers and treasure hunters for centuries. Until Arius, nobody has come close to finding the crystals. I had hoped, perhaps foolishly, that they had been forgotten by everyone outside of our circle."

"Where did he go?" asked Thomas. "Where are the crystals now?"

"America," Adelia responded. "Originally, James landed in New York. He wrote me twice after we parted ways. Once from the ship, and once about a year after landing.

After the final letter, I never heard from him again. For a long time, I assumed he had died without finding a way to awaken the crystals. That's not what happened, though."

Thomas's eyes widened. "What did happen?"

"It took us decades to piece the rest of the story together," Huxley chimed in. "Are you sure you want to jump to the ending so quickly?"

"Yes. Yes, I am."

Professor Reilly laughed. "Of course, he does. Go on. Tell him the rest of it."

"All right," said Adelia. She was smiling now. "A member of our network eventually discovered letters indicating that Jackman had left for the territories near the Great Lakes. By the time Huxley and I finally made our way to the origin of those letters, James had passed away and the crystals had been hidden yet again."

"No way! That can't be the end," said Thomas. "There has to be more to the story."

"There is more, actually," said Adelia. "In our search, we met Dark Eagle, a Sioux chief who told us what had happened. He described James as a man with extraordinary powers. Blind, but unparalleled as a Shaman and healer.

"James protected Dark Eagle and his people from the pox and settlers. As a reward, the chief offered his daughter in marriage. She and James had three sons. All had abilities, but the youngest, Jameson, had the same extraordinary gifts as his father."

"Apparently, he also had a knack for getting into trouble. The people called him the wildest one." Huxley smiled wryly at Thomas. "By the time we met him, Jameson had taken a variation of that nickname and made it his own."

"What do you mean?" asked Thomas.

This time, it was the professor who answered. "He called himself Wildus. Jameson Wildus."

"That's the beginning of your part in this story," added Huxley. "You're part of an unbroken line that dates back to James Jackman and his youngest son. And like you, many in that line have inherited a measure of his power. A few have achieved far more."

"Slow down," said Thomas. "You're telling me I'm related to James Jackman?"

"That's right," said Huxley. "James was your great-great-great-great-grandfather, with a bunch more greats added in the middle."

"We've come to understand that there is a genetic component to the thing we call magic," said Professor Reilly. "An activation of certain genes that enable a leap forward in human potential. Your dad focused a significant fraction of his research trying to find and understand the specific genes affected by the crystals. He believed, as I do, that it might be possible to activate those same genes through scientific means."

"Whatever the specific mechanism, the crystals awakened that potential in James," said Huxley. "The code has been carried through the centuries in your family DNA. It's usually around the time a child comes of age that the potential starts blossoming into tangible abilities."

"No way," said Thomas.

"Yes," said Adelia, her eyes twinkling with delight. "*The Book of Sorrows* verified your potential. Summoning the statue proves that your abilities have started to manifest."

"Whoa," whistled Thomas. A mingling rush of awe, disbelief, and even fear flooded his mind, filling his body with strange sensations. They were talking about magic. *Real magic*, based on science and history.

"My sentiments exactly," laughed Professor Reilly. "My sentiments exactly."

"So, what happened to the crystals?" asked Thomas, grasping for something concrete to hold onto. Something he could really understand.

"I wish I could say that James destroyed them." Adelia sighed and shook her head. "It's what he should have done. Instead, he did the same thing as Isham. He gave a crystal to each of his sons, along with secret instructions for where to hide them. They followed his wishes, and as far as we know, none of them told a living soul where the crystals had been hidden. We let the search go, choosing instead to focus our attention on Jameson and his remarkable abilities."

"Adelia and I have been friends of the Wildus family for more than 300 years," Huxley continued. "We've helped guard your family secret and guide those with magical abilities for that entire time. And when we said that everything you see here is yours, we weren't kidding. It's literally yours. Your great-great-grandfather built this place. Marcus Wildus."

"Mine?" Thomas looked around, his eyes wide. The living room alone was as big as his entire house, and that was just a tiny corner of the place. He gathered his thoughts and tried to refocus. "What about Arius? Why are we fighting him?"

"That's a story that goes back at least to the time of Isham, perhaps even farther," said Huxley. "Since the dawn of human history, there has been a battle between the forces of creation and those of destruction. Light and dark, as we tend to think of them, or good and evil. The light seeks to move us forward, to bring out the best in our species. The darkness stands in opposition, seeking to corrupt and destroy."

"Like *Star Wars*? The Force?" Thomas's skepticism edged up a notch.

"In a way, perhaps," said Adelia. "Countless religions, philosophies, and theories have attempted to explain these forces, but the truth is that nobody truly understands them. Not in their entirety. I've spent my life studying little else, and after hundreds of years, one of the only things I can say with certainty is that the battle is real. There is light and there is darkness. Our history revolves around very little else."

"What does that have to do with Arius?" asked Thomas.

"Arius has aligned himself with the forces of darkness," said Huxley. "The very best-case scenario is that he has been deceived. The alternative is much worse, but in either case, he is pursuing a path that will almost certainly lead to catastrophic destruction."

"Whatever else it might be, the darkness is clever, capable of disguising its influence in a million ways. Take Isham, for example. Would you say he was an evil person?" asked Adelia. "No? Neither would I, and yet because of his hunger for power, two villages were destroyed and hundreds of people died. Now, what about the stranger who gave the crystals to Isham?"

"I don't know." Thomas thought for a moment about the description of the dark gloves and gravelly voice. "Maybe."

Adelia nodded. "We can't be entirely sure, either, but we know it wasn't human, and we believe it was an instrument of darkness. That creature is one of several such beings whose appearance has been recorded over the centuries."

"You're saying that thing was real? That it wasn't just a made-up story?"

"We believe that it was," said Huxley. "Similar encounters have occurred throughout history, and each time, the aftermath has been horrific. Our species is capable of doing plenty of damage on its own, but the worst of our mistakes have been preceded by a dark visitor. We'll never know the extent of the damage that would have been caused if Isham hadn't hidden the crystals, but the destruction of two villages is insignificant compared to the horror of our modern wars."

"If Arius finds all three crystals, we might find out just how bad it could have been," said Professor Reilly.

"Why do you think he'd use them like that?" asked Thomas. "The article I read made it sound like he was doing some good."

"The darkness is like a disease," said Adelia. "The symptoms of infection are consistent and predictable. Arius has more money, influence, and power than almost anyone on the planet, and yet it's not enough. He has magical abilities, and still, he wants more. Insatiable hunger for power is one of the unmistakable signs of corruption."

Professor Reilly shuddered. "If he were able to awaken the crystals, to add that power to what he already has, his ability to cause destruction would be almost unlimited."

"Why? What would he do if he gets them?"

"Imagine that instead of a villager in a world before cities, Isham was one of the wealthiest and most powerful people alive today, on a planet with a population of nearly eight billion people," said Huxley. "Imagine that his already extraordinary resources and abilities weren't enough, that he also wanted the power to control the future for all of mankind. What would happen if you gave the crystals to a man like that and let him loose in a world full of nuclear, chemical, and atomic weapons? A world where almost every person and place is connected through technology?"

"The best case is bad," said Professor Reilly. "The worst is destruction of a biblical nature. Apocalypse."

"Obviously, we can't take that kind of risk," said Huxley. "We've faced the darkness before, but the stakes have never been higher. And because we're the only ones who know what he's after, we're the only ones who can stop him."

"That's why you're here," said Adelia. "We need you to unlock your gifts and help us."

Thomas's brain felt like a punching bag. All the adults were watching him, their expressions serious. Going up against a billionaire with magical abilities who also happened to be backed by some kind of mystical darkness? *They're messing with me. This is a joke. A big, elaborate joke.* And then, *I'm not even a teenager yet.* "You're kidding, right?"

"I'm afraid not," said Adelia. "We don't yet know how Arius learned about the crystals, but we know that he did. He recovered one of them right around the time you found your way to our shop. That's why you were led to us."

"You might have seen something about it in the news," said Professor Reilly. "A group of armed men took over a cave in Canada, and then the whole thing blew up."

"I read about that," said Thomas. "That was Arius?"

"It was," said Huxley. "We didn't immediately realize he was involved or that he was after the crystals. Now we're playing from behind."

"I thought none of the attackers made it out alive."

"Arius escaped, and probably the others as well. We don't know how much time there is before he finds the other crystals, but we have to assume it isn't much," said Adelia. "Whoever told him about the crystals also gave away your family secret. That's why he had his people watching you, and that's why we moved so quickly to bring you here."

Thomas felt numb. His mom had said he was part of something bigger, but saving the world was a whole lot more than he'd imagined. He swallowed, tried to regain his composure. "What now?"

"Now you have to learn enough magic to help us stop that maniac and save the human race," said Professor Reilly. "No pressure, of course."

"No," said Thomas. "No pressure at all."

THIRTY

"IT'S NOT MUCH TO LOOK AT, IS IT?" said Professor Reilly, a slightly horrified expression on his face.

"Are you sure this is the right place?" asked Thomas, peering past the professor into a dingy space slightly smaller than his room back home. The stone stairs and narrow hallways leading to the room had done little to dampen his mood, but the giddiness he'd felt upstairs slipped quickly away. "It looks like a prison cell."

"Marcus Wildus, your great-great-grandfather, intended for this to be a space completely free of distractions." Huxley stepped into the room and pulled a thin chain that dangled from the ceiling just inside of the heavy wooden door. A single lightbulb sputtered on, bathing the room in a dim yellow glow. "I think he succeeded."

"If he was aiming for awful, he definitely did," said Professor Reilly. "I've never seen a less appealing classroom in my life."

Thomas agreed. Aside from the solitary lightbulb, there

were a pair of small wooden chairs, a dented metal table, and nothing else. The walls, like the floor and ceiling, were carved from interlocking gray stones, cold and hard and unforgiving. There wasn't a single picture, painting, or scrap of carpet to soften things up. It felt more like a converted torture chamber than a place of learning.

"This wasn't a classroom," said Huxley. "It was the place Marcus came to meditate and train, long before he had children of his own. Later, when Thomas's great-grandfather showed promise, he used it as a teaching area. Marcus thought the luxuries of the upper rooms were fine for daily living but detrimental to deeper study. He felt the same way about American cities. That's why he built this compound, as a place of solitude and refuge."

"Well," said Professor Reilly. "If this is it, then this is it. I suppose we should get down to business."

"We should." Huxley turned to Thomas, his expression serious. "Under normal circumstances, a young magician might spend weeks or months learning and mastering a single piece of magic. Because of Arius, we don't have that kind of time."

"Not by a long shot," said Professor Reilly. "You need to learn faster than anyone in the history of magic, and for better or worse, you're stuck with us as your teachers."

"I'm afraid that's correct, on both counts," said Huxley. "Adelia and I have guided others in the past, but never under such intense time constraints or in such dire circumstances. Figuring this out is going to be a process, and one without a proper blueprint to work from."

"We'd like your permission to jumpstart the learning," said Professor Reilly. "To skip some of the preliminaries and get straight to the serious stuff."

More magic, faster? "That sounds good to me. Let's do it."

"Before you agree, we should warn you that such an impromptu and unstructured approach will come with some amount of discomfort and risk," said Huxley. "A master magician would be capable of activating certain aspects of your innate potential, speeding up your progress in a natural way. We thought we had such a teacher lined up for you, but he disappeared, literally, shortly after your arrival."

The man in the olive overcoat? A master magician? Was it possible?

"The next best approach, the one that Adelia and I have used in the past, is slow and systematic learning," continued Huxley. "Building skill and experience, piece by piece, much the same way a person is taught how to swim."

"We'd like to dispense with the preliminary steps and head directly into the experimentation phase," said Professor Reilly. "To drop you directly into the deep end, as it were."

"But people drown in the deep end," said Thomas.

"Or they learn very, very quickly," said Huxley. "We're hoping for the latter."

"Sink or swim, as the old saying goes," said Professor Reilly. "Of course, we wouldn't actually let you sink. Not all the way."

"Wow. That is totally not reassuring." The sarcasm Thomas intended was lost as the last shred of excitement gave way to fear. "Do I have a choice in any of this?"

"Not exactly," started Professor Reilly.

"Of course, you do," interrupted Huxley. "We brought you here without your consent, but you have my word that such a thing will never happen again. Not with me. You know the stakes, Thomas. The choice is yours to make. The rest of us will do the best we can, regardless of what you decide."

What if I can't do it? What if I fail? Thomas's hands clenched and unclenched. His palms felt slick with moisture. Matching beads of sweat leaped onto his forehead. An image of his mom flashed into his mind. She was shaking her head in disappointment. *What would I tell her? Oops, sorry, Mom. I know you wanted me to help, but I was too scared. Now the world is ending. My bad.*

Thomas closed his eyes and took a deep breath. Then another. He forced himself to reframe the issue. *This is it. The chance I've always wanted. I can learn magic. And how would I feel if Arius succeeded and I didn't do everything in my power to stop him? What about Enrique? What would he do if he was in my situation?*

The answer was instant. If he could, Enrique would

sock Arius in the nose and take the crystal right out of his hands. And if that wasn't an option and magic was, he'd learn magic. No fear and no hesitation. He'd do whatever he could to get the job done. Thomas opened his eyes. "Okay. I'm in. Whatever it takes."

"That's the spirit, my boy!" boomed Professor Reilly.

"I hoped you'd say that." Huxley smiled, his eyes flashing in the dim light. "Although there are hundreds of magical techniques, you've already touched on summoning. We'll start there and build quickly. You brought the Rodin unconsciously, through instinct and need. That's good, but not good enough. You have to be able to repeat the effort consciously, on command. You have to be able to summon anything you need, any time you need it."

"Your dad used to say that magic isn't a process of defying the laws of nature, but rather applying a higher set of laws *to* nature," said Professor Reilly. "Once you understand those laws, you'll be able to do it."

"What do you mean?" asked Thomas.

"Science has known for centuries that every object in the physical world is a collection of particles," said Professor Reilly. "And from our brief conversations on quantum physics, you know that it's possible for a particle to be in two places at the same time. Summoning simply takes things a step further, moving those particles from one place to another. Quantum computing is built on very similar ideas."

When he said it like that, the idea almost sounded rational. "Okay."

"The other part, the making it happen part, is more art than science," said Huxley. "Magic is not a purely detached and analytical study. It also requires intention and energy. Emotion. You succeeded in summoning the sculpture because you wanted to escape. Desperately. Intensely. Emotion energizes intention, gives it power. The ability to *feel*, combined with the ability to focus, will allow you to *create*. Our job is to help you tap into that ability. Got it?"

"I think so," said Thomas. The incident in the alley back home jumped into his mind. He remembered the swell of energy, the flash of blue, the man flying backward. *Was that magic, too?*

"Good." Huxley pulled an orange from his pocket and tossed it to Thomas.

Thomas caught it. "What am I supposed to—?"

"Look at it. Feel it. Smell it. Get to know it as well as you can," said Huxley. "In a minute, we're going to put it on the dining room table and you're going to summon it back."

Thomas lifted the fruit to eye level. His hand, slightly damp with perspiration, was noticeably shaky. He sucked in a deep breath and jumped up and down, wriggling the nervousness from his body. This time, his hands were steadier, the orange in clearer focus. It was smaller than his fist and slightly lopsided, with thin, smooth skin. He rotated it and ran a gentle finger over a small brown scar near the navel.

The lumps inside were wrinkly and almost brain-like. He cut into the skin with his fingernail and let the fragrance linger in his nose.

"Good. Now close your eyes and make sure you have a clear image in your head," said Professor Reilly. "Can you see it?"

An image of the fruit materialized in his mind, fuzzy at first, and then clear. He nodded.

"Great." Huxley took the orange from Thomas's hand and stepped into the hallway. "Sit tight and give us a few minutes to get to the dining room. This will be at the very center of the table, right across from the fireplace."

"Good luck," said Professor Reilly.

The door swung shut and a heavy metal bolt slid into place with a jarring thud.

"Wait a second! Huxley! Professor! Hold on!" Thomas's voice bounced hollowly from the stone walls. They didn't answer. He tried to open the door. It didn't budge. He was locked in. Trapped. He leaned his forehead into the heavy wood. "But what if I can't do it?"

• • •

A mental tsunami crashed into Thomas as he waited, dozens of disconnected ideas and images flooding his mind all at once. Peggy, Enrique, Akhil, Jameel, Meng. The man in the olive overcoat. The giant and the taser lady. *The Book of Sorrows*. Mom. School. Arius. The dance committee. *The dance committee! No, no, no! Peggy's going to think I flaked.*

I didn't flake, I got kidnapped. Kind of. What will I tell her? I don't know.

Peggy's voice materialized along with her imagined face. *Don't you like me, Thomas?* She looked at him with sad eyes and a hurt expression. Anguish filled his chest. *What about Enrique? We were supposed to hang out. What will my mom tell him? And Akhil. Will Parker pick on him even more now that I'm not around? What if I get home and everyone has moved on? What if I don't belong anymore?*

And then, far worse: *What if I never get to go home? What if I never leave this room?*

Thomas's breathing accelerated. His palms started to sweat again. The walls pressed in. The room blurred into an unpleasant gray swirl. Panic began to carry him in a dark and scary direction.

Amid the swirl of terror, the memory of his dad's blue eyes and bearded face materialized, firm and solid. Thomas felt a rough hand on his cheek, heard the words that had carried him through the past seven years. *Magic is real, Thomas.*

Dad! Dad's alive, and if I can figure this out, one day I might be able to bring him home. The thought pulled Thomas out of the downward spiral, refocusing him on the task at hand. *I have to learn magic! I have to!*

He stared at the empty table. It taunted him, the dented metal reminding him that he was supposed to do the impossible.

"It's not impossible. I can do this." He said the words out loud, but they came out soft, feeble, as if he didn't believe them. He smacked the table so hard his hands stung and his ears rang. Pain cut through the negative thoughts, kept his mind from slipping sideways. "I summoned *The Thinker* and I can summon the orange. Come on, Thomas. Focus! You can do this!"

The tsunami receded, making room for rational thought. He took a breath, forced himself to remember the look and feel and smell of the orange—the scar on top, the weird brain-looking navel, the slightly oblong shape. He held the picture in his mind and willed the orange to appear.

Nothing happened. He tried again. And again and again and again, each time with the same outcome.

Time passed. Minutes, maybe hours. In the bare room, it was hard to tell.

He stood up, sat back down, paced, walked in circles. He asked, pleaded, begged, demanded, commanded. Nothing worked. He thought about the professor's words, comparing magic to quantum physics. Particles in two places at once. He let the words become a mantra. Particles in two places. There and here. There and here. Now *here*!

The table was still empty.

Over and over he tried, and over and over he failed. Frustration set in, drove deeper with every unsuccessful attempt. *Appear, you stupid, stinking, dinkety little orange! Why won't you just appear?*

"Ahhh!" He banged his head on the tabletop and pulled his hair.

His stomach gurgled loudly. He tried to push the hunger out of his mind. It gnawed more insistently, intensified until it filled his thoughts and made it impossible to focus. He pushed himself up and banged on the door.

"Hey, guys, it's time for a break. I need something to eat!" He tried again, banging harder and yelling louder. "Huxley! Adelia! Professor Reilly! Somebody let me out!"

He waited, ear pressed against the door, hoping to hear footsteps. More silence.

"Huxley! Professor! I'm not kidding! I need food! Come on, let me out!" He pounded until his hands throbbed, then stepped back and kicked over and over until his entire leg felt numb. The wood was unyielding, the bolt far too strong to break.

Thomas stepped back, exhausted and in pain, and slumped into one of the chairs. The empty table stared at him, dared him to try again. He did, with the same result. More time passed. His attempts to summon the orange were met with failure, his shouts with silence. The hunger became overwhelming. Every cell in his body screamed for food.

Darker thoughts entered his mind, threatening to carry him down a nasty path. *What if I'm in here forever? What if all of this was some kind of sick game and now I'm a prisoner?* He stood up and kicked at the door. "Let me out! Please! Please . . ."

The only response was thundering silence. He kicked the door with his left leg until it ached as badly as the right. He sank to the floor and crawled to the corner of the tiny room. His hands and legs throbbed. Hunger gnawed belly. He had failed, and nobody was coming to offer any help. Tears of fear and pain and frustration spilled from his eyes, rolled down his cheeks. He wedged himself into the corner and let himself cry until exhaustion carried him to sleep.

. . .

Thomas woke slowly, painfully. If dreams had troubled his slumber, he didn't remember them. His hands were bruised and sore. His back, shoulders, and legs ached. His neck was so stiff he could hardly move. But the worst part—the absolute worst—was the hunger. Every ounce of him wanted food. His body and brain were practically screaming with the desire to eat.

He shifted position and found that his right leg had fallen asleep. He wriggled, willing the blood to return. It did, tingling unpleasantly. He climbed to his knees and tried to stand up. A wave of dizziness hit. He nearly fell over, catching himself with a hand against the stone wall. The lightheadedness passed. He walked gingerly to the chair and lowered himself into the uncomfortable seat. As expected, the table was still empty and there was no sign of help from the adults.

He closed his eyes and resisted the urge to completely freak out. Death by starvation was a fate as horrible as any he could imagine, and it felt like he was heading in that direction. Horrific images surfaced, one after another, threatening to push him into a state of total panic.

A sudden swell of resentment and anger washed over him. How dare they put him in this situation? His mom, Huxley, Adelia, the professor. How dare they fill his head with dreams then lock him up and leave him to suffer?

"Aaaaaaaaa!" A roar of rage ripped from his lungs, animalistic and wild. Fury seared through the fog of fear and pain.

Thomas willed himself to take a single purposeful breath. Then another. And another. Slowly his mind cleared. *Nobody did this to me. I asked for it. They warned me it would be hard, but I didn't care. Magic is my dream, and this is my chance to learn it.*

Piece by tiny piece, the fear and fury and hunger faded into the background. He could feel them, see them, but they no longer controlled him. Time slipped past. Hunger ebbed and flowed. Thirst parched his throat and dried his lips. Fear nibbled at the corners of his awareness. The sensations came and went.

A point of light appeared in the distant reaches of his mind, oblong and wobbling. The light came closer. He saw a splash of color in the center, a familiar object blurring in and out of focus. The orange hovered in space, growing more solid and tangible with every passing second.

"Just summon it. Quit trying to do it and do it." It was

Enrique's voice, then Master Sifu's, and finally his own. The phrase repeated, the three voices blending together. Thomas smiled. The last remnants of fear and frustration melted away. The orange was on the dining room table, and he was here. No big deal. A window opened in Thomas's mind and suddenly he saw what to do. He felt it.

He summoned the orange. He didn't try to do it. He did it.

THIRTY-ONE

THOMAS OPENED HIS EYES SLOWLY, cautiously, almost afraid to hope. The table came into view one tiny bit at a time, blurry and gray at first, and then with a sudden shock of color. He stood up so fast his chair clanged to the floor behind him. He didn't care. The orange was there, really there, a lone splash of color in the otherwise dingy room. The light refracted from its shiny skin, giving the fruit an almost otherworldly glow.

He reached out, mouth agape and heart racing. It was real. The fruit was solid. He ran his fingers over the thin skin, marveling at the slightly oblong shape and strange navel. He picked it up. It wasn't just an orange. It was *the orange*. The exact same one.

"I did it. I did it." The words came out as an awed whisper, along with a soft swear. He could practically hear his mom's reaction to his language but was too stunned to feel guilty. He ran to the door. "I did it! Huxley! Adelia! I did it! Professor Reilly! I did magic. Real magic!"

He waited, listening for a reaction, then shouted again. The hallway was silent. His stomach wasn't. A deep rumbling reminded Thomas that he needed food. He looked at the orange, reluctant to destroy the proof of his achievement.

Fresh gurgling in his gut settled the argument. He tore at the peel until the fruit was free and the first wedge was in his mouth. Sweet juicy citrus burst against his taste buds like a revelation, spilling droplets down his chin.

He wiped a sleeve across his face and took another bite. The aches and pains faded as he savored the fruit, replaced by a temporary state of near bliss. When the final slice was finished, he licked the last droplets of deliciousness from his fingers and looked longingly at the empty peel. *What now?*

Footsteps and voices echoed down the hallway, growing progressively closer until the bolt slid and Professor Reilly burst into the room. Huxley followed close behind.

"You did it! I knew you had it in you! Well done, Thomas!" shouted Professor Reilly, wrapping his arms around Thomas and lifting him off the floor in a gigantic bear hug. Thomas's lungs protested at the rib-cracking squeeze, but his joy compounded as the words sank in. *I did it! I really did it. Enrique's not going to believe this.* Enrique. A stab of sadness threatened to kill the celebratory mood but vanished as Huxley stepped into the room.

"Very well done indeed!" said Huxley. His eyes sparkled, the gold flecks shimmering in the yellow light. "Not a single one of your ancestors made their first breakthrough that quickly. Your great-grandfather Charles was the last to attempt that particular exercise, and it took him the better part of three days. Every time we tried to sleep, he'd start shouting and pounding on the door. When he finally made it, Adelia had to spend hours pulling splinters out of his hands."

"Three days?" Thomas grimaced. "Ten more minutes and I might have started gnawing on my own arm."

"Three days," said Huxley. "We had to sneak him water while he slept. I'm glad, for all of our sakes, that it didn't take that long for you."

"Me, too," said Thomas. The idea of three days without food was horrifying. "Why was he trying to learn so fast?"

"The war," said Huxley. "Things weren't looking so good in Europe, and his dad—your great-great-grandfather Marcus—had gone to England to help the Allies. He wanted Charles to be ready, in case the fighting got worse. Of course, Charles wanted to rush over and join his dad anyway. Luckily for all of us, the war ended before that was necessary."

"Oh," said Thomas. World War II.

"Come on," said Professor Reilly. "Ling Sun must have known you'd be finishing soon. There's dinner waiting upstairs. We'll pick up the practice once you've eaten and gotten some proper rest."

"Dinner?" Thomas's ears perked up. He was in the hallway without even realizing he'd moved. "Let's go! I'm starving."

THIRTY-TWO

"YOU RASCAL!" SAID PROFESSOR REILLY, his eyes wide with disbelief. "I spent hours looking for this. Hours!"

"Sorry, Professor," said Thomas, trying not to laugh. He'd practiced his new skill for almost two days, summoning a variety of items from around the compound. He'd even managed to get a couple of comic books from back home. The coup de gras was snagging the watch right off Professor Reilly's wrist. "You said to challenge myself, and that was a new challenge. I couldn't help it."

"Couldn't help it," Professor Reilly muttered as he refastened the band around his wrist. He was understandably grumpy, having just retraced every step from the past day and a half. "You might think a bit of gratitude was in order, but no, heaven forbid. Why say 'thank you' when there's a nice old man to torture. It's a thankless job, I tell you. A thankless job."

Thomas's attempt to hold back the laughter broke down in dramatic fashion. His attempt to cover it with a fake cough only brought a crankier look to the professor's face.

"Come on. Follow me. It's time to step things up a bit." Huxley glanced at Thomas as he started down the hallway, an amused twinkle in his eye. "You know, your dad was a bit of a prankster as well. Has anyone ever told you that?"

Thomas shook his head.

"Well, he most definitely was," said Huxley. "I'm not sure I've ever known anyone who enjoyed a practical joke more than he did."

"A bit of a prankster?" said Professor Reilly. "Ha! John Wildus was the king of the practical joke. Do you remember the time he materialized a bag of frozen peas in Bobby's knickers? I'm not sure I've ever seen anyone jump so high in my life."

"I do indeed," said Huxley. "And if I remember correctly, that particular prank was your idea."

"Me? I may have suggested that such a thing might be amusing—Bobby was acting like a stick in the mud, you know—but I didn't expect John to actually do it." Professor Reilly chuckled and thumped Thomas on the back. "Your dad was always willing to go after a good laugh, but he had a heart of gold and always made things right by people if they took offense. Remember that, Thomas. As someone with powers, it's doubly important to keep your heart in the right place."

Picturing his dad as a jokester was strange, but the idea of putting frozen peas in a friend's pants was easy enough to imagine. He didn't know this Bobby person, but he could practically see Enrique jumping out of his seat. Or even better, Sean Parker.

"In here." Huxley opened a door and held it for Thomas. "It's time that you try summoning something a bit larger."

Thomas stepped into a space that wasn't as large as a full-sized basketball court but wasn't all that far off either. *How big is this place anyway?* "What did you have in mind?"

"Anything you can *safely* summon is fair game," said Professor Reilly. "Just be thoughtful about it. Don't do anything that could cause harm to yourself or others."

"That's right," said Huxley. "Living things are off limits, but we'd like to see you challenge yourself. Start with whatever you can manage and work your way up to items that are larger than you are. We've put fresh fruit on the dining room table and bottles of water as well. Summon a snack when you need one."

"Got it," said Thomas. "Anything else?"

"Not a thing," said Professor Reilly. "We'll be back in a little while to see how you're doing."

. . .

When Huxley and Professor Reilly popped their heads into the room, Thomas was sitting in the bean bag chair he'd summoned from home and staring at his handiwork with a satisfied smile. A pair of banana peels, an empty carton of ice cream, and a container of chocolate syrup were on the floor next to a half-finished water bottle.

"A hippopotamus! Where on earth did you get a life-sized statue of a hippo?" Professor Reilly looked from Thomas to the giant bronze animal and back again.

"That's Earl," said Thomas. In addition to the hippo, he'd summoned his bunk bed, a potted palm tree, and a display case from Bogie's, a bookshop where the sales clerk had treated his question about magic with uncommon rudeness. "Me and Enrique met him on a class trip to the San Diego Zoo. We took pictures sitting on his back before the security guards kicked us off."

"Impressive." Huxley smiled a bit wryly. "I see you also found yourself more than just fresh fruit to snack on. It seems that your command of summoning is at a sufficiently high level to move on to the next lesson. Would you agree, Professor?"

"I would," said Professor Reilly. He put a hand on Earl's head and looked at Thomas. "And a good thing, too. Loading this fellow into a shipping crate isn't in the cards. You're going to have to put him back the magical way."

THIRTY-THREE

"BAD NEWS FROM OUR NETWORK," said Huxley. "Gareth sent a message. Arius is closing in on the second crystal."

The refrigerator door slammed shut so loudly the contents rattled. Professor Reilly turned around, his expression grim. "That is bad news. Did he give a timeline? Or see anything that can help us get to the bloody thing first?"

"I'm afraid not." Huxley pulled up a high backed-stool, set his glasses on the granite countertop, and rubbed his eyes. "But the image was clear. Arius is starting to make preparations, and Gareth wasn't able to pick up anything about a location or timeline. He's doing everything in his power to slow them down, but I'm afraid it might not be enough."

"Who's Gareth?" asked Thomas.

"Gareth Garibaldi." Huxley looked at Thomas with an expression that was both tired and puzzled. "He was here when you first arrived. I was under the assumption that you and he had been introduced. Is that not the case?"

Thomas shook his head, but one of the missing pieces

snapped into place. It was Garibaldi's office where he'd emerged from hiding. He was the man with the rough voice and thick leather boots. "He left before I came out of the ventilation system. Who is he?"

"He's one of us," said Professor Reilly. "He specializes in information retrieval and counterintelligence. He's helping us keep tabs on Arius and his crew while we try to teach you something useful."

"What can we do to help?" asked Thomas.

"Our best bet is to focus on your training," said Huxley. "The closer Arius gets, the more important it is that you be ready for action. That's doubly true if we aren't able to get our allies off the sidelines. At the moment, nobody believes us about Arius, so we may be on our own."

"I'm ready whenever you are," said Thomas. He'd managed a short nap and was itching to get to the next lesson. "Let's go."

Huxley smiled. "That's the spirit. If you're ready, we can head back to the training room. Professor, I believe Ling Sun is in the other kitchen finishing the special dish you ordered. Perhaps you could pick it up and join us downstairs."

"I'll meet you there in just a minute," said Professor Reilly.

• • •

"Making an object disappear isn't as simple as it might seem." Huxley once again pulled the dangling chain in the training room, bathing the once-forbidding room in light.

"When you send a thing away from where you are, it doesn't cease to exist. It goes somewhere. It has to. And you, the magician, have to dictate where that somewhere will be. If you just try to make a thing disappear, nothing happens. It doesn't work."

"Like sending Earl back." Thomas leaned forward and rested his elbows on the metal table where he'd made the orange appear. "He can't just disappear. I have to send him to his spot at the zoo. I get that."

"Exactly," said Huxley. "As before, we're going to start here, with small things, and work our way toward efforts of greater complexity. No matter what the size or scale, it is essential that you hold a clear image of the destination in your mind. Precision is key. Is that clear? Do you have any other questions?"

"Does it work with people?" Thomas pictured Sean Parker whisked from his house and deposited in the monkey exhibit at the zoo, the one place where he might really belong.

"You may one day learn to teleport, if that's what you're asking," said Huxley. Thomas felt a rush of excitement. It hadn't yet occurred to him that he might be able to zoom around the globe. "But the results of improperly sending or summoning a living thing can be quite horrifying. The practice requires exceptional caution."

"Why? What happens if you get it wrong?"

"Bad things," said Professor Reilly, causing both

Thomas and Huxley to turn around. Thomas was surprised he hadn't heard him coming. "Things no decent person would want on their conscience."

"Imagine what might happen if your image of the destination was incorrect, or that something had changed since the last time you saw the place," said Huxley. "Then, instead of an empty room, a person might materialize in exactly the same place as another person. Or a chair or sofa."

"Two things can't occupy the same physical space without their substance becoming entangled," said Professor Reilly. "And once they're entangled, there's no way to put either one back exactly the way it was before."

Thomas grimaced. The image was sufficiently unpleasant to discourage further discussion. "Right. That would be bad. So, where do we start?"

"Food worked pretty well last time, so we're going to try it again." Professor Reilly wore a mischievous expression as he produced a silver platter with a domed lid. A familiar and distinctly unpleasant aroma hit Thomas's nostrils. He turned from Professor Reilly to Huxley, his eyes wide and face horrified.

"What is that?"

Professor Reilly winked and whisked the lid away. "Your mom thought you might react a bit like that. She sends her sincere apologies, along with her wishes for the lesson to be learned swiftly and with minimal suffering."

Thomas stared, horrified. Spinach. An entire plate

covered in cooked spinach. *Mom!* He couldn't believe she'd sold him out like that. The very smell made him want to puke. Being the same room for an extended period would be completely unbearable. "My mom told you to torture me with spinach?"

"More or less. We wanted to find ways to motivate speedy learning. She supplied a list of your most and least favorite foods. Judging by your reactions so far, I'd say she was spot on."

The taste of bile tickled at the back of his throat, causing Thomas to gag. He covered his nose with his sleeve and took a shallow breath, silently vowing to pay them back. Some things simply can't be forgiven, and spinach is at the top of the list.

"Well, we'll leave you to it," boomed the professor. He thumped Thomas on the back and stepped into the hall, looking decidedly pleased with himself. "Good luck, my boy!"

"Sincere apologies," said Huxley, following close behind. "And speedy success."

The heavy bolt slid into place with a jolt. Thomas sat reeling, left alone in the tiny space with nothing but silence and the pile of green mush. His stomach turned. It was all he could do to keep from vomiting. "They are so going to pay for this."

Thomas muttered soft curses as he turned his mind to making the offensive stuff disappear. He closed his eyes and pictured it splattering against the hallway wall. He visualized the whole platter in the garbage can in the kitchen. He pictured the particles reassembling on the floor outside in an equally disgusting pile. The effort left him with a spinning head and a room still full of the horrific smell.

He stuck his nose into the front of his shirt and used the cloth as a filter. It helped, but each breath was still tinged with hints of nastiness. He closed his eyes and tried to gather his thoughts. Over and over, he tried to make the stuff disappear.

Hours passed, and Thomas's stomach began to grumble. He wanted to puke and eat all at the same time. His body and brain argued vehemently, but the more he tried to ignore his hunger, the more dominant it became. Soon all he could think about was food, but there was absolutely no way he'd take even a single bite of the now-cold pile of slime. Starvation would be better.

Inspiration struck. The lesson was sending, sure, but nobody told him not to use his summoning skills. A container of zipper-seal freezer bags appeared on the table, along with a large cloth napkin and a serving spoon. He wrapped the napkin around his face and shoveled the spinach into the bag. He gagged, but only a little, and managed to get every scrap of disgustingness sealed away. The bag went into the far corner of the room.

Now on to food.

He'd seen a sandwich in the refrigerator earlier. Turkey,

bacon, and avocado or something like that. It appeared, followed by a carton of milk and a package of chocolate chip cookies. There was writing on the see-through sandwich bag. *Prof Reilly.* The letters scrawled in tall black letters. Thomas grinned and took a bite. Phase one of revenging himself on the evil perpetrators of spinach torture had begun.

When the sandwich was down to scraps, he grabbed a cookie and, mouth still full of chocolatey deliciousness, washed it down with a gulp of milk straight from the carton. He ate a second cookie and took another swig.

"Errrrrrrrrrrrrrrp." His burp bounced from the walls like a ping-pong ball. He smiled and burped again. An aftershock, as Enrique would have called it. Enrique. For the hundredth time, Thomas wished his friend was with him. Together they'd figure things out twice as fast, and more importantly, they'd have a ten times better chance at beating Arius.

Thomas forced himself to change focus and found his eyes drawn back to the plastic bag. *How am I supposed to send that nasty stuff out of here?*

He leaned back in his chair and took a deep breath. The air no longer made him nauseous, and with his belly full, his eyes felt heavy. Instead of fighting the wave of sleepiness, he went with it. His eyelids fluttered shut. Strange and scattered images flitted through his mind as he slipped into the rubbery space where awake and dreaming mingle until they are one and the same.

Familiar faces blended with impossible things; Peggy became Enrique, who became Akhil. All of them were looking for him. Mr. Dilstrom stood in front of the class and repeated his name, over and over. *Wildus. Wildus. Wildus.* His mom sat on the couch, holding his picture with tears in her eyes. His face in the photo became his dad's, bearded, with piercing blue eyes. A giant hippopotamus charged out of the picture frame and into their living room, which was really a bookstore. The shelves warped around the rumbling beast. The hippo transformed into Sifu, who was actually Yoda—walking stick, robe and all. Sifu-Yoda whacked Thomas over the head with his stick. "There is no try."

Thomas's eyes flew open. There was a subtle ache where the dream-stick hit him, but he suddenly knew exactly what to do. He thought for a moment, but the destination was a no-brainer. He closed his eyes and sent the spinach to its new home. Then he kicked his feet onto the table, leaned back, and waited.

THIRTY-FOUR

"OF ALL THE SNEAKY, low down, dirty magician tricks! Spinach! In my pants! It's a bloody miracle I wasn't sitting down!" Professor Reilly's face was red and flustered. He held the bag of spinach in the air, his eyes wide and wild-looking.

The reaction was even better than Thomas could have imagined. He tried to keep a straight face, but the giggles came on strong. He squawked, a choked gurgling sound, and covered his mouth, trying to hold back the tide. The professor's expression fluctuated between fury and disbelief. Thomas broke into full-fledged laughter.

"Funny, is it? Messing with an old man's britches?"

Thomas nodded, his arms and legs pumping with glee. He tumbled from his chair and rolled on the floor in hysterics. The laughter came so hard Thomas could barely breathe. Professor Reilly stared at him. His mouth opened, closed, opened again. Like a fish. A big bearded fish. Thomas laughed harder. He fell back to the ground, his arms and legs jiggly.

"Did I hear correctly? Spinach in the pants?" Huxley

walked into the room and looked down. "Thomas, what on earth are you doing on the floor?"

"He's having a poke at an old man whose only fault is trying to teach him a bit of magic," said Professor Reilly. He mock-scowled at Thomas, one eyebrow raised. "I suppose I should be grateful that the stuff was in a plastic bag, but on the whole, it wasn't a particularly nice gesture."

"Not nice at all." Huxley's lips turned up at the corners, just a touch. "We're going to have to keep a close eye on you, Master Wildus. That much is for certain."

Professor Reilly's eyes settled on the table. They widened, and he stared at Thomas once more. "Is that my sandwich? The one with avocado and bacon? I've been looking forward to that all day."

Thomas's laughter redoubled, and this time even Huxley joined in.

• • •

The afternoon sun descended toward the peaks of the distant mountains, bathing the sky in bright blue as Thomas finished his Ba Gua form. He'd only done a few minutes of work, but as usual, the practice left him feeling better than when he started. He sat down on the wooden bench at the edge of the garden and picked up the book Professor Reilly had given him. *Quantum Physics and the Quest for Infinity.* Not exactly light reading, but an interesting way to fill the time between practice sessions.

"Thomas! How are you?"

Thomas looked up. "Adelia. Hey! I'm doing great. How about you?"

"I'm doing wonderfully, thanks." Adelia smiled, her brown eyes twinkling. "I hear your training is coming along quite nicely."

"Thanks," said Thomas, suddenly aware that Adelia hadn't been around for any of the instruction. *When was the last time I saw her? Two days ago? Longer?* "We sent Earl back to the zoo today. Huxley had a friend text pictures. It looks like we got him to the right spot."

"Earl?"

"A statue from the San Diego Zoo," said Thomas. "A hippo. I summoned him a couple days ago and was finally able to send him back."

"Oh, right. Yes, Huxley told me about that," said Adelia. "Very nicely done. It's hard to imagine all that many reasons to summon something larger than a hippo. You've made even faster progress than we hoped."

"What have you been up to?" asked Thomas. "It feels like I haven't seen you since the training started."

"That's because you haven't." Adelia's smile had a playful quality to it. "How do you feel about surprises?"

"Depends on the surprise, I guess," said Thomas. "What is it?"

"Something I've been working on. I think you'll like it. Come on, let me show you." Adelia took Thomas by the hand and pulled him to his feet.

"Where are we headed?" Thomas asked, thoroughly intrigued.

"This way." Adelia led him into the house, through the dining room, around a corner, and into a familiar hallway. She finally stopped outside of the office where Thomas had come out of hiding. He still hadn't met Mr. Garibaldi. Maybe that was the surprise, finally getting to talk to the mysterious surveillance expert.

Adelia grabbed the doorknob and flashed a smile so bright it literally seemed to glow. The door opened, and a familiar figure sped at him like a torpedo. Before he had a chance to react, he was being lifted off his feet and squeezed by a pair of wiry arms.

"Enrique! What are you doing here?"

THIRTY-FIVE

"SO, THIS IS SCIENCE CAMP, HUH? Doesn't look like much of a science camp to me," said Enrique.

"Science camp?" Thomas's brain was three steps behind, still trying to get a handle on the fact that Enrique was actually there.

"Yeah. Science camp for gifted kids," Enrique answered. "That's what your mom told my mom, anyway. She said she'd arranged a scholarship for me to come, too."

"My mom said I was at science camp?" said Thomas.

"Yeah. I knew that was BS, but I had no idea where you really were. Obviously, I had to find out."

"I'm totally and completely lost." Thomas looked at Adelia for help, but she just smiled and shrugged her shoulders.

"Of course, you are." Enrique jabbed Thomas in the arm. "You can't just disappear and expect me not to come looking for you. I came over to hang out and nobody was home. You didn't answer your phone or return any of my calls. Then you weren't at school, which never happens, so

I called your mom to see if you got sick or something. She didn't answer either, so I waited at your house until she came home. She said you were visiting relatives on the East Coast, but I wasn't having any of that. You'd have told me if you were going out of town."

"Of course, I would've," Thomas replied. "But how did you end up here?"

"It's kind of a long story," said Enrique.

"I've got time, I think." Thomas looked at Adelia for confirmation.

"You do," said Adelia. "Come on. You can talk while we walk. Enrique hasn't seen this place yet. We can give him a tour while he fills you in."

"Sounds good to me," said Enrique.

"Ditto," said Thomas. He followed Adelia and Enrique into the hall. "So, what happened?"

"I ask your mom more questions, and she starts acting all weird and sad, like she might cry or something. She said you were at camp and that she didn't expect you home for at least a couple of weeks. I asked if 'camp' had something to do with the book you'd shown me. Her eyes got all big, and she said, 'What book?' I said the weird little book you kept in a box under your bed."

"You told her I showed you the book? That was supposed to be a secret!" Thomas was horrified, but Enrique didn't seem to mind.

"Interrupting again, are we?" Enrique quipped, his left

eyebrow raised. "Anyway, I told her you'd shown me the book and how the next day it changed a bunch. She said, 'Interesting,' and asked if I'd be around for the next couple days. I said yeah, of course. The next day, she shows up with Adelia."

Adelia shrugged her shoulders and looked pleased with herself.

"They talk to me for a while about my family. You know, a whole bunch of questions about my mom and dad, aunts, uncles, grandparents. Weird stuff, like if anyone ever told stories about people in our family having unusual abilities. I never heard of anything like that, but at the end, they give me a wooden box and tell me there's a book inside like the one you had. Adelia gives me the same spiel you got. Keep it hidden. Don't tell anyone. Read it only when you're alone. Yadda yadda yadda."

Thomas could hardly believe his ears. *Could this possibly be going where I think it is?* "Then what?"

"Your mom sends me to your house to start reading the thing. You know how it is at my place. It would have been impossible to ever get a minute alone. So, I start reading the book, and within a couple days the cover starts changing. At first, it's little stuff like you said. Pictures moving around, but only a tiny bit. Then the color started showing up."

Thomas's eyes got big. "Seriously?"

"Yeah, seriously," said Enrique. "I still don't know what any of that means, but I tell your mom what's going on—they said it would be okay to do that, so long as I don't tell anyone else—and next thing you know, she and Adelia show up at my place again. I get home from class, and there they are, sitting in the kitchen talking to my mom."

"No way!" exclaimed Thomas. His heart was racing now.

"Yes way. They were telling her about a scholarship to a special science camp. Super fancy and exclusive. At first, my mom didn't want to hear it, but they kept telling her what a great opportunity it is, and I start begging, so eventually, she says yes." Enrique paused and looked around the room. "Now, call me crazy, but this ain't science camp. What is this place, and what are we doing here?"

Adelia looked at Thomas. "Maybe you should tell him?"

"For real? You're sure?" Thomas could hardly believe what was happening. It was literally a wish come true.

Adelia smiled and nodded. "Positive."

"Tell me what?"

"You're here to learn magic," said Thomas. "Real magic."

Enrique stared at Thomas as if he was looking at a crazy person. "Great. Now you've lost your stinking mind. Let's try this. Repeat after me. There. Is. No. Such. Thing. As—"

"You know your favorite comic book?" interrupted Thomas. "The first run *Ghost World*? Where is it right now?"

"On the top shelf in my closet, like always," Enrique replied. "Why?"

Thomas closed his eyes and took a breath. When he

opened them, the comic was on the desk in front of him, still in its thick plastic case.

"H-how? What the—?" Enrique's jaw dropped to the floor. He looked from the comic to Thomas and back again. His mouth opened, closed, opened again. "Are you telling me you can do magic? For reals?"

Thomas nodded. His smile practically cracked his face in half. "For reals. And making things appear is just the beginning."

"Sweet mother of guacamole! You can do magic." An uncertain expression flashed across Enrique's face. He looked questioningly at Adelia. "Are you saying I get to learn magic? That I might be able to do that, too?"

Adelia's smile was both amused and radiant. "And yes, that's exactly what we're saying. You're here to learn magic."

"B-but how?" asked Enrique. "How is it possible?"

"Magic? Or your ability to learn it?" asked Adelia.

"Both. Either. All of it. I don't know."

"Magic is real. It's existed for thousands of years, if not longer. As to why you have the ability to learn it, we're not yet sure," said Adelia. "In every case Huxley and I ever studied, the gift has been acquired from an object of power or passed down genetically. We haven't yet figured out where in your family history such an event occurred, but *The Book of Sorrows* is never wrong. You have the gift. It's only a matter of time before we figure out how and why."

"Ah, there they are," said Professor Reilly as Thomas

stepped into the great room. "This must be the infamous Enrique Rodriguez. Enrique, I'm Professor Reilly, and this fine gentleman here is Huxley. You've already met Adelia."

"It's very nice to meet you." Huxley smiled and extended a hand toward Enrique. "We haven't managed to scare you off yet, have we?"

"Nice to meet you, too," said Enrique, though he shook hands with the look of someone who wasn't quite sure he was actually awake. "Not yet."

"Good! We have work to do, and not much time to do it in. Are you ready to get started?"

THIRTY-SIX

"ARIUS HAS THE SECOND CRYSTAL." Adelia's expression was grim. "I don't know how he got to it so quickly, but we're running out of time."

"Are you certain?" asked Huxley. "That would be incredibly bad news."

"Gareth is certain," said Adelia. "And I trust him implicitly."

"I thought those things had been hidden for hundreds of years? How is he finding them?" Enrique had been brought up to speed on their situation between training sessions. Much to everyone's surprise, including and especially his own, he'd picked up summoning and sending almost as quickly as Thomas had. Thomas, meanwhile, was struggling to make any new progress. Teleporting had thus far proven impossible.

"Arius has a seer on his side," said Huxley. "A very talented seer at that. The fact that she's found two of the crystals is a testament to her abilities. I wouldn't have expected anyone to find the second so quickly after the first."

"A seer?" said Enrique. "You mean like a psychic or something?"

"Exactly like that," replied Professor Reilly. "Only Arianna is much more than a psychic. Her gifts run deep and wide, far more so than those of her brother, though he's the one who draws all the attention. Being a billionaire does that, I suppose. Whatever the case, Arius is far more dangerous with Arianna at his side than he would ever be on his own."

"What are we supposed to do if we can't find the last crystal before he does?" asked Thomas. "Can we take the ones he's already got? You know, summon them or break into his house or something?"

"You're welcome to try summoning them, but I'm afraid it won't work," said Huxley. "Objects of power are almost always resistant to magic. They work on their own laws. Laws I don't fully understand."

"We can't risk an attack on Arius's compound," said Adelia. "It's too well-protected, and we don't have enough support. Nobody wants to believe the crystals still exist, much less that Arius has a real chance at recovering them. Our only hope is to find the third crystal and destroy it, like James should have done centuries ago. If it can't be destroyed, we at least have to find a way to keep it out of Arius's reach."

"That sounds great, but how are we supposed to find the thing?" asked Enrique. "I'm not psychic. Are any of you?"

"I'm afraid not," said Huxley. "But we do have a seer on our side. Gareth Garibaldi. Aside from Arianna, I'm not aware of anyone on the planet with more psychic ability. Gareth is searching for the last crystal even as we speak. With a little bit of luck, we'll hear from him with a location before Arius and Arianna can find it."

"I thought Garibaldi was some kind of spy." Thomas looked at Professor Reilly with a touch of annoyance. "Counterintelligence and information retrieval. How come you didn't just say, 'He's a psychic'?"

"Apologies, my boy," said Professor Reilly. "It's an old habit. I've gotten so used to talking around these things that sometimes the metaphors come out more naturally than the plain truth. Gareth is, as Huxley said, a seer. Or psychic, if you prefer. In either case, he is a gatherer of information and intelligence of the highest order."

Thomas scowled for a second, then decided to get over it. "All right, fine. What can we do to help?"

"Focus on your training," said Huxley. "Right now, the most important thing you can do is prepare yourselves for action."

"He's right," said Adelia. "Time is short. The very instant that Gareth finds the location, we have to be ready to move, and you have to be ready. And on that note, we have another surprise."

"Another surprise?" said Enrique. "How many more surprises are there?"

"At least one." Adelia smiled, but to Thomas, she looked nervous. "Come on. He's waiting for us down the hall."

• • •

Thomas stopped abruptly, only halfway into the richly appointed office. Enrique bumped into him, pushing him the rest of the way into the room. A flush of adrenaline hit Thomas's system. "You."

"Me." The man with the olive overcoat leaned back in a reclining chair, his shredded boots resting on the top of the desk. He was even more unkempt than Thomas remembered. His black hair hung in greasy locks around a gnarled beard. His face and hands were smudged and dirty. His head lolled to the side, almost as if he were drunk. Only his piercing green eyes gave any hint that he was more than he appeared to be. "Me, me, me, me."

Adelia stepped forward and put a hand on Thomas's shoulder. "Thomas, Enrique, I would like you to meet—"

"Squattapus," said the man. His voice was soft, but with a harsh edge. "Long for Squat."

Thomas lifted his hand in a half wave. "I, uh, I'm Thomas."

"Squat?" mouthed Enrique, flashing Thomas a skeptical look. He looked from the man to Huxley and Adelia. "No offense, but how is this guy supposed to teach us magic?"

Huxley smiled. "Things aren't always what they seem, Mr. Rodriguez. You should know that by now. Squattapus—Squat—is a magician of unparalleled ability. He guided

Thomas to our shop before we'd even learned about Arius's pursuit of the crystals. As of today, he will take over your instruction. If we're to have any chance of success, you're going to need every bit of his skill and experience."

Squat's lips parted in a smile that showed yellowed and uneven teeth. He glanced at Thomas and Enrique as if contemplating a meal, his green eyes narrowed and blazing. Enrique stared back, his chin jutting defiantly forward. Thomas shifted uneasily on his feet, hardly able to meet the magician's gaze. If Squat noticed their discomfort, he gave no outward sign. Instead, he looked lazily away and picked at his teeth with a long and filthy fingernail.

"Well, I suppose we should leave you to it." Adelia looked decidedly nervous.

"Best of luck," said Professor Reilly. He clapped Thomas and Enrique on the back. "I have a feeling you're going to need it."

The other adults filed out of the room, leaving Thomas and Enrique alone with the unkempt magician. Squat looked down at his hand, silently contemplating the extracted contents of his jagged teeth. Apparently satisfied, he reached back and ran a grubby finger over the wall. A dark smudge appeared on the otherwise pristine surface.

"Gross," whispered Enrique.

Thomas agreed, but was too focused on their alleged teacher to respond. Squat spun around in his chair, stood up, and strolled to the door. He paused, flashed an almost predatory smile, and disappeared into the hallway with a contemptuous snort. The door swung shut and the lock engaged from the outside.

"What the heck was that?" said Enrique. "What are we supposed to do? Just hang out in here and twiddle our thumbs? I thought he was going to teach us something."

"I don't know," said Thomas.

"Are you sure they didn't just grab some nutjob off the street?" Enrique looked uneasily at the locked door. "I know it's not cool to judge people by their looks, but if he really is some kind of heavy-hitter magician, why doesn't he summon himself some clean pants and a toothbrush? It's like, come on, man, how about a little personal hygiene? You know what I mean?"

Thomas's mind zoomed through his various encounters with the man, settling on the quasi-attack on his ride home from Enrique's house. He heard the words in his head, remembered the rush of shapeless energy and the flash of blue light, saw the man flying backward through the air. *Was he already teaching me then?* "I don't know. I saw him a couple times back home. I think he might be the real deal."

"You sure he's not just some crazy?" Enrique looked skeptical. He glanced past Thomas. His eyes narrowed, then widened. He stepped toward the big desk where Squat had been sitting. "Hey, what's that?"

Thomas followed Enrique's gaze and felt a momentary buzz of confusion. The smudge on the wall was no longer a smudge. It was a pitch-black circle almost half the size of a baseball. And it wasn't a dirt stain. It was a hole. A hole that was growing larger with every passing second. As Thomas watched, the opening continued to increase in size, swallowing the fragments of plaster and drywall around it. "I don't know, but I don't like it. Come on, let's get out of here."

Enrique nodded. "Yeah. Yeah, I think that's a good call."

More and more wall disappeared, revealing a darkness so deep it seemed alive, hungry. Thomas's stomach clenched as he backed away. He yanked on the door handle, hoping to force the latch. The door was stuck solid. "Come on, give me a hand."

Enrique gripped the handle and they both pulled. Same result.

Thomas put a foot on the wall for leverage and yanked with all his might. His fingers screamed in protest, but the door didn't budge. The darkness was nearly the size of a person now, and an audible sucking sound accompanied the accelerating collapse of the wall. Larger and larger chunks disappeared every second, as if the thing was getting stronger. He pulled again, straining until his back ached, but to no avail. He stepped back and kicked at the doorknob. It didn't budge.

Enrique pounded on the door. "Hey, guys! Guys! Open up. Let us out of here!"

The sucking sound increased as more of the room

crumbled. The darkness seemed to take on a palpable, almost living form as it grew. Tendrils of pure black wisped into the room, hungry tentacles bent on pulling everything into the gaping abyss.

"We've got to get out of here," shouted Thomas. "I'll try to send the door down to the training room. Summon us a hammer or an ax or something, in case that doesn't work."

"Got it!" yelled Enrique.

The sound was a jet engine and growing louder by the second. One of the bookshelves disappeared, a few stray books at first, and then in a single massive collapse. Thomas closed his eyes and focused on the training room. He tried sending the door again and again. It refused to move. With a sense of horror, he realized something—or someone—was stopping him. "I can't do it! Something is blocking me. Any luck?"

"No!" shouted Enrique. He shook his head. "It's not working."

Darkness reached the floor, devouring carpet and ceiling, bits of wall and floor and ceiling crumbling on all sides. Thomas backed away, watching in shock as a leather chair sucked into the growing abyss and disappeared. Thomas and Enrique stared at each other with wide, horrified eyes. The far wall was completely gone, and now the floor was crumbling at an increasingly rapid pace.

"Try again!" shouted Thomas. He closed his eyes, drawing every bit of focus and concentration he could muster.

The door wouldn't budge. Neither would the doorknob or bolt.

"I can't summon anything!" shouted Enrique. "We have to teleport!"

"Teleport?" yelled Thomas, hardly able to hear himself over the deafening roar. "But I haven't figured out how."

"Me neither! We'd better learn fast!"

The abyss was closing in, a giant mouth coming closer and closer as it swallowed more of the room. *Quantum physics.* Thomas closed his eyes and tried to focus. *Particles in two places at the same time. Here and there. Here and there.* He imagined the hallway, pictured himself standing outside of the room. *Now go!*

It didn't work.

He tried again. Nothing.

"I can't do it!" Enrique's voice was full of fear and frustration.

Thomas opened his eyes. Wisps of blackness were closing in, the darkness beyond deeper and more terrifying than anything he had ever seen. He moved away until his back pressed into the wall and there was nowhere left to go. He stared into the abyss, found an infinite void staring back, horrifying in its absolute emptiness. Fear flooded his system, filling him with terrified energy. He heard Enrique scream, but the sound was distant, almost from another world.

Here and there. Here and there. There. Just there. He didn't move.

Thomas suddenly felt something in his mind, a voice or presence. Energy rushed up his spine as the wires connected. A window opened in his mind, a pathway forward. He grabbed Enrique's arm and focused on the hallway with every ounce of his strength. The darkness gobbled the carpet, moving greedily toward his feet, threatening to swallow him whole.

Thomas stepped forward, mentally and physically.

There was a sudden rush, and then silence.

THIRTY-SEVEN

THOMAS OPENED HIS EYES and found himself standing in the hall. His hand was so tight on Enrique's arm that his knuckles had turned white. Enrique's face was a mask of fear—his eyes squeezed shut and jaw clenched against the imminent onslaught of darkness. Thomas took a step back, half expecting the door to crumble as the terrible darkness continued its onslaught of the house.

He waited. Nothing happened.

"Are—are we alive?" asked Enrique. His eyes squinted open, just a fraction.

Thomas nodded. The hall was silent, the door held, and the walls stood strong. There was no sign that anything strange had happened at all. "I think so."

Enrique took in the hallway with a look of complete disbelief. He stepped hesitantly forward and pressed his ear against the wall. He pulled away with a puzzled look on his face. "I don't hear anything. Literally, not a single sound."

Thomas tried, with the same result. "Me either."

"What the hell was that?"

"I don't know."

"Should we look inside?" asked Enrique.

"I don't know," repeated Thomas. He closed his eyes and listened again. There was nothing. Pure silence. A thought cut through the lingering haze of fear and adrenaline. *I just teleported. This is crazy! I teleported, and I took Enrique with me.* The last remnant of fear gave way, replaced by excitement that bordered on giddiness. "Yeah. Definitely."

Enrique stepped tentatively to the door and pressed his ear against the heavy wood. Thomas followed suit. Inside it was silent. Thomas reached down and slid back the heavy bolt. He grabbed the doorknob and looked at Enrique for affirmation.

Enrique nodded. Thomas twisted the knob. The latch clicked, and the door swung inward with a soft creak. Thomas flinched backward, bracing himself against what he might see.

The room looked exactly as it had before the abyss nearly devoured them. The walls and bookcases were back, books on the shelves and papers in neat piles. The chair was at an odd angle to the desk, just the way Squat left it. It looked like nothing out of the ordinary had happened at all. The air whooshed out of Thomas's lungs. He hadn't even realized he was holding his breath. Only a small dark spot on the wall remained as a reminder that Squat had ever been there.

"Right." Enrique glanced at Thomas and ran a tentative

finger over the smudge. "I, uh, I guess the guy might have some skills."

"Yeah," said Thomas. "I think he might."

• • •

The adults were gathered around the fireplace in the great room when Thomas and Enrique found them. Huxley, Adelia, and Professor Reilly huddled with their heads together, talking in hushed tones. Squat lay on the long couch nearby, sprawled out with his feet up and filthy boots wreaking havoc on the soft leather. He didn't seem the slightest bit concerned about the mess or the nearby conversation.

"Hey, guys," said Thomas. Three heads swung around instantly. The fourth didn't react at all.

"You did it!" exclaimed Adelia. She stood and rushed toward them, a look of profound relief on her face. "Oh, thank goodness!"

"Barely," said Enrique, allowing Adelia to guide him forward. "What was that in there?"

"An illusion," said Huxley. He glanced at Squat, who continued his lounging as if there were nobody else in the room. Apparently, the ceiling was more interesting than the people. "A powerful illusion, but an illusion nonetheless."

"Right. If it was an illusion, how come you all look so relieved?" said Enrique. "What would have happened if we didn't escape? Or if we'd messed up the teleporting."

"Hard to know," said Squat, still staring into space. "But don't worry. I'm sure we'd have sorted it out. Eventually."

276

"Eventually?! What? Are you psychotic or something?" said Enrique.

Squat let out a dismissive snort and continued his study of the ceiling.

"I can understand why you might be upset." Huxley put a hand on Enrique's shoulder. "I admit that the technique was unorthodox. But time is short, and you just learned something in minutes that most magicians struggle with for months or years."

"I didn't learn it. Thomas did," said Enrique. There was a hint of jealousy in his voice.

"You'll get it," said Thomas. "Don't worry. I had a four-day head start on training."

"He's right," said Adelia. "You'll figure it out soon enough."

"You will," said Thomas. "And think about it. We just teleported. You and me. Literally teleported. How cool is that?

"Pretty cool." Enrique grinned. "Teach me to do that, and I'll forgive sorcerer psycho-pants for giving me a heart attack."

"Done deal," said Thomas. "Come on. We'll see the rest of you at dinner."

THIRTY-EIGHT

"ENRIQUE. HEY, ENRIQUE. YOU UP?"

"Go away. Too early. Tired."

Thomas waited a minute, then flipped the light switch. "Enrique. Let's go. It's time to get up."

Enrique groaned and pulled a pillow over his head. "Noooo. Need sleep. Tired."

"Come on. Let's get some breakfast and start training. Enrique."

Thomas leaned against the door, thrumming his fingers against the frame. He could teleport at will now, but Enrique's progress had been painfully slow. Two days of struggle and still he hadn't made the breakthrough. Thomas kept hoping Squat would intervene, but the unkempt magician had been a non-entity. He'd hinted at the next lesson—something to do with projecting energy from the hands—and then retreated without demonstrating or offering specifics. Not super helpful.

Meanwhile, the tension in the house was mounting

rapidly. There was no word from Garibaldi about the location of the last crystal, and every hour felt like a steady march toward doom. Thomas couldn't help feeling that Arius had the more powerful seer on his side and would find the crystal first. Whatever the case, the adults were hardly talking anymore, and everyone seemed stressed. "Yo, 'Rique. Time to get started."

"Bad friend. Go away," grunted Enrique. "Enrique tired. Need sleep."

"Lazy friend, wake up," said Thomas, smiling in spite of his impatience. "Eat food. Practice magic. Have fun."

Enrique sighed and peered out from under the pillow. "Ugh. What time is it?"

"Magic time."

"That's not what I meant." Enrique yawned and rubbed his face. "It feels early."

"I know," said Thomas. Enrique was right. It was still dark outside, but he needed his friend to catch up so they could both move on to the next challenge. "But I'm up, and now you are, too. Exciting, right?"

"Exciting isn't the word I'd use," said Enrique. "What's the hurry anyway?"

"Don't know," said Thomas. He did know. Kind of. An intense dream had pulled him from sleep—the last clear image was a flash of purple light silhouetting a man with a coat billowing around him. The rest of the details had scattered, but now he was wide awake and had a gnawing compulsion to visit the kitchen. "Come on, let's grab breakfast and get back to work."

Enrique sat up with a grunt. "Fine, but you owe me. I could have slept another ten hours. Easy."

"Deal," said Thomas. "Now come on, let's roll. I'm hungry."

"You're hungry? How about I feed you a knuckle sandwich?" said Enrique. "What time is it, anyway? For real? It feels early. Sleep spoiler."

Thomas shrugged and stepped into the hallway. It was empty, as was the great room when he got there a minute later. He glanced at the grandfather clock in the corner. 5:57. It was too early for a rational human being to be awake, and he couldn't logically explain the compulsion to go to the kitchen, much less the need to have Enrique come along. He didn't even try to defend himself when Enrique muttered "knucklehead" and thumped his shoulder.

"That's my bad," said Thomas. "I'll get breakfast."

He pulled a pair of cereal bowls from the cupboard and set them on the granite island, then grabbed spoons from the drawer. As he set the spoons down, a box of Life cereal and a carton of milk appeared on the table. Enrique flashed a victorious smile, pointed at his own chest, and mouthed the word "magic."

Thomas mentally kicked himself. He could have summoned the gear himself. Rookie mistake.

An almost musical rattle accompanied the clatter of cereal tumbling into his bowl. The sound disappeared so quickly he didn't bother turning around. Instead, he handed the box to Enrique and poured himself some milk. The rattling came again, slightly louder this time, and clearer.

"What's that?" asked Thomas, his mouth full of the still-crunchy cereal. A thin trickle of milk escaped his lips. He wiped at it with his sleeve.

Enrique glanced over his shoulder. A puzzled look crossed his face, and then surprise. His eyes widened. He scrambled onto the granite countertop, pulling his legs up so quickly his chair clattered to the ground. The rattling became a chorus, no longer distant and musical, but angry and close.

"T-thomas," stammered Enrique. "Y-you have to get up here. Now!"

Thomas's heart jumped into his throat. A giant snake had coiled just a few feet away, head raised and knobby tail rattling dangerously. At least four more were slithering into the kitchen from the great room. All of their tails were equipped with the same telltale rattle. Thomas fought the urge to panic and forced himself to climb slowly onto the granite. His eyes never left the nearest snake. The thing seemed poised to strike at any second. "Those are rattlesnakes."

"No kidding, Sherlock," whispered Enrique. He had slid as far back from the coiled snake as the narrow strip of granite allowed. "What are rattlesnakes doing in here?"

"I don't know." Thomas watched as the other snakes coiled, their tails lifted into the air. "Can rattlesnakes jump?"

"Don't know, and I don't want to find out," said Enrique. "Let's teleport out of here and call for help?"

Thomas shook his head. "The others could wake up any minute. What if one of them came in here before we could warn them?"

"That'd be bad." Enrique looked down, his eyes fearful. "There's no way I'm trying to jump past those things. What's your great idea?"

"We blast them with energy," said Thomas. "Squat says it's possible. Maybe this is some kind of training exercise."

"Yeah, sure," said Enrique. The nearest snake hissed and shook its rattle. He kicked a stool away from the island. It clattered over with a bang, nearly landing on the smallest snake. The serpent lunged, striking at the leg of the chair with his venomous fangs before coiling once more. The rattling doubled in intensity, taking on an almost frenzied quality. "One minor problem. We don't know how."

"We'd better learn—" Thomas froze mid-sentence. There was rattling coming from behind him now, too. He looked over his shoulder and saw a thick snake slithering along the countertop, tail shaking as it approached. A second was close behind, making its way up the leg of the tilted stool, using it like a makeshift ramp. Within seconds, the deadly creatures would be separated from the granite island by only a few feet of empty space.

Enrique pulled himself to the center of the granite. "This is bad. Really, really bad."

Fear and anger mingled in Thomas's chest. He aimed his hands at the snake closest to him, his eyes scrunched up with concentration. "Fire!"

Nothing happened.

The snake began to coil. Enrique aimed his hands and grunted. "This isn't working."

"Figure it out," said Thomas. "Fast!"

"I'm trying!" Enrique pounded his hands into the granite. A fresh round of rattling erupted, angrier and closer than ever.

The diamond-shaped head wobbled back and forth, beady eyes fixed directly on Thomas. Blood and adrenaline pounded through Thomas's veins. He aimed his palm at the creature and yelled again. "Fire! Shoot!"

He felt a spark kindling in his gut, energy flushing into his hands. The snake hissed, its mouth opened, revealing fangs dripping with deadly venom.

"Something's happening," shouted Enrique. "I can feel it."

Thomas could, too. An image flashed in his mind—particles flowing through his body into his hand and blasting outward with a burst of blue light. The spark took on fuel, feeding on energy and adrenaline until there was a fire raging in his belly. The synapses clicked into place. He *felt* the answer in his body. His hands relaxed.

The snake pulled itself into a tighter coil, its head recoiling even as its slithering tongue forked between deadly fangs.

A white-hot sensation burned in the center of Thomas's forehead, building in intensity as the creature prepared to strike. Suddenly it launched into the tiny space that divided them, its jaws open and fangs dripping with venom.

"Eeeyaaii!" shouted Thomas. Sizzling fire blazed in his mind, burning a trail to the palm of his hand. A burst of blue light exploded outward, striking the creature mid-flight. The snake collapsed into a heap on the floor.

A wordless and primal scream issued from Enrique as a green flash lit up the kitchen.

The second countertop snake launched itself at Thomas. Another ball of light exploded from his palm, blazing outward until it struck the airborne creature. It thudded to the floor as if it had slammed into a pane of glass. Like the other, it was either unconscious or dead.

Enrique shouted again, and another green flash lit up the kitchen. And another. Thomas turned. Three snakes lay on the ground, their bodies limp and unmoving.

Enrique looked at him with wide eyes. "Did you see that?"

Thomas shook his head. His palms burned with the lingering traces of energy. He jumped to his feet, eyes locked on the last two snakes. They were coiled just inside of the door, their tails rattling furiously.

Enrique flashed a fierce grin and stood beside him. "You

take the one on the right. I've got the one on the left. On three."

"On three."

"One. Two. Three." Their voices blended, and then blue light ripped from Thomas's palm, thudding into the coiled body of the larger snake. The thing tumbled backward even as a matching ball of green energy blasted from Enrique's hand and slammed into the other.

"Bam!" said Enrique. "That's what I'm talking about."

Thomas's entire body tingled, head to toe. Even his hair felt alive and vibrant. The bodies of seven snakes littered the kitchen floor.

A hulking shadow suddenly materialized in the great room, lumbering forward. Thomas almost let fire with another blast of energy. "What's with all the commotion? Folks are trying to get some shuteye around here."

Thomas lowered his hands. It was Professor Reilly, his voice grumpy and tired. "Sorry, Professor. We had a little incident with snakes."

"With what?"

"Snake!" shouted Enrique.

An enormous rattler slithered out from behind a trash can a few feet from Professor Reilly, tail rattling like a maraca. The professor cried out and took a stumbling half-step back, his face a mask of pure fear. The rattling intensified as the creature pulled itself into a swift coil, its head cocking back as it prepared to strike.

The snake launched itself toward the professor, fangs aiming at the open flesh of his hairy legs. Professor Reilly screamed and fell backward onto the floor.

Thomas's hand was up and aimed on pure instinct. Green light exploded into the serpent, followed almost instantly by a burst of blue. The creature tumbled forward, moist fangs clacking on the hard floor inches from Professor Reilly's bare feet. He scrambled backward, a whimpering moan of terror tumbling from his lips as moved into the giant living room.

For a long moment, there was silence as the professor's mouth worked wordlessly. "Bloody hell! Rattlesnakes in the kitchen? What in the name of Moses is happening around here?"

"Training." Squattapus appeared in the corner of the kitchen, materializing as smoothly as the Cheshire cat. His voice was amused, his lips pulled into the ghost of a smile.

"Training?" Professor Reilly's eyes widened. "This was your doing? That bloody thing nearly bit my bloody leg."

"Then it's a good thing they learned quickly." Squattapus snapped his fingers and the snakes disappeared. He vanished as well, but not before Thomas saw the half smile on his face. A second later, Squat's disembodied voice echoed through the kitchen. "Lesson over. Now practice."

THIRTY-NINE

"HE'S FOUND IT!" Huxley's voice penetrated Thomas's dream even as a pair of hands shook his body. "Get up. Quickly! It's time to go."

"What? Huh?" Thomas looked up groggily, torn between the haze of sleep and the jarring intrusion of sound and feeling. Someone flipped a switch, triggering an onslaught of bright light.

"Up and dressed. Hurry," said Huxley.

Thomas blinked his eyes open and found Huxley leaning over him. "Dressed for what?"

"Gareth found the third crystal." Adelia was holding two pairs of jeans and a couple of long-sleeved shirts. "We've got to get moving. Come on. There isn't a minute to lose."

"What?" Enrique sounded awake now. "Now?"

"We have the location of the third crystal," said Huxley. "And if Gareth found it, it's only a matter of time before Arianna does as well. We've got to get moving if we're to have any chance of getting to it first."

Adrenaline shook the remaining fog from Thomas's

head. He jumped out of bed and pulled on a fresh pair of jeans. "Where is it?"

"Sumidero Canyon," said Adelia. "Come on. We've already loaded backpacks for you. The jet is fueled up and ready to take us there now, but the airstrip is forty-five minutes away."

"Sumi-whatty canyon?" asked Thomas as he climbed out of bed.

"Sumidero Canyon," said Enrique. "It's in Mexico."

"Very good, Enrique," said Huxley. "Quite right. Sumidero Canyon is in Southern Mexico, near the border of Guatemala."

"How did you know that?" asked Thomas. He pulled on his shirt.

"My dad's from Chiapas. My mom went down there to look for him once, right after he took off," said Enrique. "I guess she was hoping to find him and bring him home. Obviously, that didn't happen."

"Sorry 'Rique. I didn't know," said Thomas.

"I'm sorry, too," said Adelia, pushing them toward the door. "But right now, we've got to get moving. We can talk during the flight, but we don't have even a minute to spare. Let's go."

"Why don't we teleport?" asked Thomas. "We could be there in ten seconds."

"Teleport?" Professor Reilly shook his head vigorously and headed toward the great room. "Not me. No thank you."

"We can't," said Huxley. "Not without knowing exactly where we're going and precisely what that location looks like at the very moment we intend to arrive. It would be far too dangerous."

"He's right," said Adelia. "We simply can't risk it. Come on. We'll drive to the airstrip."

"Maybe," said Thomas. "But I have an idea. Let's go, we can try it on the way to the plane. If it doesn't work out, we'll fly. If it does, we teleport."

"What's your idea?" asked Enrique.

"You have the class roster loaded on your phone, right? The one with everyone's number and email address?"

"Yeah, but how's that going to help?" asked Enrique.

"I need the phone number for Akhil Nagarajan," said Thomas.

"Who?"

"Akhil Nagarajan," said Thomas. "He's a year ahead of us. Skinny. Glasses. Into computers."

"Oh, right. The new kid. What's he got to do with anything?"

"I'll explain on the way." Thomas followed Adelia out the front door and into the courtyard where a large SUV was waiting with the engine on. Vapor streamed from the exhaust pipe into the cool night air, floating upward into a sky still dotted with thousands of visible stars. The moon was hardly more than a silver-white sliver above the nearby mountains, reflecting a sun that was still hours from rising.

"Just find me the number. Please. I have to get him on the phone."

"All right, I guess," said Enrique.

Thomas climbed into the third row and strapped himself in next to Enrique, who had his phone out and was tapping on the screen. Adelia and Huxley took the middle row. Squat was in the front passenger seat, staring idly out the window. It was the first time he'd surfaced in days, and even now, he seemed only half present. For the hundredth time, Thomas wondered who he really was and what he wanted.

The SUV shot forward and bounced down the dirt road, reminding Thomas there was work to be done. "Adelia, can your phone make international calls?"

"Yes, of course," she answered.

"Okay, great. Can you please punch in the country code for the US and 714 for the area code? Enrique will give you the rest of the number as soon as he can pull it up on his phone."

"Got it. Enrique, I'm ready when you are."

"I can't get any signal." Enrique smacked his phone in frustration. "This thing isn't going to work out here."

"Keep trying. Maybe you'll get lucky," said Thomas.

"Zero bars," said Enrique. "I never downloaded the roster, so unless there's a town or cell tower between here and the plane, it's not happening."

"My mom has a printed copy in her emergency folder in the kitchen. Hold on." Thomas closed his eyes, and a thin white binder appeared in his hands. He flipped through the pages. "Yes! Okay, okay. I've got it. Akhil Nagarajan."

Thomas called out the numbers, and Adelia tapped them into her phone. When the last number was entered, she handed the device to Thomas. Booop. Booop. Booop. After three seemingly endless rings, a small voice picked up on the other side of the phone.

"Hi, may I speak with Akhil?" asked Thomas. "Oh, hey, Akhil. It's Thomas, from school. Thomas Wildus."

"Oh, hi Thomas. I haven't seen you at school. Where have you been? Is everything okay?"

"I'm okay. I guess you could say there was an emergency," said Thomas. "No, I don't know when I'll be back. It's a long story. Right now, I have a huge favor to ask, and I wouldn't do it unless it was totally urgent. It involves that special skill you told me about and probably means breaking a whole bunch of laws. I'll stop talking if you don't want to hear more."

"What is it?" Akhil's voice was louder and more excited.

"You know how you told me about the backdoor in Google's satellite control system? Do you think there's still a way in? I need real-time images from a specific set of coordinates."

"Why?"

"I don't have time to explain right now, but I promise I will as soon as possible. Can you help? Will you?"

"This is an emergency?"

"Life and death," said Thomas. "Seriously."

There was a pause. Thomas felt the entire car straining to hear the other side of the conversation. "Okay. I'll do it. How soon do you need this?"

"Now. As soon as possible."

"Can the images be from yesterday? It will be much easier to pull information from a database than take control of an entire satellite."

"No, that won't work. The images have to be real time. A couple of minutes of delay at most."

"I'm not sure it's possible. If it is, and I get caught, I'd be in really big trouble."

"I know," said Thomas. "I wouldn't ask if it wasn't an emergency, but this is super important. You can blame me if things go wrong. Can you do it? Will you?"

"What's he saying?" whispered Enrique. Thomas held up a hand for silence.

"Okay. I'll try."

"Yes! Do you have something to write with? Okay, great." Thomas read out the coordinates Garibaldi had provided. "Akhil, you're a rockstar! I'm hanging up, but I swear I'll fill you in as soon as I can. And, Akhil? I owe you big time. Seriously."

Thomas handed the phone back to Adelia and let out a long breath.

"Wait a second," said Enrique. "Take over a satellite? Why? What are you talking about?"

"If we can get our hands on real-time satellite images, would you guys be willing to teleport?" asked Thomas. Enrique had only been able to teleport to places within plain sight so far, but that wasn't a good enough reason to kill the idea. Speed was too important.

"I would," said Huxley. "Under these circumstances, it's entirely reasonable to take on a bit more risk than we normally might."

"Are you mad? If you think I'm going to teleport halfway across the world with a pair of two-week-old magicians, you must be out of your bleeding minds," sputtered Professor Reilly. "No offense intended, of course."

"None taken," said Thomas. The idea was terrifying enough for him, and he would be doing the magic.

"You can stay behind with me if you'd like," said Adelia. "But keep in mind that Squat has been at this a bit longer than two weeks."

Professor Reilly flashed a grumpy look at Adelia, then looked to his side where Squat was staring out the window. He shook his head, as if unable to believe he was even considering the idea. "Bloody hell. If I get my bum planted on a cactus, none of you is going to hear the end of it."

The car bumped along the rough dirt road for what seemed like an eternity. Thomas felt like he was going to crawl completely out of his skin. He looked at the clock on the dashboard. Thirty-seven minutes had passed since the call with Akhil, and still no updates. They slowed down, turned onto an almost invisible dirt road that branched into the darkness. The car hit a hidden bump, sending him bouncing in his seat.

"Ow," said Enrique, rubbing his head where it had thudded into the ceiling.

"Sorry," said Professor Reilly. "Didn't see that one coming."

"It's okay. We're almost there," said Adelia. "Another ten minutes, give or take."

She was right. They bumped through the darkness for exactly ten minutes before a row of small blue lights appeared on the ground in a narrow valley down below. The road wound steeply, forcing them to a near crawl as they navigated a series of sharp S-curves in the hillside. A long dirt runway materialized at the bottom, lit by the blue lights. At the far end of the landing strip was an airplane, and on either side of that, cell and radio towers with blinking red lights on top.

Enrique whistled as they approached the plane. "Whoa!"

"Is that yours?" asked Thomas. It was a sleek black machine with huge jet engines and room for at least two dozen passengers.

"Ours," said Huxley. "Not too shabby, is it?"

"Ours?" said Thomas.

"Technically, it belongs to a trust," said Adelia. "The plane, compound, car, and a few other useful resources are maintained through a fund we established along with your great-great-grandfather Marcus. One day, you'll assume joint ownership of everything."

"Are you kidding me?" said Enrique. He jabbed Thomas on the shoulder. "That's yours? Seriously?"

"Uhhhh." Thomas stared, his mouth half open. "I, uh, I . . ."

Adelia's phone beeped, interrupting as the SUV skidded to a stop twenty feet from the plane.

"Come on, let's move!" boomed Professor Reilly.

"Hold on. It's a text message from Akhil." Adelia swiped and then tapped her screen. "Three encrypted files and a note. He says the images came from a spot about three miles north of the coordinates. It was as close as he could get before a systems administrator booted him out of the system. The password is the last name of the bully from school, followed by Thomas's GPA from last semester."

"Parker3.9," said Thomas. He felt Enrique's eyes on him and shrugged. "What? I got a B+ in English. Latin cognates."

"Slacker," said Enrique.

Squat grabbed the phone from Adelia before Thomas could get a peek at the photos. Professor Reilly and Huxley opened their doors. A blast of sound enveloped the vehicle. Even idling, the roar of the jet engines was nearly deafening.

"What should we do?" shouted Thomas, his voice hardly audible.

Adelia put a hand on Squat's shoulder. "What do you think? Are the pictures good enough?"

Squat nodded and handed the phone back.

"Great! Adelia, you head back to the compound," shouted Huxley. "Set up the medical room and make sure you have supplies ready in case things go wrong. We'll do our best to get in and out cleanly, but let's be prepared. If the news articles are any indication, the other crystals were extremely well-protected."

"Got it," yelled Adelia. She flashed a thumbs up and jogged around the back of the car. She reappeared a few seconds later with a pair of backpacks, which she handed to Thomas and Enrique. "These have bottled water, protein bars, bug spray, and a few basic supplies. If there's an emergency, teleport back to the training room. We'll move out the table and keep the space clear until you're home."

"Thank you!" shouted Thomas.

Huxley, Squat, and Professor Reilly grabbed similarly equipped packs, then moved to the side of the SUV opposite the airplane. Squat held out his right hand, palm up, and snapped his fingers. An overhead picture of a lush canyon materialized, as clear and solid-looking as a poster-sized photograph. A thick blue ribbon of river ran straight through the middle.

"Is that the picture Akhil sent?" yelled Thomas. "How'd you do that?"

Squat ignored the questions and gestured with his left index finger. The image zoomed forward to a flat patch of earth on the banks of the river. Squat pointed at the open piece of land and zoomed even closer. He tapped Thomas on the forehead, right between the eyes, and pointed at the spot again. "Right there. Focus."

Squat repeated the same sequence with Enrique. Thomas stared at the hovering image, unable to take his eyes off the spot where the wizard had pointed. The picture imprinted itself so clearly in his mind it felt as if there were literally a reproduction inside of his head. He blinked slowly, and it was still there. Every rock, leaf, and blade of grass, as clear as when his eyes were still open.

"Link hands!" shouted Huxley. "We need to be touching to teleport together."

Squat stared at the image, his expression focused, his eyes clear. He looked from Enrique to Thomas, the hint of a smile on his face. His presence and demeanor had shifted, as if a hard edge had begun to soften in a barely perceptible way. "On three. Focus!"

"This better work!" shouted Professor Reilly.

Thomas ignored him and kept his mind fixed on the idea of materializing in the open space near the winding river. "One!"

Thomas kept his eyes locked on the patch of flat ground as all five voices blended together. "Two!"

"Three!"

FORTY

THE ROAR OF ENGINES DISAPPEARED, replaced by the warbling rush of the nearby river. Dense heat enveloped Thomas, the fresh humid air tousling his hair and moistening his cheeks. He looked around in amazement at the landscape captured by Akhil's photograph. Craggy walls sheared upward on either side of the canyon, angling into a deep blue sky. The river rushed past, partially hidden by the tangle of trees and bushes.

"Well, I suppose that wasn't so bad," said Professor Reilly, patting himself up and down as if to make sure all his parts had arrived intact. "Better than riding in that clunky old jet, anyway."

"Yeah, 'cause that would have been awful," said Enrique. "I mean, who needs the hassle of riding in a luxury jet. Maybe you guys should just give it to me. You know, to save you all the headache of having to take care of it."

Thomas laughed. "Fine with me. I didn't even know the thing existed ten minutes ago."

Squat stood silently, surveying their surroundings. A

lush jungle landscape sprawled on all sides of them, with trees climbing the steep canyon walls almost as high as the eye could see. Tropical flowers bloomed everywhere, tiny explosions of purple, red, blue, orange, yellow, and dozens of other shades. Huxley ignored the scenery, focusing instead on the GPS unit in his hand.

"The crystal is that way," said Huxley. "We're just over three miles from the coordinates Garibaldi gave us."

Professor Reilly groaned.

"Three miles? I can't see past the first thirty feet." Enrique looked skeptical. The terrain was intimidating, covered with thick shrubs, jagged rocks, and narrow passes. If there was an easy path to their goal, Thomas didn't see it.

Squattapus was undaunted. He was peering into the distance through hands that had been curled up like a child's telescope. His head shifted back and forth, then stopped on a massive stone that jutted through the trees and shrubbery just above the banks of the river. "There."

"How in the blue blazes are we supposed to get there?" asked Professor Reilly. "It's a bloody jungle in between. Snakes and bugs and poisonous plants and what not."

"Hold on," said Squattapus. His voice was cool, his expression calm. Without waiting for a reaction, he disappeared, materializing on the stone almost instantaneously. He looked around for a moment and was back with the group almost before Thomas could blink. He took Enrique by the wrist and nodded for the others to link up. "On three."

"What?" Professor Reilly's eyes were wide, his expression fearful. "Again?"

Squattapus started the countdown without hesitation or explanation. Thomas stared at the top of the wide stone, willing himself to focus.

The countdown hit three, and Thomas projected himself forward. The ground under his feet shifted from loose dirt to solid stone. He opened his eyes and had a moment of vertigo. The wide stone rose above the river, which plunged through a maze of boulders. The whitewater tumbled over stones, sending a thin mist into the air. Sunlight caught in the spray, creating a shimmering rainbow.

"Bloody hell," breathed the professor. "You should give a little more warning before whisking me through space like that. I almost wet myself."

"You're in the company of magicians, Professor," said Huxley. His smile was amused but genuine. "Lord only knows what they might do next."

"The drawing, please." Squat stood motionless, his right hand extended to Huxley. His voice was soft and confident, his presence strangely powerful. There was a freshness about him, as if the layers of grease and grime were falling away. For the first time, Thomas felt like he might be seeing hints of the man behind the untamed and grubby exterior. Sensing the attention, Squat glanced at Thomas and winked. It was a subtle gesture, accompanied by the faintest of smiles, but it was enough. A fresh wave of vertigo washed over

Thomas, as once again his world shifted in a meaningful but indescribable way.

Squat shaped his hands into a telescope and stared into the distance. Thomas watched, motionless, suddenly realizing that he didn't know anything about his unlikely teacher.

"There's a cave," said Squat. "You can see the edge, hidden in the rock wall about halfway up. We're going to have to get closer to find a way in."

"Through that mess?" said Enrique. The underbrush was thick and tangly, without the faintest hint of a proper path.

"Unless you'd prefer to teleport blind," said Squat.

"Blind?" Professor Reilly shook his head so vigorously his beard shook. "Absolutely not!"

"I'm with the professor on this one," said Thomas. One of his mom's pet phrases popped into his mind. *Risk can be managed. Stupidity can't.* "I'd like to get there in one piece."

"Agreed," said Huxley. "It's a mess, but we'll manage."

"Follow me," said Squat. "Carefully."

Thomas followed, climbing and scrambling down the rocks to the ground below.

Squat ducked between the trees and kept going. The vines and shrubs warped around him as he walked, shifting and moving until the way was clear and passable. The rest of the group followed, moving into the canopy of trees. The shrubs and vines sprang back into shape behind them, erasing the opening as if it had never existed. Squat walked forward, slowly, the path forming around him like a bubble.

"Okay, that's a cool trick," said Enrique.

"Super cool," agreed Thomas.

Squat glanced over his shoulder, a half smile playing at his lips, then angled through the trees, climbing over rocks and skirting around deadfall even as the path took shape around him. The sheer canyon walls flickered in and out of sight, disappearing and reappearing as they passed through the lush foliage.

The group paused frequently, allowing Professor Reilly to catch his breath and wipe his brow. Thomas didn't mind. The constantly changing landscape was fascinating. Vibrant and unfamiliar flowers appeared at every turn. Strange birds sang as they fluttered through the canopy, their wings flecked with color. Bizarrely large insects climbed the trunks of the multivariate trees. In the background, constant yet ever-changing, the rushing of the river made fresh music. Thomas had never been in a place so spectacularly vibrant with life and color.

By the time they reached a clearing below the three-rock formation from Garibaldi's drawing, the sun had moved past the upper edge of the canyon. Thomas stared at the massive stones jutting out from the canyon wall. They were tall and jagged, the top edges piercing the sky at least two hundred feet above them.

There was only a tiny corner of the cave visible amongst the crags, its dark entrance almost indistinguishable from the shadows cast by the shifting light. As far as Thomas could tell, there was no way up to climb up the face of the rocks without proper gear, and climbing down from the upper rim of the canyon seemed equally unlikely. The cave was inaccessible, and even the ledge in front of it impossible to see.

"What now?" asked Enrique.

"Wait here." Squat looked strangely renewed, as if the hike had washed away another layer of grime and enchantment. "Rest. Have a drink. I'll be back in a few minutes."

He vanished almost before the last syllable was out of his mouth. Thomas squinted up at the canyon entrance but didn't see where the magician reappeared.

"Finally, the man says something sensible," said Professor Reilly. He plopped down on a rock and wrung out his handkerchief. "I've never been so hot and exhausted in my life."

"Snack, anyone?" asked Enrique. He dug inside his backpack and pulled out a bag of trail mix.

"Yes, please." Thomas scooped out a handful and chased it down with an entire bottle of water.

"We can get to the cave from up there," said Squat, reappearing as quickly as he'd vanished. He pointed at a boulder at the top of the steep slope. "From the top of that rock, we can see directly across to the entrance. It's not an easy climb, but we can teleport from there."

"Not bloody likely," said Professor Reilly. "Look at me. There's no way I can climb up there."

"No, I imagine not," said Huxley. He flashed a wry smile. "I'm not sure I'd do much better. I think, Professor, that you and I should stand watch and leave the retrieval to those with magical abilities. We'll all meet here afterward and teleport home."

"Praise the Lord!" said Professor Reilly. "I mean yes, right. That's a very good idea. We'll stay here and keep an eye out for Arius. Team spirit and all that."

"Come with me," said Squat, gesturing for Thomas and Enrique to follow. "Take a drink and leave your backpacks here. Where we're going, you aren't going to need them."

FORTY-ONE

THE ENTRANCE TO THE CAVE was a jagged gash in the rock wall, dark and forbidding. Like a mouth. A giant, sideways mouth. Thomas shivered. In spite of the heat and sunshine, goosebumps covered his skin from head to toe.

"In there?" Enrique looked as uneasy as Thomas felt.

Squat stepped forward with his palm up. A glowing ball of light appeared above his hand as he crossed into the darkness, illuminating the entrance and casting shadows onto the walls. He looked back with a smile that made him look youthful to a degree Thomas wouldn't have considered possible just a day earlier. Even his hair and beard looked different, less tangled and greasy, as if he'd snuck off for a quick shower while they weren't looking.

A question-thought popped into Thomas's mind. *The Book of Sorrows* had revealed its true colors slowly. Was something similar happening with the strange magician?

Unable to answer his own question, Thomas followed quietly into an unexpectedly large interior chamber.

Instantly, he found his eyes drawn to the cavern walls. In the glow of Squat's magical light, surprising shapes took shape on the streaked gray stones, partially hidden beneath a thin layer of lichen. He stepped closer. Primitive figures danced behind the living cover, dozens of images and scenes, maybe more. *How did cave paintings get up here? And when?*

"Do you see this?" whispered Thomas. He lightly brushed at the wall, his voice hushed instinctively, as if he were in a church or library. The light shifted, the ochre and charcoal images blurred into shadow. "It's amazing."

"Totally," said Enrique. "Now come on, before he gets too far ahead."

Thomas turned. Squat was moving deeper into the cavern. Almost reluctantly, he turned to follow. "Where's the crystal?"

"Over here, I think," said Squat. He beckoned them deeper into the shadows. Thomas followed until they stood in front of a narrow stretch of stone that looked like every other part of the cave, with one exception—it was missing the lichen and paintings. Squat stared at the wall for a long moment, his head tilted slightly. He took a half step back and smiled. "Stand back."

Thomas tried to make out the words of the singsong humming, but to him, they were nothing more than jumbled sounds. He met Enrique's eyes and lifted his shoulders. Enrique raised his eyebrows and shrugged back.

Still humming, Squat traced a pattern in the air in front of the stone and snapped his fingers. Thomas's vision became suddenly blurry. He blinked, shook his head, blinked again. It wasn't his eyes. The wall itself was blurring, fading, beginning to melt away. The section of stone vanished, revealing a narrow alcove that stretched beyond the circle of light.

The magician walked forward, hugging the right-hand wall. "This way. Follow me."

"Whoa!" said Thomas, squinting into the shadowy corners.

"Okay, I did *not* see that coming," said Enrique. Eyes wide, he started toward the back of the hidden recess.

"Careful!" said Squat, pulling Enrique forcefully to the wall. He gestured at the ground. A sharp chasm opened abruptly into an even deeper darkness. Squat knelt and peered into the depths. Suddenly, and without warning, he grabbed Enrique's hand and jabbed a long fingernail directly into his palm.

Enrique cried out in pain and tried to wriggle away. Squat held firm, pressing down until blood spilled from the wound.

"What are you doing? Let me go!" shouted Enrique.

Thomas felt a surge of adrenaline and started forward, ready to defend his friend.

Even as he struggled, a faint ball of light appeared above

Enrique's bleeding hand. He stopped fighting and stared, eyes wide. Squat tapped him on the forehead, right between the eyes. The light grew brighter, intensifying until it nearly matched the orb glowing in front of the older magician.

"What the—? H-how did you do that?" stammered Enrique.

Squat ran a hand over Enrique's palm. The wound closed, but the orb remained, casting fresh light on the magician's face. Perhaps it was a trick of the shadows, but it seemed to Thomas that his smile had an almost soft quality to it. And were the once-jagged teeth straight? They were, and his clothes looked less grungy.

The magician extended a hand toward Thomas, as if asking permission. Thomas let his hand rise with more than a touch of trepidation. He was promptly rewarded with stabbing pain and an answering twinge at the center of his brow, faint and buzzing. He stared at the blood pooling in his palm, resisting the urge to yank his hand away.

A faint glow appeared above the red droplets. Squat tapped Thomas's forehead, sending vibrations rippling through his mind. With a sudden flash, Thomas understood how to pull light from thought and memory, to shape it even in the darkness. He gathered luminous threads in his mind until the orb glowed and his thoughts thrummed with an inner flame.

"You can call on the light whenever you need it," Squat

said softly. "It will be there for you always, to illuminate your path when the world grows dark."

Thomas caught a hint of emotion in the eyes and face of the magician. Sadness, perhaps a touch of something deeper. Before Thomas could think or speak, Squat was climbing into the dark hole. Light reflected from the narrow walls, revealing the thinnest of grooves on either side of the channel. After perhaps fifteen feet of descent, Squat reached the floor of a second chamber and looked up.

"Come down. Carefully."

"After you, amigo," said Enrique, gesturing toward the hole.

"Brains and beauty first. Got it."

"Knucklehead."

Thomas wiggled his eyebrows and started his descent. The orb of light hovered just above his head, illuminating the narrow handholds. He wedged his toes into the nooks and managed to climb down with relative ease. His feet hit the ground in a chamber a fraction the size of the one up above. He turned around and flinched, a fresh jolt of adrenaline pumping through his veins. On the other side of Squat a brightly dressed woman knelt on the floor of the cavern, her eyes staring right at him.

Not a woman. A mural so lifelike it seemed ready to climb from the wall into the chamber. The woman's hands were open in a gesture of prayer, her body wrapped in a flowing red robe with gilded hems. Moisture bled from the wall below her eyes, creating a trail of tears from her cheeks to the cavern floor. The droplets collected into a pool at her feet.

Thomas stepped closer. The breath caught in his throat. At the bottom of the pool was a shimmering black crystal.

• • •

Thomas felt drawn closer, pulled by a force he was powerless to resist. He moved past Squat and peered into the water. Light caught and gathered at the heart of the crystal. Light that wasn't a reflection but rather a collection of lights moving in an intricate and dazzling dance, constellations whirling at a microscopic scale.

He reached out, compelled to touch the magnificent crystal. His fingers met water. Icy flames shocked through his system, with the jolt a thousand times more intense than grabbing the metal key. Terrified, he jerked back, tumbling to the cavern floor.

"Are you all right?" Squat's voice sounded thin, distant.

Thomas lifted his hand, half-expecting to find it burned or frozen. It was neither. He stared again at the dark crystal, the breath rattling through his lungs. Feet dropped to the floor behind him. He looked back, blood thundering through his ears.

"What's that?" Enrique peered into the water. "Oh. Oh, wow."

Thomas looked tentatively at Squat. The wizard was staring at the crystal as intently as Thomas had. His face was frozen, his body tense, as if he were forcibly restraining himself. He pulled his eyes away and met Thomas's questioning stare.

"It can't be me," said Squat. There was strain on his face and perhaps a hint of desire. "It has to be one of you."

"Rock paper scissors?" Enrique made a fist with his right hand and held it over his left. "Best of three?"

"Deal," said Thomas. "Rock. Paper. Scissors. Shoot."

Thomas's rock crushed Enrique's scissors. They went again. Enrique sliced Thomas's paper with his scissors. The next round was a draw, paper versus paper. Then again, scissor versus scissor.

"You're going down, Wildus. Rock. Paper. Scissors. Shoot." Their hands shot forward. Enrique raised an eyebrow. "Or not."

Thomas's paper folded over Enrique's rock. A nervous shudder ran through him, tensing his chest and belly. He'd won, but it didn't exactly feel like victory. "I guess it's me."

"I guess so," said Enrique.

"That seems fitting." Squat put a hand on Thomas's shoulder, his expression soft, almost gentle. "That pool is enchanted, which means it was almost certainly Jameson Wildus who hid this crystal. Your blood connection is interesting, perhaps even a key to making it through the defenses. Either way, Enrique and I will be here. We'll help in whatever way we can. Okay?"

"Okay," said Thomas. The idea that it might have been his ancestor, the very first Wildus, helped ease his mind. He faced the praying woman and peered into the pool of tears. The butterflies multiplied, swarming through his chest and belly. Forcing himself not to think about the imminent shock, he took a breath and stretched out his hand.

His fingers touched water. The shock jolted his arm and shuddered through his body. His nervous system lit up as if he'd grabbed a live wire, sending spasms through every inch of his body. Every instinct screamed for him to pull back. He fought through the fear and pain, reaching deeper into the pulsing water even as tentacles of ice burned inside of his arm, creeping upward, freezing him from the inside out.

His fingers grasped for the crystal and found only liquid. *Where is it?*

It felt like he should have reached the bottom, but the water was pulling him now, yanking him forward with irresistible force. His shoulder touched and still the pulling grew stronger. As if from a distance, he heard someone screaming for help. In the back of his mind, a second voice answered. *That's me. I'm the one screaming.*

Other voices answered, shouting. Hands grabbed him, tried to yank him backward. The momentum continued, pulling his head downward. He sucked in a last gasping breath before his face plunged into the impossible depths. Deeper and deeper he dove, until his lungs screamed and the voices grew faint above him.

The burning in his lungs suddenly stopped. Stillness wrapped itself around him. Panic and fear disappeared. There was no water, no cave, no crystal. He was somewhere else, something else.

A presence filled the space around him, strange and yet somehow familiar. Thomas searched for the source. He felt as much as saw a flash of wild blue eyes and blond hair. *Dad? No, someone else. Jameson?* The image disappeared, leaving him in a void free of all physical sensation. He was a mind, nothing else. Another mind reached into his own, filtering through his thoughts and feelings. The rawness of his unfiltered emotions left him feeling naked, insecure.

The mind-touch faded, and something exploded inside of his head. He felt himself sucked backward, rushing through space until frozen water filled his mouth and lungs. He grasped for solid ground, felt his fingers on the hard, black edges of the crystal. Fire ripped up his arm, burning a trail from his fingers to his heart. He grabbed even as hands pulled his shoulders, his back, his legs.

Suddenly, he was free, sprawled out on the cavern floor with lungs full of water. He couldn't breathe, couldn't move. Dark spots clouded his eyes. He heard voices, frantic. Enrique and Squat. Hands thumped his back, pumped on his chest.

A flash of purple lit up the cave. Something pierced his chest, opened a path to his lungs. His body spasmed. Blackness filled everything, devouring his field of vision. Another flash, this one faint, distant. Something shifted, like a dam breaking loose.

Thomas retched, spewing water from his ragged throat and lungs. He gasped for breath, retched again. His body curled into a ball as he coughed and sputtered.

"Thomas! Thomas, can you hear me?" Squat's voice was intense, insistent.

Enrique sounded panicked. "Thomas, are you okay?"

Thomas tried to answer and coughed instead. His body clenched from head to toe. Droplets of water sprayed from his mouth in a fine mist. He rolled onto his stomach, still wracked with coughs. He pressed his hands against the floor, trying to get his knees under him. Something hard pressed back, the sharp edges stabbing into his palm. He rocked back, managing to sit without falling over.

He lifted his hand. The black crystal shimmered in the soft light.

"You got it!" whispered Enrique, his voice hushed. "I thought you were toast, but you got it."

Squat looked at Thomas through eyes that were more lucid and powerful than any Thomas had ever seen. The dirt and grime were completely gone from his face, and with them, the last traces of seeming insanity. "What happened? What did you see?"

Thomas did his best to describe the experience, but his words were woefully inadequate. When he finished, Squat put a hand on his shoulder and pulled him up to his feet.

"Very, very interesting. It's surprising that Jameson was able to make magic of that quality without any kind of formal training. I wonder . . ." Squat's voice trailed off.

"Wonder what?" asked Thomas. He thumped himself on the chest and coughed more.

Squat shook his head. "Nothing. Just a wild thought. Come on. Let's move."

"What was that?" Enrique whipped his head around and stared at the opening into the upper chamber.

"What was what?" asked Thomas.

"I don't know. I thought I heard something up there. Voices, maybe."

Squat put a finger to his lips and tilted his head. "Put the crystal away. It's time to go. Hurry."

They climbed quickly, Squat first followed by Thomas and then Enrique. The upper cave was empty and quiet, but something felt amiss. A distant thrumming stirred the air, faint but somehow familiar. Even Thomas could sense it.

"We've only had a short time together, but you are ready for this. Both of you are." Squat knelt between Thomas and Enrique, his hands firm on their shoulders, his green eyes almost imploring.

"Ready for what?"

The magician ignored the question and intensified his

grip. "No matter what happens next, I want you to promise that Arius will not get the crystal. No matter what. Promise me."

"I promise," said Thomas, staring into the intense eyes.

"No matter what?"

"No matter what."

"Me, too," said Enrique, his jaw set and his eyes hard. "He's not getting the crystal."

Squat held their gaze a moment longer. "Good. Then it's time. Follow me."

FORTY-TWO

SQUAT TURNED TOWARD the jagged opening. As he moved, Thomas realized that even the wizard's clothes had changed. The grimy olive overcoat was now a rich green cloak that shimmered in the half-light. His once-scraggly beard was trimmed and neat, his dark hair groomed and smooth. He turned around and met Thomas's gaze. His eyes were the same, green and fiery, the only part of him unchanged by the transformation.

"What you see now, just as what you saw before, is only skin deep," said Squat. "A man is more than his appearances, and more, I hope, than his past mistakes."

"Scott Alpheus! My oldest friend." A figure materialized in the entranceway, backlit by the afternoon sun, his voice rich and melodious.

"Arius." Squat's voice was tight, his posture tense.

"Scott Alpheus?" whispered Enrique. Thomas shrugged, his eyes locked on the silhouetted figure at the mouth of the cave.

"I hear you've been playing homeless again." The tone

was friendly, almost jovial, but was laced with an undercurrent of contempt. "Why? You and I could still be doing great things together. Changing the world."

"What do you want, Arius?"

"You know what I want and how important it is that I get it," said Arius. "Come, step into the light so we can talk like civilized beings. All of you, so that I'm not forced to do things we'll all regret."

Arius disappeared from the mouth of the cave without waiting for a response. Squat looked from Thomas to Enrique, his eyes pained but hopeful. "Remember what you promised. No matter what you hear or see or think, Arius does not get the crystal. No matter what."

Thomas nodded. Enrique followed Squat through the jagged opening and into the light. Thomas followed, shielding his eyes against the onslaught of brightness. As the world came into focus, his heart nearly pounded out of his chest. An enormous man was holding Huxley in one hand and Professor Reilly in the other. Both had tape across their mouths and dangled like rag dolls. Their toes barely skimmed the rock ledge, but the giant showed no more strain than an ordinary person lifting a glass of water.

"Thomas Wildus. I've been looking forward to meeting you."

The rich voice brought Thomas's attention to the man standing just a few feet away. His brain skipped. This was Arius Strong? He'd expected a monster, but Arius was handsome, with dark-hair, smooth skin, and hazel eyes. In spite of their situation, his posture was relaxed, his smile easy, as if they were old friends meeting for a pleasant afternoon. His eyes sparkled. He looked genuinely happy.

"You recovered the crystal," Arius continued. It was a statement rather than a question, and his tone conveyed sincere appreciation. "Very impressive. Arianna was certain this would be the hardest of the three, and the others were anything but easy. A truly remarkable accomplishment. You should be extremely proud."

"Where is she?" asked Squat. "I know she's here."

"Let's not worry about Arianna," said Arius. He turned his gaze to Squat, his expression holding a hint of contempt. "I think it would be more appropriate to take a moment and focus on you. How much do our young friends know about you, Scott? Have you bothered to tell them anything important at all?"

"Like what?" said Enrique. "That you're an evil bastard?"

"Enrique Rodriguez." Arius's smile returned, widening until he positively radiated joy. "What an extraordinary and wonderful surprise! Young men with abilities like yours are extremely rare, Enrique. I wish the circumstances were more fortuitous, but I couldn't be happier to meet you."

Enrique crossed his arms, but his scowl softened.

Thomas felt an unexpected twinge of envy. *I thought I was the special one.* A muffled grunt brought his attention back to the canyon ledge. Professor Reilly writhed, his face red and his voice muted by the duct tape. The giant silently swung him until his feet dangled over the canyon ledge. The professor looked down, his eyes bulging, and stopped struggling.

"I'm sorry, Professor, but our young friends deserve to know the truth about the company they keep," said Arius. "It seems that a few important details have been neglected, and it is only fair that they have a complete picture before making such a monumental choice. The crystal is far too important to risk on partial information. Once I've had my say, Heinrik will happily return you to your friends. You as well, Alchemist."

"They do deserve the truth." Squat looked at Thomas, his green eyes imploring, his face pained but determined. "Try not to judge me too harshly."

"Very well," said Arius. "First, I must apologize. Thomas, Enrique, I'm sorry for using your friends as leverage like this. It's unfair to put you in such a position, but it is imperative that you hear me out. Please, accept my most sincere apologies."

Thomas felt helpless, confused. Arius was so different than he expected. He seemed so genuine, so sincere, and yet he was threatening to kill Huxley and Professor Reilly. These were people he had chosen to trust—people his mom believed in so deeply she let them take him from his home and help him unlock his magical powers. Then there was Squat. He was an enigma, far more complex and deep than

Thomas had imagined. He had obviously kept his past hidden, but why? Nothing was clear. Nothing made any sense.

"I understand how you must feel," Arius continued. "Secrets can be confusing. If these people are truly your friends, why have they kept so much from you? One has to wonder if they are just using you to get what they want?"

"And you aren't?" said Enrique. The defiance had returned to his eyes and voice.

Arius looked at Enrique and laughed gently. "Very insightful, Enrique. You're quite right. Yes, of course, I'm trying to get what I want. We all are, aren't we? You, me, everyone. The question is what do you *really* want, and whose interests are best aligned with your own?"

"Then what are you trying to get?" asked Thomas. "What are your interests?"

"I want the crystal," said Arius. "And I want it because I want the power to shape the future of this planet. We have allowed weapons and war and environmental destruction to dominate for far too long. The time has come for a new era, and I want to be part of bringing it forward."

"Why? So you can take more for yourself?" said Enrique. "Being a billionaire isn't good enough for you?"

A look flashed across Arius's face, dark, dangerous. He composed himself quickly, but his smile took on a new, almost wolfish quality. "Money has nothing to do with it, but we'll come back to that shortly. First, let's talk about your friend and teacher. How much do you really know about Scott Alpheus? Or should I call him Squattapus?"

"He taught us magic," said Enrique. "That's more than you've done for us."

"Of course. Scott is a magician of unparalleled ability. In a life spent seeking out extraordinary people, I have yet to come across anyone with more innate talent," said Arius. "Until today, perhaps, but that is still to be seen. Unfortunately, he is also a traitor, and worse. Far, far worse. He's a—"

"That was a long time ago, Arius." Scott sounded pained, almost desperate. "I'm not that man anymore."

"You will always be that man." Arius's voice was hard, sharp. "Some sins cannot be simply washed away. Some sins are forever."

Scott looked at the stones near his feet, the lines of his face suddenly deeper, more pronounced. His hands hung at his sides, loose and helpless, but he didn't argue.

Arius shifted his gaze back to Thomas and Enrique. "Are you sure you want to know the rest?"

Thomas felt himself nodding, unable to resist. Enrique's head lifted and lowered at the same time.

"Scott Alpheus," said Arius, leaning forward and lowering his voice to a near whisper, "is a *murderer*."

The final word twisted from Arius's lips like poison, saturating the air with venom. Thomas stared at Squat— Scott—his mouth open, revulsion roiling his gut. The look on Scott's face was as much an admission of guilt as anything he could have said or done. The magician didn't even try to protest.

"Oh, yes, a murderer," said Arius. "When we were younger, Scott was my closest friend and most trusted advisor. Our work together was extraordinary, and our goals perfectly aligned. We were going to change the world, create a better future for all of mankind."

"That's BS. The only future you care about is your own," said Thomas. But his voice was weak, uncertain. He felt sick, confused. Nothing made sense.

"Is that true, Thomas?" asked Arius. "The Alchemist and his wife have lived far beyond the years nature intended, using their craft for long life and financial gain. Your professor's research has been used to create weapons of mass destruction, and Scott *is* a weapon of mass destruction. How sure are you that you have chosen the right side in this exchange?"

Thomas's brain felt scrambled, overloaded. He looked at Professor Reilly and Huxley dangling from the hands of the giant, at Scott standing in shame, at Enrique, who seemed just as confused as he felt. Then there was Arius. Handsome, confident, composed. What if he hadn't chosen right? What if he was on the wrong side? He didn't know what to think or believe.

"Good. You should be questioning your alliances," said Arius. "Did you know Scott had a family once? No? He didn't mention that, either? Interesting. Well, he did. He was married to a lovely woman, Maritza, and together they had a son. Jamie was a beautiful boy, bright and full of life. Jamie was like a son to me, and for Scott, he was far more than that. He was the center of the universe, the sun and moon and stars."

"Enough," whispered Scott. "Please. Enough."

"One day little Jamie got sick," continued Arius. "When his fever rose, Maritza took him to the doctor, as any good mother would do. And as any good doctor would do in the same situation, the good man prescribed antibiotics. How was he to know? How were any of them to know?"

A cry pierced the air, the forlorn call of a bird lost above a distant sea. Scott dropped to his knees, a trail of tears dripping silently down his cheek.

"By the time they realized that Jamie was allergic, it was too late. He was gone." Arius paused for dramatic effect, pulling Thomas closer. "In her agony, Maritza took her own life, then and there. When Scott came home, he found them together, cold and lifeless. His whole life, suddenly shattered. I can't possibly imagine the horror he felt in that moment. So much pain would be enough to drive any man mad, but knowing Scott's power, can you imagine what happened next?"

Thomas shook his head, but his mind danced with dark suspicions.

"No, no," Arius continued, shaking his head. "No, it is far worse than you can possibly imagine. By the time I arrived, the doctor's entire building was in ruins, crushed to dust and rubble. My friend, your teacher, had destroyed everything and everyone. Not just the doctor but also the nurses and staff. More than a dozen dead, and not a single survivor. That is the person your alchemist calls upon to teach magic to children."

Thomas stood in shock. He had seen, through Arius's speaking, a reflection of the destruction Scott caused. The scene played through his mind like a movie. Dust filtering through the air above a building that had been completely leveled, neighbors streaming into the street to see what had happened, the sounds of shouting and terror. The heartbroken wails of those whose family members had been inside.

"Heinrik, please set them down," said Arius, addressing the giant. "Now you know the truth, Thomas, and it is time to make your choice. Will you stand beside a murderer, or will you join with me and help to truly change the world?"

FORTY-THREE

THOMAS'S MIND WAS NUMB, shell-shocked. He turned to Squat—Scott—as the giant dropped Huxley and Professor Reilly onto solid ground. The magician was still on his knees, tears streaming down his cheeks. Scott didn't argue or attempt to defend himself, only looked back, the agony etched into the subtle lines of his face. Thomas looked away and found Enrique in a similar state of shock.

"What Arius said is true." Huxley picked himself up from the ground and ran a hand over his lips, massaging the place where the duct tape had covered his lips. "In a moment of unbearable pain and grief, a young and incredibly powerful magician made an unforgivable mistake. A mistake so horrible it hardly bears imagining. But that's not the end of the story. Scott has spent decades helping those without power, trying to find redemption through service to others. Arius has done nothing but expand his own power, and he still hasn't answered the questions that matter most."

"Scott Alpheus is a murderer, and you, Alchemist, have far outlived your natural time on this planet," said Arius. "What other questions are there?"

"Quite a few," said Huxley. "I think it is rather important that Thomas and Enrique know what you would do if you acquired the third crystal. You have everything— money, power, magical ability. What more do you want?"

"To fulfill my destiny and reshape our world," said Arius. "Look at this planet. Billions of people competing for resources. Pollution choking our oceans and filling the sky. Nuclear stockpiles adequate to kill every last human a hundred times and still growing. And things are only getting worse. Every day the population increases. Consumption increases. We're destroying the future faster with every passing day, and soon there will be nothing left for anyone. Someone has to make it stop."

"We are facing extraordinary challenges," agreed Huxley. "But how will you stop them? How *exactly* do you plan to make things better?"

"First, by putting an end to weapons, nuclear and otherwise," said Arius. "After taking away our capacity for self-destruction, we will have the freedom to create a new future, to restore balance and sustain life on this planet."

"Disarmament is a noble goal," said Huxley. "But at what cost? And even if you succeed, how will you prevent people and governments from making new ones?"

"By any means necessary," said Arius.

"That's not an answer," said Huxley.

"It is an answer," spat Arius. There was an edge to his voice, a hardness in his eyes. "I'll do whatever I have to, however, it needs to be done."

"And what does that mean for the rest of humanity?" asked Huxley. "What about the people who share this planet with you? How many of them have to die for you to fulfill your destiny?"

"As many as it takes," said Arius. "Look around you, Alchemist. You've lived long enough to see that, on their own, people do nothing but cause destruction. They seem to welcome it even, through their ignorance and greed. They buy their precious devices and stare at the stupid screens, never considering that these are tools of control, created at the cost of lives and resources. Their cars spew poison even as they consume the garbage corporations call food, all at the cost of the planet that keeps our species alive. They never consider the true cost of anything, and it will cost us everything."

"Then help them make better choices," said Huxley. "Give them better options. You have the resources and power to make real progress. Work with us to create a better way."

"It's too late for that." Arius shook his head and turned to Thomas, his eyes full of emotion. "The adults may be blind, but even a child can see that we've gone too far.

There is no choice but the one I am making, and nobody else capable of making it. I *need* the crystal, Thomas. There is no other—"

"Stop!" Scott's command cut through the air, echoing from the canyon walls. He was on his feet, a fiery purple glow around his hands. "That's far enough, Arianna. Show yourself, and step away from the boys."

Arius smiled, but his eyes turned hard. "As you wish, *murderer*. Arianna, if you please."

The air to Enrique's right rippled and bent, revealing a woman with short black hair and bright red lipstick. Her almond shaped eyes were the same multi-hued hazel as those of Arius, her skin a slightly deeper brown. Black leather hugged her curvy figure, but Thomas found his eyes drawn to the pulsing red and white energy crackling above her hands. He took an instinctive step backward.

"Away from the boys, please," said Huxley. Arianna took a silent step toward Arius, the deadly energy continuing to sizzle over her palms. "That's better. Thank you. Scott?"

The trail of tears had dried on Scott's cheeks. The purple glow above his hand disappeared, replaced by a translucent field that sprang from his open palm, expanding until it enveloped the entire ledge in a shimmering bubble-like sphere. Thomas felt a faint tickle run up the back of his neck and shivered as a web of goosebumps covered his body.

"A truth field?" Arius rolled his eyes. "Is there no trust among us?"

"Thomas and Enrique deserve honest answers, from us as well as from you," said Huxley. "Are you concerned?"

"Of course," said Arius. His eyes widened at his own answer. He recovered his composure and smiled. "Very well, Alchemist. Truth it shall be. Let's start with you, shall we? The crystal is my destiny. Why are you so intent on stopping me?"

"Because I have seen what happens when men of power make choices for the rest of us," said Huxley. "You may not see it, but you are walking the path of darkness, Arius. Putting the crystal in your hands would create a greater threat than any weapon that exists on this planet. I have lived through too many wars and fought against too many tyrants to stand by and allow that kind of destruction to unfold."

"The path of darkness?" scoffed Arius. "Please. There is action and inaction, progress and obstacle. The real threat to humanity is the failure to act intelligently on our own behalf. If we do nothing, our species and planet are doomed. Surely even you can see that."

"Perhaps, but I choose to believe in the creativity of mankind, and in the goodness of the force that created us," said Huxley. "I believe we have time to heal the earth, and that there is abundance in this universe beyond what any of us can imagine—if we work together. Look to the stars. We live in one solar system among trillions, in a universe with far more to offer than can be found on this truly remarkable planet."

"Without action, we'll destroy ourselves before finding another home," said Arius. "And then what? We destroy that one as well? No, that's not a solution. We need time, and I can create that. You lack will, Alchemist, but I do not. I *need* the crystal."

"About that," said Professor Reilly. "How exactly did you learn about the crystals?"

"From someone who believes in me," said Arius. "Someone who sees what I can do, who understands my vision for the future."

"Who?"

"He calls himself the Sumerian," said Arius. "I've never known him by any other name."

"And what did this Sumerian tell you?" asked Huxley.

"He told me about the crystals," said Arius. "Of their existence and also where to begin my search. He told me about Thomas and the Wildus family, about *The Book of Sorrows*, and about Enrique's emergence as a magical adept. Most importantly, he told me of my own destiny, of my power to reshape the future of this earth."

Professor Reilly looked at Huxley, his expression shell-shocked. "Outside of our circle, who knows these things?"

"Nobody," said Huxley. "How is this Sumerian getting his information?"

"He knows more than you can imagine," said Arius. "And he chose me to claim the power of the crystals. Me, and me alone."

"Yes, but why?" said Huxley. "If he knows so much, why not claim the power for himself?"

"Because it is *my* destiny," said Arius. His expression was haughty, almost gleeful, as if his own excellence was sufficient to answer the question. "The Sumerian knows that if I harness the power of the crystals, every weapon on this planet will turn to dust. Governments will fall, and in their absence, I will have the power to create a better and more beautiful future."

"Better for who?" asked Huxley. "Others have made that claim before and it didn't work out particularly well. Not even for themselves."

"Why does this Sumerian character want you to do that?" said Professor Reilly. "What's in it for him?"

A look flashed across Arius's face, swift and almost imperceptible. Confusion? Uncertainty?

"Enough questions." Arius turned to Thomas, all traces of haughtiness and uncertainty wiped away, his face and eyes smoldering with sincerity that bordered on angelic. "What will it be, Thomas? Help me transform the world and save our planet, or cast your lot with a murderer and start a war you can't possibly win?"

Questions twisted Thomas's mind and roiled his gut. He didn't know what to think or believe. It didn't take a genius to see that getting rid of nuclear weapons was a good idea, or that over-consumption was destroying the environment. Maybe Arius was right. His hand ventured into his pocket, his fingers wrapping instinctively around the crystal.

"Search your heart, Thomas." Huxley looked at Thomas, a tiny smile at the corner of his gold-touched eyes. "We are your friends, truly and genuinely. All of us. Deep down, you know that. Your mother would not have trusted you into our care if she had any doubt about our motives or character. But she did, and not just you. She trusted us to teach and take care of Enrique as well. She knows what is at stake and made her choice."

The logic rang true, cutting through the fog and confusion. Thomas could doubt almost anything, but not his mom. His grip on the crystal loosened.

"Huxley is right," said Professor Reilly. "We're on your side, Thomas, and the side of humanity. Scott as well. His penance isn't finished, not by a long shot, but he's trying. You have to believe us. Giving the crystal to a man like Arius is asking for disaster at a scale you can't possibly imagine. Gareth has seen it. The consequences are far more serious than you can imagine."

Thomas let go of the crystal.

"Time's up," said Arius. "Make your choice, Thomas."

"No, it isn't," said Huxley. "A decision of this magnitude shouldn't be taken lightly, and it shouldn't be rushed. Millions of lives are at stake, maybe billions. Take your time, Thomas. Think through the consequences of your choice."

"Says the man who has lived for centuries," said Arius. "If you have such love for the common man, Alchemist, why don't you share the secret of your arts and help everyone live forever? Or if you believe that death is a natural and inevitable process, why don't you join in the habit of dying like the rest of us?"

Huxley stared back. "Death is a natural and inevitable process, Arius, and one day my time will come. Until then, I will stand against the darkness. I will fight against tyrants and tyranny until I have breathed my last breath. No one person should control the fate of humanity, and certainly not one so foolish as to follow a guide with unknown motives."

"Such passion," said Arius. "If you're lucky, you'll live long enough to see the outcome of this little exchange. Nothing fatal, Arianna. Not yet."

Reddish white lit up the ledge as a flash of electric energy blazed from Arianna's hand and slammed into Huxley's left shoulder. A sizzling snap reverberated from the canyon walls as the alchemist staggered backward, a spout of red blossoming at the point of impact. He let out a pained cry as he dropped to his knees, his right hand covering the expanding patch of red. A thin trail of smoke rose into the air.

"Violence is crude but sometimes necessary," said Arius. He stared at Thomas, his eyes blazing. "As much as I despise these ridiculous displays, I will do what I must to fulfill my destiny. Hand over the crystal, Thomas, before I am forced to take further action."

"Don't do it, Thomas," said Professor Reilly. "What happens to us is insignificant compared to—"

A second flash shattered the last syllable. Electricity blazed from Arianna's hands, arcing across the ledge. The professor's eyes widened, and his face wrenched in agony. Blood gathered around a smoking hole in his pants, spilling down his thigh in a crimson swath. The professor groaned, clutching his leg as he fell to the ground. "Argghh. Bloody hell!"

Thomas stared at the crimson liquid spilling onto the professor's khaki pants, at the growing patch of blood on Huxley's shoulder. He felt shocked, numb, unable to form a clear thought. Light gathered above Arianna's hands, crackling with explosive potential. She ran her tongue slowly over the red lipstick as if savoring something wickedly delicious.

"Last chance, Thomas," said Arius. "Hand over the crystal or one of them dies."

"Don't give it to him," groaned Professor Reilly. "Don't give the bastard a bloody thing. Go! Now!"

"The clock is ticking, Thomas. You have ten seconds to decide. Ten!"

"Don't do it," said Enrique. "This guy is sick in the head."

Thomas looked at his friends bleeding on the ground. It was an impossible choice. He couldn't leave Huxley and

Professor Reilly to die any more than he could turn over the crystal to Arius.

A sharp jab thumped his shoulder, jarring him back to the present. Enrique shook his head. "Don't do it. Me and Scott can fight these clowns. Go. Get the crystal out of here."

"Eight!"

Remember your promise. The voice was a whisper in his mind, distant but familiar. He looked up. The voice came through again, louder this time. It was the same voice he'd heard in the alley back home. Thomas looked at Scott. The magician's face was open, vulnerable. The tears had dried on his cheeks, but the hurt and shame were clear in the subtle lines around his eyes. *It's okay. I don't blame you for judging me. I deserve it, and far more. But please, please don't give Arius the crystal. Remember your promise, Thomas. No matter what.*

"Six!"

Enrique looked from Arius to Scott, his head tilted as if he could hear the voice as well.

We have to destroy it. I can't do it myself. It has to be all three of us, together. Blink if you can hear me. Thomas blinked. *Good. Now take the crystal out of your pocket, but don't let on that you hear me. Quickly.*

"Five!"

Thomas reached into his pocket. The crystal slid smoothly into the afternoon light, the shiny black glistening in his hand. He lifted it into the air, watching as the inner lights danced. Arius took a half step closer, his eyes wide and the count momentarily forgotten.

"Don't give it to him, Thomas," said Huxley. His face was anguished, his voice weak but determined. "No matter what happens to us, don't give it to him."

"Go!" groaned Professor Reilly. "Get out of here. Now!"

"Three!" called Arius, his hand extended toward Thomas. "Hand it over and your friends live, Thomas."

Thomas willed himself to focus, commanded the energy inside of himself to build as he listened to Scott's final instructions.

"Two!" Arius's shout carried across the canyon, echoing from the rocks and trees.

The light above Arianna's hands crackled. Her eyes gleamed and her fingers tensed. Her palms were aimed at Professor Reilly and Huxley. A fiery spark flickered in Thomas's belly, kindling into a furious flame.

Arius's mouth opened to shape the final number, his eyes blazing with hungry light as Thomas's hand dipped down in preparation for the throw.

Thomas tossed the crystal into the air, high above the canyon ledge. Arius's eyes widened. Arianna turned to follow the path of the shimmering stone, her focus shifting away from the professor and Huxley. The crystal caught and reflected the afternoon light, blazing as it reached the apex of its flight.

Now!

Energy exploded out of Thomas's hand in a flash of electric blue, brighter and more powerful than any attack he'd ever managed. Matching blasts ripped upward, purple and green, as Scott and Enrique added their firepower to the attack. All three blasts hit the crystal at the same time. The dark material hovered for a moment, then descended toward Arius.

Arianna wheeled, energy arcing from her hands. Scott reacted so quickly the only thing Thomas saw was a burst of purple and Arianna flying backward across the ledge.

Thomas let fire again. Blue energy thumped into the crystal, which only seemed to shine brighter as it fell toward Arius. Time slowed to a crawl. Fresh bursts of purple and green flashed past, speeding toward the dark magician. A shimmering barrier materialized around Arius's body, shattering the attacks into diffuse and useless fragments. The crystal fell into his grasping fingers.

Arianna scrambled sideways, fire blazing from her hands. Her attacks were deflected, but this time, Scott's counterattack didn't catch her off guard. The purple blast shattered into the rock wall as she dove forward, pulling herself into a somersault that ended at Arius's side.

A thought flashed through Thomas's mind, awful in its impact and clarity. *I just gave Arius the power to take over the world.*

FORTY-FOUR

A PRIMAL SHOUT ECHOED through the canyon. Arius held the crystal in his upraised hand like a trophy, his face reflecting furious triumph. Fresh bursts of purple, blue, and green shuddered into the shimmering barrier in front of him. The giant strode toward Arius. Arianna raised a hand and the barrier expanded to protect all three.

Thomas fell to his knees. The plan had failed. Instead of destroying the crystal, he'd given it to a madman. As if from a distance, he heard Enrique swear. Professor Reilly's shout of "No!" trailed off into a pained whimper. Huxley's cry was wordless, a wounded seagull lost in the canyon.

Arius suddenly looked up, his eyes wide, a look of shock and pain flashing across his face. He dropped the crystal into his other hand, then passed it swiftly back and forth as if it were suddenly on fire.

And it was.

The crystal was glowing, the black material blazing like a meteor crashing through the atmosphere on a moonless night. Beams of blue and green and purple shone from the center of the crystal, radiating outward until the canyon ledge was a symphony of light and color. Arius gasped in pain as he struggled to keep hold of the blazing crystal. The giant stared, his face as impassive as ever. Arianna's lips curled in a snarl of confusion.

A blinding flash exploded outward as the crystal shattered into ten thousand tiny pieces. A thunderous crack split the air.

Thomas flinched, half deaf and two-thirds blind. He stumbled to his feet, trying to catch his balance. The sound of Arius's scream and the deafening echo of the explosion overwhelmed his senses. Enrique grabbed him by the arm. Thomas turned and saw his friend's mouth moving. He could make out the shape of the word even though the sound was lost. "Go! Now!"

Thomas took two steps and then dove, sliding across the rock surface as Arianna blasted red-white fire across the ledge. He reached for Huxley's hand, grabbing hold of the alchemist as he visualized the training room and projected himself forward. The damp heat vanished, replaced by the shocking cool of a stone floor and conditioned air.

Thomas opened his still-stinging eyes. Huxley was on the ground at his side, blood oozing from the gash in his shoulder. He looked weak, hardly able to keep pressure on the wound.

"Help! Adelia! Adelia, we need help! In the training

room. Hurry!" Thomas pressed his hands against the wound and shouted again. "Adelia!"

"It's okay." Huxley grabbed Thomas's arm with his left hand, groaned, and pulled himself to a sitting position. His face was pale, but his hazel-gold eyes crinkled with the touch of a smile. "It's been a long time since I was last blasted like that. I'd almost forgotten how much a magical injury can hurt."

Enrique materialized across the room with Professor Reilly. The professor's face was pale and clammy, his eyes blinking open and shut. A crimson stain covered the lower half of his pant leg. Droplets of fresh blood pooled at the cuff and splashed onto the floor, forming a rapidly growing pool at his feet. Enrique stripped off his shirt and pressed it against the wound.

Professor Reilly groaned. His voice was weak, full of pain. "Oww! That bloody hurts."

"You're gonna be okay, Professor," said Enrique. He looked at Thomas and Huxley, his face strained with fear. "He needs help. Fast."

"Adelia!" Thomas shouted so loudly his voice cracked and his throat burned.

"Help! We need help in here!" Enrique took over, his voice thundering in the little room.

Footsteps pounded on the stone slabs and the door flew open. Adelia rushed to Huxley's side, Ling Sun following close behind.

"What happened?" asked Adelia. She moved Thomas's hands out of the way to look at the damage. Her voice was shockingly steady as she reached into her medical bag. "Gunshots? Both of you?"

"Not gunshots." Huxley grimaced and held his shoulder. "Arianna. She and Arius tried to use us as leverage."

"He didn't get the crystal, did he? No? Oh, thank goodness!" Adelia's fearful expression shifted to one of concern. She turned her attention back to Huxley and Professor Reilly. "We need to disinfect and close these wounds. Magical injuries fester if they're not treated quickly. Thomas, hold Huxley while I work on his shoulder. Enrique, you help Ling Sun with the professor. Okay?"

"Will it hurt?" asked Professor Reilly. He looked as if someone were already jabbing him with needles.

"Buckle down, you big baby," said Adelia, grabbing a bottle of disinfectant and a pair of scissors from a tray of medical supplies. "This is the easy part."

"Baby?" Professor Reilly groaned indignantly. He lifted his head, a touch of color flushing his pale cheeks. "I got blasted by magic, for crying out loud. If this isn't the time for a bit of sympathy, I don't know what is."

Huxley gritted his teeth and squeezed Thomas's hand as Adelia poured disinfectant over his shoulder. When the area was soaked, she quickly cut away the surrounding cloth and dumped a second splash directly onto the wound. She handed the bottle to Ling Sun and grabbed a fresh gauze pad.

"What's that—yeeoowwww!" shouted Professor Reilly. Enrique grunted as the professor squeezed his arm. "Bloody hell!"

"Sorry," said Ling Sun. "Disinfectant hurts, but better to hurt now than lose leg later."

Professor Reilly gasped and let his head fall back to the floor. He looked up, his eyes suddenly wide again. "Wait. Did you say that was the easy part?"

Ling Sun handed the professor a piece of wood. "Bite on this. I have to check inside before we stitch you up."

Professor Reilly's eyes widened, but he took the wood and clamped it between his teeth. Ling Sun cut the cloth around the professor's wound and poured another splash of disinfectant. Satisfied, she inserted long tweezers into the holes. Professor Reilly squirmed and groaned.

Ling Sun lifted the tweezers, bringing with them a fragment of cloth. She patted Professor Reilly on the stomach. "You're going to be fine. A little bit of bleeding, but the extra padding protected the bone."

"I've been saying for years it's a good idea to be a bit husky." The professor's voice was a pained whisper, but Thomas felt a wave of relief at hearing the man joke.

"Wood back in," said Ling Sun. "One more time with the disinfectant, and then we'll do the stitches. Bite on that wood, husky man. Hard!"

"You, too, Huxley," said Adelia. "Come on. Let's get you sewn up."

When the last stitch had been tied, Professor Reilly pulled the wood from his mouth and lay back on the hard stone floor. "Arius is going to pay for that. Blasting a couple of old men with magic! The next time I see that power-hungry jackal, I'm going to shove this wood so far up his arse he'll be farting splinters for a month."

"Farting splinters?" said Enrique. "Ooh! That sounds awful."

"A woodblock-wedgy is the least the man deserves," said Professor Reilly. "I have half a mind to do him worse than that."

Relief spread through the room, which filled with gentle laughter.

"Oh, oh, no more," whimpered Huxley. He gripped his shoulder. "It hurts too much."

As the laughter tapered off, Thomas felt a sudden stab of fear. "Hey, what happened to Scott? Where's Scott?"

FORTY-FIVE

"I'M RIGHT HERE." The air shimmered in the empty doorway. Scott was there, but to Thomas, the wizard looked lighter, more relaxed. Even his face and eyes seemed softer, less etched with guilt and pain. "Sorry. I didn't want to distract anyone from getting these two stitched up."

A fresh wave of relief washed over Thomas. "What happened? How come you got here later than the rest of us?"

"Arius needed some straightening out," said Scott. "Heinrik and Arianna, too. We had a nice chat and came to a few agreements."

"What did you do?" asked Professor Reilly, a hopeful expression on his face. "Was it painful?"

"To Arius? Yes, I suppose so." Scott pulled a device from his pocket. "This recording would put him on every terrorist watch list in the world, and every last asset he owns would be frozen. That's a solid deterrent, but for him, I think the blindness will be much worse."

"You blinded him?" said Professor Reilly, suddenly sitting up a little.

"The explosion did," said Scott. "At least temporarily. I simply made sure the condition would stick. Not forever, of course, but long enough to remind Arius what it means to depend on other people. If and when he proves himself worthy, Arius will be able to see as well as ever. Until then, he is strongly incentivized to stay out of trouble and allow Thomas and Enrique to go back to their lives."

"So what now?" asked Enrique. "Me and Thomas just go home and pretend we've been at science camp?"

"Pretty much," said Adelia. She smiled, amusement sparkling in her eyes. "But first, I think we should head upstairs and find you something to eat."

"That sounds perfect," said Thomas. "I'm starving."

EPILOGUE

THOMAS STEPPED OUT of his classroom and into the afternoon light, squinting as his eyes adjusted to the brightness. A wave of students rushed toward the front gates, excited voices and hurried footsteps announcing the arrival of the weekend. Thomas allowed himself to be swept past his locker, carried forward in the stream of his classmates toward the line of buses waiting out front. A hand grabbed his arm and pulled him suddenly sideways.

"Hey, stranger. Where you rushing off to?" Thomas turned and found Peggy's hazel eyes staring directly into his own. A radiant smile illuminated her elfin features. Thomas tried to reply, but the words failed to form properly in his mouth. Peggy laughed, took his hand, and pulled him toward the exit. "Come on."

"What's up, y'all?" hollered Enrique. "It's weekend time."

"Hey, Enrique," Thomas and Peggy answered in perfect unison. They looked at each other and laughed.

"All right, that's just creepy," said Enrique. "You two

just started going out last week, and already you sound like the same person. Cut that out."

"I don't know," said Peggy. "I kind of like it."

"Gross," said Enrique. "So what's up? Are we doing something tomorrow or what?"

"Yeah," said Thomas. "I thought we'd head down to San Clemente. My mom said she'd drive. I talked with Jameel and Meng earlier. They're going to meet us there. Akhil, too."

"The beach sounds good," said Peggy. "I'm in."

"Ditto," said Enrique. A blue-eyed girl with sandy-blond hair slipped into the group and bumped Enrique with a hip-check. He bounced sideways, then stepped back and slung his arm around her. "How about it, Celeste? Are you in?"

"In for what?"

"Hitting up San Clemente. Thomas's mom is driving."

"Sounds like fun," said Celeste. "What time?"

"We'll meet at my place around ten," said Thomas. "Do you think you can make it?"

"I hope so," said Celeste. "I'll have to ask my dad when I get home."

"Would it help if I call and invite you once you're home?" asked Peggy.

"For sure," said Celeste. "Thank you!"

"What? You think her dad wouldn't want her to come

if it was just me?" Enrique rolled his shoulders, wiggled his eyebrows, and did a goofy salsa dance step. "Maybe he'd be intimidated by all this awesomeness?"

"I *know* her dad wouldn't want her to come if he saw that." Peggy flashed a wicked smile.

"Definitely not," said Celeste. "And come to think of it, I'm pretty sure I've got an appointment in the morning. A root canal."

Enrique pulled his mouth into a wide "O" and looked hurt.

"All right," laughed Thomas. "The bus is about to take off. Let's get you over there."

"Aren't you coming?" asked Peggy.

"Not today," said Thomas. "Enrique and I have a little project to work on. I'll call you later, okay?"

"On a Friday? Really?"

"I'm sorry," said Thomas. And looking into her hazel eyes, he really was sorry. "When you see Akhil, make sure he knows to meet at my house at ten."

"I will," said Peggy. She met his eyes, holding him transfixed for an endless second. She leaned closer, her lips gently brushing his cheek. Thomas locked up, his body and brain equally frozen. The bus horn blared, a deep, booming sound that put an abrupt end to the moment.

"Hey, are you kids coming or what?" hollered the driver.

"See ya," said Peggy. She flipped her auburn hair and

followed Celeste up the steps, leaving Thomas on the sidewalk in stunned silence.

Thomas's mouth opened, but his mind was completely incapable of forming a response. He tried raising a hand to wave, but his arm had turned to spaghetti. All he could do was watch as she melted into a cluster of friends.

"Man, that girl's done a number on you," said Enrique. "I can't believe she asked *you* out. I did not see that coming."

"Me either," said Thomas. "It's like she knows a whole different kind of magic. Where do you think she learned how to do that?"

"You're asking the wrong guy," said Enrique. "Come on, let's get moving."

"Out of the way, geekwad." Sean Parker rumbled past, thumping Thomas's shoulder with a stray elbow.

"Yeah, geekwad, out of the way," repeated one of Parker's mindless friends. The others chuckled as they filed onto the bus. Thomas rubbed his shoulder and watched the bully drop heavily into his normal seat.

"Hey! Hey, what the heck?" Parker's voice rose dangerously, booming through the open windows. "What is that? Spaghetti? That's not funny! Which one of you idiots put spaghetti on my seat? These are new pants, guys. Who did that? WHO?"

A chorus of laughter erupted as the door swung shut with a mechanical whoosh. Parker's angry shouting persisted as the bus pulled away from the curb, carrying over the sound of the grinding engine.

"Was that you?" asked Thomas, though he already knew the answer.

"What? Me?" Enrique feigned shock. "I'm out here. How could I possibly put a pile of old cafeteria spaghetti and meat sauce on Parker's seat? Must have been someone else."

Thomas laughed. "I almost feel sorry for his friends right now."

"Not me," said Enrique. "They deserve each other. Come on, it's almost 3:30. Let's get going."

"Deal," said Thomas. He and Enrique walked side by side to a place where a row of tall shrubs met a windowless corner of the building. Thomas slid past the barrier and looked around to make sure nobody was in sight. Satisfied, he squared up in front of Enrique and extended his right arm. "Training room on three."

"To the training room on three," Enrique agreed. He grabbed Thomas's forearm. "One."

"Two. Three."

Halfway across the world, in a dimly lit room carved of ancient gray stones, Thomas and Enrique materialized, their arms still linked together. A man in a rich purple robe sat waiting, his tall frame perched on a spare metal chair. A miniature galaxy shimmered above his left hand, an impossible orchestra of whirling stars that bathed the room in living light.

Scott gestured to a pair of chairs that might or might not have been there a second earlier. Mischief and magic danced in his green eyes, and the hint of something that might have been peace.

You've learned how to survive, the magician's melodious voice whispered in Thomas's mind. *Now it's time to learn some magic. Are you ready to get started?*

If you enjoyed THOMAS WILDUS
AND THE BOOK OF SORROWS,
make sure to order:

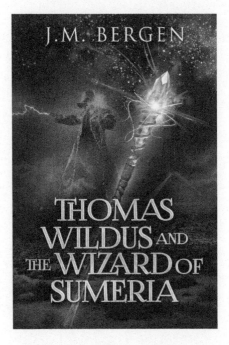

ACKNOWLEDGMENTS

BRINGING THIS BOOK TO LIFE has been a wonderful challenge, and it would be impossible to thank everyone who deserves appreciation for their contributions. Even so, special thanks go to Amy for the gifts of time and children, to my parents and brothers for their insight and support, to Matty and Emma for general awesomeness, and to Mikey for motivating the creation of the *Thomas Wildus* series. Thanks also to Brittany Harrison for editorial excellence, Susan Gerber for a wonderful interior, Dan Van Oss for a gorgeous cover, Mason and Braden for positive and insightful feedback, and to the many writers and storytellers who have inspired me with their beautiful work. Finally, to PJ for a lifetime of friendship, and to JC, Jesse, Ace, Dave, Carp, Mike, Joe, Glenn, Shrfu, Aunt Shar, Ann, Archie, Jennifer, Belikos, Boyer, Brian, Tiffany, Adam, Fred, Brenda, Ram Das, Karen, John, my extended family, and the countless others who have traveled with me on this strange and sometimes wonderful journey through life. You are more loved and appreciated than you'll ever know.

Made in the USA
Las Vegas, NV
02 May 2021

22385378R00215